Älvor

Älvor

LAURA BINGHAM

Sweetwater Books
Springville, Utah

The views expressed within this work are the sole responsibility of the author and do not necessarily reflect the position of Cedar Fort, Inc., or any other entity.

This is a work of fiction. The characters, names, incidents, places, and dialogue are products of the author's imagination, and are not to be construed as real.

ISBN 13: 978-1-59955-272-9

Published by Sweetwater Books, an imprint of Cedar Fort, Inc., 2373 W. 700 S., Springville, UT 84663
Distributed by Cedar Fort, Inc. www.cedarfort.com

LIBRARY OF CONGRESS CATALOGING-IN-PUBLICATION DATA

Bingham, Laura.
Älvor / Laura Bingham.
   p. cm.
   Summary: While hiking in the hills behind their Pennsylvania home,
teenaged twins Erin and Bain discover their magical abilities, enter a
fantasy fairy world, and train to become elves.
   ISBN 978-1-59955-272-9 (acid-free paper)
   [1. Brothers and sisters--Fiction. 2. Twins--Fiction. 3. Magic--Fiction. 4.
Elves--Fiction. 5. Fairies--Fiction. 6. Fantasy.] I. Title.
   PZ7.B5118169Al 2009
   [Fic]--dc22
                    2009006053

Cover design by Angela D. Olsen
Cover design © 2009 by Lyle Mortimer
Edited and typeset by Melissa J. Caldwell

Printed in the United States of America

10 9 8 7 6 5 4 3 2 1

Printed on acid-free paper

For Parley, who dares me to dream
and my children, who inspire me

CONTENTS

PROLOGUE

ADARAE WAITED. THERE WAS STILL a chance. She couldn't shake the feeling that she was close. So close. She had been looking at every new face for the last year. As of yet, she did not feel drawn to anyone, but she couldn't resist trying to find whoever the chosen one would be. She wasn't sure even when things would happen, only that they surely would. And she was certain that she would know when the right person appeared.

Just coming over the crest of the hill was a man pushing a stroller. Adarae had been looking at new little faces for so long, she teased herself that she should probably give up, but she couldn't. She would see this one last child.

The old man whistled softly as he pushed the stroller down the sloping hill. She could hear the sweet melody even from here. Soon the stroller was only a whisper's distance from Adarae.

The man's words pierced the moment. "Would you take a look at that? Just when you think you've seen them all, something new pops up. Now, isn't that a pretty one." He let out a low whistle as he stopped the stroller. "It came right up to you and everything. In all my years, I do believe this is the first time I have ever seen such a thing. You two must be pretty lucky. Butterflies always bring good luck, but if they sit by you they leave a blessing."

Adarae jolted as the feeling surged through her. She looked

carefully at not one, but two little faces and felt the warm power within them. No one suspected it could be two, but the strength pulsing from them was undeniable. They stared back into her eyes. They could *see* her, more than just the butterfly wings. The baby girl had curly red hair and blue eyes that were showing hints of green. Her full pink lips broke into an angelic smile, and her chubby finger reached out as if to touch her. The boy's deeper blue eyes locked on hers with a knowing gaze.

Adarae drank in the moment. It had been so long since one of their kind could *see* her. She was so mesmerized by the two beautiful babies that she wanted to look at them all day, but she knew she must keep moving. At last, she could tell the others of her success.

Chapter One

A NEW BOOK

ERIN SAT ON THE BACK seat alone. The sound of laughter drowned out the drone of the school bus. It was amazing how much noise two fifteen-year-old boys could make. Soon it would be just her and her brother left for the thirty-minute drive home.

She thumbed through the yearbook. Grandpa Jessie always insisted on buying them each their own.

"See you in the fall, man. Woo-hoo! It's finally summer!" the boy shouted as he stepped off the bus.

"Yeah! Have fun in Florida, you lucky dog!" Bain called back.

The bus jerked down the street again. Bain got up and walked to the back. He sat backwards in the seat and looked at her.

"Trade you," he said. "I didn't get to sign yours yet."

She handed him her book as he let his bounce on the seat next to her. She picked up his yearbook and let it open randomly. Colorful permanent ink graced the page with hearts, smiley faces, and lots of exclamation points. She turned the pages looking for a blank space.

"I think I'll just sign over the top of my picture. It could only improve it." Erin looked for the section where the black and white photo of her stared out. She took her red marker and wrote, "Here's to the summer!"

"Erin, didn't you even go outside for the yearbook signing?

There's practically nothing written in here."

"Oh, I was talking to my chemistry teacher about my grade. I didn't expect to see an A-. I was sure I had an A in there."

"The last day of school and you spend your time talking to a teacher on purpose? I think you might need professional help."

"Thanks."

"Anytime, little sister."

"Hey, only by ten minutes."

"I'm still bigger than you." He smiled with a crooked grin.

He had her there. He was already almost six feet tall. At this rate, she was never going to catch up. He flipped back around in his seat so he was facing forward.

She stared out the window. The trees walled the sides of the street in green. As they approached their village, the familiar Pennsylvania misted hills came into view. She loved seeing them every day from the bus after school.

A purple butterfly flickered into view before it was gone again. That was the thing she loved most about her home. There were more butterflies here than in any of the neighboring little towns. She never understood why there were so many gathered in her tiny village when only a few strays could be seen anywhere else. Maybe there was some kind of plant they loved in the hills.

The ride home made her feel as though she was ominously leaving her familiar school. She loved school. It wasn't that she really had very many friends, she just felt like she was somewhere when she was there. During the school year, she had to live in an empty house only at night. With Grandpa Jessie gone every Monday through Friday for work, the summer days dragged on in the quiet house.

She watched as the houses began again to pass by her window and imagined what it would be like to have her mom greet her at the door. How many times had she let herself slip into the same daydream? She had to stop. It wasn't like she should really miss her parents. She never even knew them.

"Wait up!" she called. "I can't believe you still have so much energy after your run." She could feel herself pant as she jogged to meet him.

Bain didn't even glance back.

"It's right over there," he pointed. "I've never really gone this way before, but I found if you climb through a few bushes it opens up on the other side."

The landscape here was full and green. From the road they could only see a few feet into the foliage. High humidity and plenty of precipitation encouraged the trees, grass, and plants to thrive.

"Right," she offered as she eyed the bushes. She hesitated.

He just chuckled quietly and moved in.

Beautiful as the greenery was, Erin was not fond of climbing through the mountain laurels that reached taller than she was. Bain held the branches for her and helped her through the thick shrubs, all the while somehow avoiding scratches from the dense vegetation.

She was grateful he didn't tease her when she tripped twice and then accidentally smacked him right in the face with a stray branch. He just laughed good-naturedly and kept going.

"How far did you get this morning?" Erin asked as she tried to calculate the forest waiting for them.

"Not too far, really, I just followed a trail for a few minutes. It kept going though, and we haven't seen a new trail for a long time." He gave her a smile as if trying to reassure her. "Don't worry; this is going to be great."

"You didn't waste any time finding a new place to explore this summer," she said, trying to stall the hard hike ahead. "Did you bring all the regular gear in your backpack? We're going to need to mark the trees so we can find our way back."

"No worries. I'm totally prepared, as always. There's enough food to last a couple of days. What else could we need?"

She couldn't help but smile. It would take an enormous amount of food to actually satisfy him for a couple of days.

After two hours, Erin was glad that Bain had come through

with the water. They tied red twine around a few trees along the way so the trail back would be easier to find. The trees all seemed the same to her, and Erin was sure she would never find her way back without the marks. Bain was a born compass though. He always seemed to know which direction they were going and how to find their way around.

The bushes finally gave way into a clearing where the view made her stop in astonishment.

She had seen many houses that the founding fathers of this country built. Century-old homes could be found in their own village even. Some were fancy, and some were not. But nothing she had ever seen could even begin to compare to the stark beauty that stood before them now.

There in the lush grass stood a small cottage. It was petite, but astounding. The eaves were carved with skill into a curling Victorian pattern. Each window was framed with a lace-carved shutter. The whole structure was in different shades of wood. There was no paint to be found, but the colors that exuded from it were vibrant and contrasting.

"Oh, wow," she breathed. "What? How?" She looked at Bain. He was just as mesmerized by the work of art as she was.

"I've never seen anything like it," he said. "It looks brand new but it can't be. All around the grass and trees are untouched. There's not even a worn path on the ground."

"What do you want to do?" She wasn't sure if their adventure was at an end.

"Eat lunch."

"Are you serious?"

Bain just smiled. "Sure. I'm starving, and if there is anyone in the house maybe they'll see us and come out. Besides, I need some time to figure out what this place is and the easiest way to get in."

"You could try knocking."

He was already sitting on the grass pulling out the bag of food. She gave in and sat down too. They ate peanut butter and grape jelly sandwiches while they puzzled out the little house. It could have been a miniature mansion. The detail suggested that the cottage was built by someone who wished to explore all the avenues of master wood carving. It must have taken ages to chisel the wooden swirls and delicate squared patterns. The oddest part was that it looked brand new. She had seen the graying effect time had on some of the older wood houses in her village, but this place looked like it had been completed just yesterday. It was perfect.

"Do you think anyone lives here?" Erin asked. She picked up an apple and took a bite.

"I was wondering that too. There's no electricity. No phone line. There is a chimney, but no wood pile. The grass looks like it has never been walked on. It's maybe the weirdest thing I've ever seen. It doesn't make sense to build this place and not hook it up at least to electricity."

"Maybe they're not done yet. It could be a rich person's summer cabin that they haven't finished yet."

"I don't know. It still doesn't make sense. I think we should look around. I seriously doubt this place has been lived in."

"Well, I'm still going to knock on the door," Erin said. She got up, brushed off her pants, walked up to the rich mahogany door, and knocked loudly. "Is anyone there?" she called. It didn't surprise her that no one answered.

She tried the door handle just to see. The knob turned easily in her hand. "It's open."

Bain started packing everything into his backpack.

"What are you doing?" she asked. Knowing Bain, he would assume that this was their invitation nailed to the front door.

"I bet no one is here. Don't you want to take a look at the inside too? It's not like we're going to hurt anything, just look around."

He walked up to the door and winked at her as the brass knob turned smoothly under his hand.

They stepped inside onto the shiny hardwood floor. There was a stone fireplace on one wall and several wooden chairs seated around the room. There were no switches or light fixtures on the golden pine ceiling. In the corner sat a small tree with delicate leaves of bright lime green that fluttered against the white bark without the benefit of a breeze. An oil lamp sat on a small table next to one of the chairs.

"Who do you think owns this?" she asked.

"I don't know." He inspected the chairs around the room.

"You have to try this! The chair is so comfortable—it's like it was built just for me to sit in!"

She just watched him, not sure what to make of this place yet. The next room appeared to be a historical museum's kitchen display. In one corner sat an old-fashioned oak box with a door. The inside was lined with metal.

"I think I found the fridge," she called.

"And the stove," he said as he leaned against the doorway. "I think you actually have to build a fire in the bottom of that thing for it to work. I don't think I would want to bake cookies here."

He walked around the room inspecting the ancient appliances. "Check this out! It looks like this floorboard lifts up." The wooden floor was shiny and smooth with a barely recognizable handle just large enough for him to fit his fingers in.

Erin knelt down and tried her fingernails in the crevice. A door began to rise when she tugged on it. She quickly let the floor drop back into place.

"What are you waiting for?" Bain asked. He crouched down and pulled the door all the way open.

She stared at the dark staircase and imagined rats and snakes below the unoccupied house.

"Are you feeling brave?" he asked. His eyes shone with excitement as he grabbed the oil lamp from the table and lit it with one of his matches. He didn't wait for her reply before descending the stairs.

Erin wasn't sure what would be worse, waiting alone in someone else's cabin or following Bain into the cool dark cellar. She took a deep breath and started down the stairs. "There better not be any spiders," she called as she caught up to the torch light.

The walls were made of the same gray and white granite as

the stairs. Specks of mineral reflected in the lamplight on the marbled walls. She touched the cold, flat wall. It felt as smooth as ice. It unexpectedly sparked a memory, like she had been here before. But before she could grasp it, it was gone.

She couldn't help but notice that each step was carved with straight, perfectly squared edges. It was nothing like the cement steps that led down to the coal room in her house.

Bain's voice pierced the silence when he called up to her. "There are forty-nine steps! That's a pretty big cellar."

"What do you think they keep down here?" She hoped she sounded braver than she felt.

Before she made it to the last step, Bain lit several torches that lined the hallway. At least she would be able to see where they were going. Already, she could see a hallway extending impossibly far with openings leading into even more corridors.

"It looks like an underground maze," he said.

"I wonder who lives here. Maybe they actually live underground." It seemed reasonable enough. There was far more room under the house than above.

Down the hall just a few feet from the stairs stood a grand-looking entrance. It was the only door in sight. The tall double doors bore the same exquisite carving as the front of the cottage. Above the door, swirling letters formed words carved in several languages.

Erin recognized the German and French, but was only sure of the one in English. " 'Room of Truth,' " she read out loud. "What is that supposed to mean?"

" 'To enter here you must tell a truth. The inner eye sees only truth. What do you wish to see?' " Bain read. "Maybe we should knock."

"*Now* you want to knock?"

"Maybe you have to tell the door what you wish to see if you want to enter." He continued as if he hadn't heard her.

"You can't be serious. We're going to talk to the door?" But even as she spoke, an odd sensation enveloped her. The cool stone cellar no longer seemed imposing, but like something she had

seen in a dream. Even the door was tugging at a lost memory. How did she know this place?

She stepped forward and closed her eyes. "I wish to see the truth," she spoke in an even tone. She wasn't sure why she knew what to say, but it all was so familiar.

The towering double doors opened. She stepped inside the cavernous room, and the doors immediately closed behind her. The walls were the same granite stone as the stairwell had been. The large room was empty with the exception of a podium that stood in the center. On it sat a large leather bound book. The cover was decorated in scrolls and patterns similar to the ones on the house and door. Letters moved before her eyes, and suddenly the cover read *The Book of Knowledge.*

Just then the doors swung slowly open and Bain stepped into the room. His broad grin clearly marked how pleased he was to have won the contest with the door.

"Bain, what happened to you? You're glowing white!"

"What are you talking about? I'm not glowing, but that book is. Do you see that? It's shining bright blue! How is it doing that?" He walked over to the table.

She couldn't keep her eyes off of him; a white halo engulfed his whole body. What had that door done to him? She checked the book to see if it had started to glow, but it sat there just as before, a beautiful brown leather book.

"Why do you think it's glowing like that?" he asked. "Do you think this place is radioactive or something?"

"I can't see anything coming off the book, but you are still glowing white. Can't you see yourself?" She was starting to wonder what was wrong with both of them. She spotted a mirror on the far wall and grabbed Bain's arm. "Come look at yourself," she insisted.

She pulled him in front of the mirror and watched his face. He did seem to look worried.

"I look the same, Erin. Something must have happened to us when we came into the room. I'm not sure what, but we'll figure it out." He put his arm around her shoulder. "Don't worry, I'll

still love you even if you do think I'm a glowworm."

"Maybe we should check out the book."

"At least we won't need a flashlight to read it. It has its own supercharged light."

She tried to give him a stern look, but he seemed convinced. Shrugging, she touched the butter soft cover and pulled it open. It seemed to set itself open to the first page.

> *You have entered into the first steps of becoming a new creature.*
>
> *Only truth will allow you to enter here.*
>
> *An honest heart is the only key to opening this book and new doors.*
>
> *The gifts you received in this room are yours to prove.*
>
> *Choose wisely.*
>
> *We are seeking the pure in heart. Your journey begins.*

She tried to turn the page, but it was as if it had turned to stone. She couldn't even lift a corner.

Chapter Two

BUTTERFLIES

THEY WERE PANTING FROM THE exertion of scaling the tall stairs at top speed. Even if it was the coolest thing Bain had ever seen, he had agreed with Erin about being officially freaked out. And there was only so much trespassing he was willing to do in one day.

"Please tell me you can see the Christmas lights, too," Bain said as they stepped back out into the sunshine. He craned his neck to get a better look at the trees towering overhead.

"Sorry, you're the only Christmas light I can see." Erin was still looking at him funny. She didn't seem to believe him. He wasn't sure why he could see little lights either.

He jogged to one of the trees and started climbing. After ascending to a sturdy limb, he crawled out a little ways and straddled the branch. There, on a leaf, sat a tiny figure with wings. A soft blue glow surrounded the delicate girl wearing a deep blue gown and rich blue and black butterfly wings. She stared at him with her large dark blue eyes, her shiny black hair reaching past her wings.

"Salutations, youngling. You are the first of your kind to see our world in many years." Her voice sounded like little bells as she spoke.

"I'm Bain," he answered. He couldn't think of anything to say. Even though he could see her with his own eyes, it seemed

impossible that something like this could exist. A tiny girl with butterfly wings. And the glow around her was so much like the book. He was struck with wonder that such a thing could exist, and that he could see their lights but Erin couldn't. As he glanced around, he could see different colors glowing through the trees. Could every glow be another one of these tiny creatures?

The tiny girl interrupted his thoughts. "Tread carefully then, Bain—your world has changed." Then, she flitted high into the air.

"Wait!" he called.

She fluttered closer and looked at him with her exotic blue eyes.

"What is your name?" he asked.

"We have been called many things over the centuries—fairies, pixies, and sometimes other less attractive things. We call ourselves the älvor. But my name is Adarae." Her voice sang as she spoke. She lifted off again and was suddenly out of sight.

He had made it back to the yard where Erin waited, excited about his latest discovery.

He looked up again at the colorful lights that dotted the branches. "Do you think every single little light in these trees is another fairy? Or I guess they call themselves älvor."

"I don't know. I still can't see any lights, Bain."

He watched her search the trees and wondered why she couldn't see the obvious lights. The balls of light illuminated in spite of the sun shining.

"Do you think I could see one up close?" she asked.

"I don't know. Let's see what we can do."

He walked around looking for the closest glow. He only had to wander into the trees a short distance. "Right there, in the bush." He pointed out an orange glow.

"Are you sure? All I see is a monarch butterfly."

They stepped closer and Erin gasped.

Bain smiled as the details of a tiny girl came into view. She had short red hair and golden brown eyes. Her gown seemed to be made of an autumn leaf and matched the wings that sprouted from her back.

"We respectfully request to speak with you," Bain said as he drew slightly closer.

The little älvor inspected them both carefully. "You may speak youngling." Her voice rang like a small melody.

"Do you know who lives in this cottage?" Erin asked, pointing back to the wooden art.

"It is not a home to anyone now, except perhaps to you," the älvor said in a harp-like voice.

"Do you know who built it?" she pressed.

The orange and black wings blurred as she flitted from leaf to leaf. "I know many things youngling. I believe your journey has only begun." With that she darted over their heads and then quickly out of sight.

All at once the sky filled with glowing butterflies, and they rushed over the treetops and out of sight. Not a single glow remained in the forest.

"I think we should head back home. I don't think they want to talk right now; they all kind of left," Bain said. He was disappointed that he wouldn't be able to approach another one of the strange butterflies. Talking to them felt so surreal. He was surprised to hear the words that had popped out of his mouth when he first saw them. He hadn't talked to anyone like that in his whole life. But somehow he just knew what to say.

"Are you sure?" Erin asked as she looked again through the trees.

"Trust me. They aren't here anymore. I'm kind of surprised you want to stay. Aren't you afraid of getting caught?" Bain watched her look through the trees. Sometimes he was surprised at what she would go along with. Maybe she was more afraid of being alone than of getting caught doing something wrong.

As they approached their home, they could see Mrs. Hammel

next door mowing her lawn. She waved at them and cut the engine.

"Hello Mrs. Hammel!" Erin called. Mrs. Hammel was already halfway to them through her enormous green lawn. Erin noticed the white aura that surrounded Mrs. Hammel just as it did Bain. She wondered if everyone she saw was going to glow white from now on.

"You kids have big plans for your summer?" Mrs. Hammel asked with a bright smile.

"We thought we would hike around a bit. Soak in a little sunshine," Bain answered.

Erin watched as Bain's aura descended to a barely misted gray. It was bad enough to see the glow, but now it seemed to change colors.

"Is that what you did today?" Mrs. Hammel eyed Bain's backpack.

"Yeah. We tried out a new trail. I think we're going back again tomorrow. We marked out the trees, so it should be pretty easy to find."

"Just watch out for the weather. I don't want to have you two stuck out in a lightning storm," she said. "I see that Jessie is still out. I made some bread today and there is really nothing better than fresh warm bread with butter and homemade raspberry jam. I won't be seeing Stan until later tonight and it would be such a shame eating it all alone. You two go on home, and I'll meet you there."

After dinner they sat around the table laughing and talking. Mrs. Hammel had so many stories to tell that most of the time Erin and Bain just sat back and listened and laughed as she filled the silence with her tales.

The whole thing seemed too normal for the kind of day they had just had. And there was no way she could tell Mrs. Hammel about it. She could only imagine what she would say. "Yeah, today we broke into a cottage and found a seriously big cellar. Then we went outside to find little fairies in the trees. By the way, did you know you glowed white?" Erin silently did the dishes.

"Well, I better finish the lawn before it gets dark," Mrs. Hammel said after the dishes were cleaned up. "Just give me a call if you need anything."

Erin shut the door behind Mrs. Hammel and sighed as she sank to the floor. She leaned back against the door and played the day over in her mind. If Bain hadn't been there too, she would have been sure she had dreamed the whole thing. She closed her eyes and tried to think.

"Do you want to talk about it?" Bain asked. He sat on the steps next to her. He twisted a loose thread on his shirt while he waited.

"Mrs. Hammel glows white too," she said.

"I almost forgot about that. Ever since we left the cottage, I haven't seen anything glow," he answered. "I've been trying to figure that out."

"I think I have an idea. I have a little test for you. Tell me something that's not true, make up some kind of lie."

"Okay. Grandpa Jessie eats ice cream for breakfast almost everyday," he said with a perfectly innocent expression.

She watched as the white glow around him darkened into a misty gray. "You turned gray instead of white. Now I will always know if you're telling the truth."

"I'm hoping that's a good thing," he said thoughtfully. His aura turned bright white again.

"What about you? What's the deal with the book and the fairies? Why do they glow for you?"

"I don't know," he answered as he weaved the string around his fingers.

She thought about it for a moment. "What did you tell the door you wanted to see?"

"I wish to see that which I have never been able to see before," he answered. "I wasn't entirely sure what I meant by that, though. It seemed like there could be so many possibilities."

"Well, you could see the älvor. That might be· the coolest thing I've ever seen. I want to go back. Do you really think we can? It seems impossible that no one lives there."

"Well, I'm going with what the little orange fairy said."

"Do you think that will hold up in a court of law?"

"You never know. Maybe we can go first thing in the morning. I'll pack plenty of food. We could spend all day there. I wonder what else there is downstairs."

"Just let me sleep long enough that I don't have to sleep walk all the way there," she said as she stood up.

"Only halfway there," he answered before bounding up the stairs.

It was a while before Erin's restless mind stopped running through the possibilities, and she could finally fall asleep. Dreams of butterfly-winged fairies in different colors filled her mind before other dreams of gray and white auras took their place. As her mind swirled around the memories, she felt someone take her hand. Her eyes blinked open to see Bain dressed and smiling at her. He already had his backpack on.

Chapter Three

RIGHT, A FAIRY GODMOTHER

ERIN COULDN'T BELIEVE THEY WERE really going back. What were they thinking? Even though the curiosity was killing her, her logical side was trying to right the situation. They really had no business going inside a stranger's cabin. And the auras she could now see around Mrs. Hammel and her brother were not exactly settling either.

She watched Bain as the trees opened up to the clearing. "Do you see the älvor?"

"I've been watching for them our whole hike, and this is the only place I've seen their light," he answered. "There are so many of them, probably hundreds, maybe more."

She wished she could see them too from this far away. As it was, she could only detect brushes of color against the trees and sky.

"Let's go in," he called as he raced to the cottage.

She sprinted to catch up with him. He was faster, but she wasn't going to let him off the hook without a fight. He started laughing, and it slowed him down just enough for her to seize the opportunity for a heated sprint. He managed to open the door just in time for her momentum to carry her into the pine room.

"Ah!" She tried to catch her breath and stifle a scream.

In one of the sculpted wooden chairs sat a tall, exquisite lady. Her dark chocolate brown hair came down to her elbows as she sat watching them expectantly. She wore an orange-red gown trimmed in gold that fell to her wrists and feet. Her brown eyes flecked with green looked much like the älvor's in their exotic shape, but showed soft welcoming light as she looked at them. In front of her sat the small table with a pitcher of lemonade and three glasses.

"Please sit down," the elegant stranger invited in a melodic tone.

Erin was at a loss for words as she fumbled for a chair facing the table of lemonade. She watched the lady pour lemonade into the glasses and then sit back with a glass in her hand.

"I am Ella. Please feel free to join me in refreshment," she said and drank some of the lemonade.

"Uh, I hope we didn't intrude," Erin said.

"Not at all," said the lady with a smile. Her aura remained white.

"I'm Bain, and this is Erin," Bain started as he took a glass from the table. After a few quick gulps he continued. "We didn't think anyone lived here. We came yesterday and no one was here. We thought we would come see it again."

"Of course," the lady said. "That is why I am here."

"So, do you live here?" Erin asked. The lady's white glow had not faltered yet.

She laughed softly and shook her head. "It might be hard to explain who I am, but perhaps the easiest way is to say that I am your Fairy Godmother." She sipped her lemonade again. "But you may call me Ella."

"Do you mean like Cinderella's fairy godmother?" Erin asked. As long as they were speaking in fairy tales, she may at least continue the conversation. Not that she was going to believe any of this.

"The very same, although they do get the story mixed up a bit. I don't believe I ever sang 'Bippety Boppety Boo.' And her name, well, I think they confuse it with my own. Her name was Amerelle—such a lovely girl," Ella said.

Bain finally spoke again. "So, if the fairies outside call

themselves the älvor, why do you call yourself the Fairy Godmother? And why are you our Godmother? I thought you had to be in utter distress or something to get one."

Erin tried not to laugh. It was too perfect that someone wanted to dress up to be a Fairy Godmother, but to watch Bain sit there and have a perfectly normal conversation with her was too much. *Utter distress.* She smiled. That was a good one.

"Now that is a very revealing question indeed," Ella said and she surveyed them carefully. "There is much about this world that you are about to discover. I will start by answering your question in the most basic way.

"First, I am your Godmother because I was given charge over you just after you passed the test of the door. And as for the fairy part, that is much more complicated. The fairies you have already met are called the älvor. I am an älva and our men are called the älv.

"The centuries and languages have changed what we are called in your world. You know the älvor as fairies in your land. I was given a special ability, a rare gift from them. It allows me freedom that others of my kind do not have. This gift from the älvor, or fairies, grants me the title of Fairy Godmother." She sipped her lemonade.

"Let me get this straight," Bain continued. "You are our Fairy Godmother?"

She nodded. She made the whole exchange seem perfectly normal.

"You were given some special power from the älvor that makes you different from everyone else?" he asked.

Ella nodded again.

"You were saying something about others of your kind. What exactly is an älva or älv?" he asked.

"That is for you to find out one step at a time, Bain. Although I think it will not take you long with your sharp mind," she answered.

Erin was impressed that Bain did not give up so easily. And that he could carry on the conversation without even a hint of sarcasm. But Ella did look impressive. Erin had never seen anyone so intimidatingly beautiful.

"Can you tell me why the älvor and the book glow for me but not for Erin?" Bain asked.

This made Erin's head come up. For some reason that question made everything seem real. The glow that she could see around Bain and this lady were impossible to deny. It was the contradiction to her hope that maybe none of this was real. She swallowed and tried to steel herself for the answer. She wasn't sure she was ready to hear it.

"And I presume you detect a glow from me as well," Ella said as she looked penetratingly into Bain's eyes. "You have discovered a gift that was given to you from the Room of Truth. It seems that you are able to see the aura of magic.

"Anything that is of magic will show itself to you with its own light. It is a rare and valuable gift. You should guard it well. It will serve you in ways you can only begin to imagine." She set her glass on the table.

"Now that you have passed the test of the door, none but the two of you from your world can enter here. Other humans will not be able to see this house. It is protected by a spell that allows only a few to enter. As your Fairy Godmother, I have passage. There will be others, as well, on occasion.

"For now, your quest is to seek out the knowledge in the book and to find the gifts behind the doors. Also, this house belongs to you as long as you are in training here. Feel free to use it at your discretion."

Erin watched as Ella stood. Her gown sparkled in the light and her tall, slender frame was imposing.

"One more thing before I depart. Our world now knows of you. There will be those wishing to persuade you to join their side. Be aware and be wise," Ella said. She touched the pitcher of lemonade, and it disappeared along with the glass she had been drinking from. "Take care until I see you again."

"Wait!" Erin called. "Why us? What is so special about us that we can be here? And the fairies. Can everyone see them?

Why haven't I ever seen them before?"

"Erin, there is much about you that you are only beginning to understand. You have always been able to see the älvor. They have just stayed far enough from you to keep you from recognizing the truth. But since you were both mere babies, you could see them. There is something special about the two of you, something that you were born with. For now, that is all you need know." She opened the door and left them sitting in the room alone.

Erin watched the empty doorway. "Can you believe that? Do you really think she is a Fairy Godmother?"

Bain just smiled back at her and shrugged. "I really want to see that book again." He lit the lantern and opened the trap door.

Chapter Four

THE STEEL DOOR

It was unsettling how the book had changed from stone back to the aged pages it was when Erin first saw it. Now she reached out with trembling fingers and turned a yellowing parchment page while Bain hovered close by. Erin caught her breath as, once again, the book seemed to transform into stone as the page settled open.

Speed and strength are yours to find.
Choose the door that greets you with steel,
For, like steel, you shall be strong.
Take heed to learn much from this room and its gift.

Bain was out the door in seconds. He seemed completely unaffected by the strange book. Erin chased after him as the hallway opened into a labyrinth. After a while they started taking turns guessing directions. This time there were no trees to mark the way back. It seemed like it would be a miracle if they didn't get lost in the underground maze.

Along one of the long halls, a metal door seemed to suddenly materialize. Erin was sure she didn't see it until they were just beside it. The steel door was fairly plain. There were no scrolls to grace the front. Metal rivets were the only feature other than the cold, flat gray surface. Bain turned the handle, and they stepped into the room.

Even with so many surprises in the last day and a half, she felt overwhelmed with what lay before them. The room stretched out impossibly large. It could have easily fit the pumpkin patch, the corn field, and most of the potato fields that landscaped the ground near her home, not to mention half of the village. And the ceiling suggested that a hill would have fit under its trusses. She walked into the room where the rubberized floor bounced ever so slightly with each step.

"Can you believe this?" she asked.

"It's pretty cool. I think there's an archery range over here." He was already headed towards the shelves of large bows.

They found a complete archery field with equipment and targets. Erin picked up a bow and some arrows and set out to test the targets. She had always wanted to try it out. She had only ever watched others, but the bow felt natural in her hands.

Bain just stood and watched her. "This place is so big."

She nodded and let the arrow spring from her bow again. It jetted towards the target and embedded itself nearly at the center. Pleased with herself, she smiled and placed another arrow onto the bow.

"I'll leave you to it then," Bain said.

She couldn't help but stare as he plunged through the open room. He ran almost daily, but it was never like this. It seemed as though he was flying over the ground, and she was certain his speed was more like a car than a human. When he reached the other side of the room, she saw him laugh out loud.

He bounded toward the open space ahead. He performed a round-off from which he began to fly high through the air. As his feet touched the ground again, he pushed off and shot his hands above his head. Now it seemed that time itself had slowed. She watched as he controlled every angle while sailing backwards through the air. As he pushed against the floor, he knew precisely what to do to land in a standing position on both feet. He made it look too easy. And yet, for as long as she had known him, he had never done anything like this before. She couldn't even get him to do a cartwheel with straight legs. She watched as he tried out a few new combinations to cross the room to her.

"Do you want to see the rest of the room?" he called as he approached her at his newfound speed.

"Sure," she answered, and set her bow back on the shelf.

"Race you to the other side!" he called, and set out in a full sprint.

Erin felt a jolt as Bain seemed to disappear beside her. She raced after him. Her legs pumped impossibly fast, and as she pushed them harder, they responded effortlessly. Air rushed past her ears and the room rushed by. She laughed as she pounded through the incredible speed. Maybe she would even be able to outrun Bain for once. She concentrated on the wall ahead and it rushed at her with impossible speed. It seemed instantaneous that she was there, and she was relieved that she could stop before she slammed into the brick wall.

"Tied," he said, sounding a little disappointed. "I thought I had you beat for sure!"

"Can you believe that?" She laughed again as she realized that she was not even out of breath.

She followed him to the opposite side of the room where they found swords and fencing gear with an oversized jungle gym nearby. It seemed that this structure was as big as ten houses sprawled next to each other. And it was so tall. The towering trees where she lived were the only thing that compared to its staggering height

They couldn't resist climbing aboard and soon games of tag and keep-off-the-ground followed. Having their exaggerated speed and strength quickly diminished the size factor in the equipment. The monkey bars were spaced so far apart that they would have been impossible to reach before, but now they almost flew between each bar as they propelled themselves along. The game escalated into an all-day event.

"You're it!" Bain called before disappearing to the rafters above.

"Not for long, monkey boy!" Erin laughed as she swung

herself over the rail and caught him off guard on the other side of the complex. She grabbed at his arms, "Okay! I think that's the end of this one."

They looked out from the second story height of the jungle gym at the sprawling room.

"What time is it?" Erin asked. She was sure they had been here for hours. She wanted to be sure they made it home for dinner so Mrs. Hammel didn't worry about them.

Bain tapped the glass on his watch. "It's broken. My watch says 11:30 and that's what time we got here. The second hand isn't moving either." He pulled his watch off and inspected it. "I guess we should go. We can come back tomorrow. There's still so much here we haven't even seen yet."

"Do you remember how to get back to the stairs?" she asked. She knew she couldn't find her way in the twisting halls.

"No worries," he said, and headed for the metal door.

Chapter Five

TIME STANDS STILL

ERIN WAS HAPPY TO SEE that the rocky path and the branches no longer posed a threat to her as they headed for home. "I might have to start running with you in the mornings," she called. "I never knew it could be this much fun!"

"I didn't either. I think we just ran a couple four minute miles," he said when they reached the house. "We better not go much faster than that or people will notice. Still, I could run this fast all day."

"Bain, this is super weird," Erin began as they came into the kitchen. "Did you notice the time?"

"I've been trying to figure that out too. My watch didn't work in the cottage, but as soon as we left it started working again. Now it is exactly the same time as the house."

She picked up the phone. It always showed the correct time. It too agreed with the house. She sat down at the kitchen table and watched Bain pace the kitchen.

"Time just stops," he finally said. "We go in the cottage, and time stops until we come out."

"Do you really think so?" she asked. But a warm rush came over her and somehow she knew it was true. "You're right. I know it. I can't explain why, but when you said that, it's just true."

"Maybe that's part of your gift too," he said as he pulled up a chair across from her. "Maybe you know if someone is telling the truth even when it's just a guess. That is definitely cool."

"We still have all day."

"Do you think we could spend a week there and no one would even know?" he asked. He got up and started rummaging through the fridge.

"Sounds really crazy." But she was considering the implications. "This could be the longest summer in the history of time."

"If we do want to spend more time there, we definitely need more food." He was still standing there with the refrigerator door open. "We should go to the store and buy some supplies. I wonder how well the ice chest at the cottage works." In his hand was rolled up lunch meat with mustard inside.

She smiled. It was fitting that his number one concern was food. "Okay, but we're going to need the wagon if you plan on bringing a bunch of stuff."

"You think it might look conspicuous if I just balance everything on top of my head?" Bain smiled. "I probably could, you know."

"I think we'll have to save that trick for later."

The local store was really more like an over-sized gas station that sold groceries. When Grandpa Jessie took them grocery shopping on the weekends, they had to drive for forty-five minutes to get to the nearest town. They bought most of their fruits and vegetables from the little stands the local farmers set up.

As they walked through the doors, Erin was instantly aware of the other people in the store. She had grown so accustomed to Bain's white aura that she didn't notice it that much anymore. Here she observed various shades of gray. Some were almost white, while others looked more like a storm cloud. She tried not to stare at people while she noted the gray shades that surrounded them. No two were exactly the same. She just felt disappointed that Bain's was the only white aura to be found.

It was puzzling to determine the cause of the shades of gray. She watched the other shoppers. They seemed very normal, just picking up milk, or comparing prices for the bread, nothing out of the ordinary. She was so distracted that she didn't notice that Bain had already taken his load to the check-out counter.

They filled the wagon with goods and started back down the road. She explained the experience with the shaded auras to Bain and he promised to think about it. When they reached the side street, they broke into a run. The wagon didn't slow them down. It seemed like only a few minutes before they reached their neighborhood. Erin had to remind Bain to walk at a regular speed.

"There was something else that I have been trying to figure out," she said, then took another bite of her orange popsicle. "When we were talking to that älvor yesterday, I couldn't see her aura at all. Why do you think that is?"

He looked over to her. "There's a lot I don't know, but we can guess around. I've been thinking about the people in the store though. Let's say that the auras you detect tell the truth from the lies. That much we're pretty sure of. What if someone has told quite a few lies? Would that change the color of their aura even when they aren't lying at the moment?

"And could there be other things that change your aura? I bet anything you do wrong affects it. But you must be able to make it white again, like when you try to right your wrongs. That's the only reason mine could be white. I know I'm not perfect. And you said that Mrs. Hammel glowed white too. I guess she's practically perfect though." He was kicking a rock back and forth on the street as they walked.

"You're right," she said staring at him. "Don't let it go to your head though. If it weren't for me you wouldn't know for sure."

"Hey, you're the one with the gift. I don't think I would want it. I wouldn't want to know just how good and bad everyone is." He kicked the rock and it flew into the air. "Oops. I didn't mean to kick it all the way to the hills. Did you see that?"

"I guess you don't know your own strength."

He flexed his arms and she rolled her eyes.

"But it can be pretty distracting, the glowing." She tried to bring the conversation back around. "What do you think about the älvor? You guessed everything else right so far."

"Sorry, still not sure. Maybe they're immune to you," he looked at her with a crooked smile.

"Great!" she said, and stopped walking.

"What?"

"You're right, again," she muttered. "How do you do that?"

"I must be a genius." He smiled back at her.

"Don't worry, you're not," she countered. She stopped with her mouth gaping open. "Do you see something in our yard?"

"What do you mean?"

"I could have sworn there was a huge mountain lion. It just ran through our front lawn and out towards the trees."

"Should we follow it?"

"Are you kidding? And get ourselves killed? I have never seen anything that big before. And fast. That thing could run as fast as us."

"Nothing can run that fast. You must be seeing things."

"Right," she answered. But she wasn't convinced. Whatever it was had streaked so fast across their lawn that she would have missed it if she hadn't been looking at just the right moment. Maybe a cheetah could move that fast, but this thing was definitely not a cheetah.

Chapter Six

SWORDPLAY

ERIN WATCHED THE CONVERSATION BETWEEN Bain and Adarae. She sat quietly, still trying to get over her latest dream. Last night was filled with the sound of screaming and the view of an airplane rocketing towards a vast ocean. It was the same short dream running over and over again in her head.

There was a lady who kept yelling, "No! Not Robert! You can't take him from me!" In her dream she never got to see the lady's face, only the bright auburn curls flying around her as they fell to the earth. Robert was her father's name.

Her thoughts were interrupted by Bain's voice. "The book said we are becoming new creatures. What is it that we're supposed to become?"

Adarae smiled. "This you must work out on your own. But you have done well so far." With that she fluttered up into the trees and out of their view.

As they headed to the steel door, the underground maze didn't seem as mysterious. But Erin still wasn't entirely sure what to make of everything. When the blue fairy talked to Bain, it seemed like a miracle all over again. Was she ever going to get used to this? And now they were treating the cabin like a second home, which would be extremely cool, but still really strange. She was pretty sure she wasn't going to tell Grandpa Jessie or Mrs. Hammel about this. Even with permission from their so-called Fairy Godmother, it still seemed like trespassing. Not that Bain seemed to share that sentiment.

When they opened the steel door, the gigantic room seemed just as amazing as it was the day before.

Erin grabbed Bain's hand.

"Bain," she whispered. "There's someone here."

A tall man stood a little ways off in the room and looked as though he had been waiting for them. She watched the stranger with his misty aura that hung like a shaded light around him. It wasn't as dark as some of the shoppers at the store, but it couldn't compare to the brilliant aura around her brother.

Bain gently tugged on her hand, and they made their approach. The stranger gave no indication that he would come to them.

She studied the man as they cautiously closed the distance. The stranger stood taller than Bain by at least six inches, and he looked to be about twenty years old. His hair was longer and fell in honey brown waves around his shoulders. Although his jaw seemed set and angular, his eyes twinkled with amusement.

He bowed when they finally stood before him. It was hard to define how he appeared different from other people. Maybe it was how angular his features were, or perhaps the uncanny grace even the smallest moves were executed with. He certainly wasn't dressed in ordinary clothes either. His top was a muted green tunic that laced in the front. His pants were almost ordinary, but his boots were unlike anything she had seen before with unfamiliar designs in the leather.

"Greetings. I have been sent to oversee some of your training here." He reached out his hand to Bain and shook hands. "My name is Agnar," he said, and took Erin's hand and quickly kissed her fingers.

Erin's cheeks burned in embarrassment.

Agnar did not seem to notice and went on smoothly. "I am a sword master. We will be studying swordplay from the rudimentary to the subtle. I expect you have already discovered their location."

She nodded glancing at Bain.

"Shall we then?" he said, and then suddenly disappeared.

It took a second to realize that he was running towards the jungle gym complex. Then, with a start, Erin remembered her own abilities as Bain tugged on her arm and raced after him.

Agnar began the lesson by introducing the swords and their uses. He showed them the proper ways to hold and carry each weapon.

Erin was fascinated but almost horrified when Agnar explained the purposes of each kind. She didn't feel compelled to use the instruments against any living creature. The worry grew when he announced that they were ready to learn defensive movements.

"What do we need to use swords for?" she finally had the courage to ask.

Agnar stepped towards her, brandishing a long, slender blade. "To keep you safe. One must not enter our world in ignorance. Why don't you start with this," he said, handing her the sword.

They began by practicing movements in the air aimed at imaginary attacks. She was pleased that her arm did not grow tired as she swung the sword forcefully in the patterns he described.

Agnar demonstrated footwork, and then had them practice using both the sword and their feet. Erin thought it had looked easy in the movies, but now she realized that speed and strength alone was not enough to make her good with these weapons. She watched her twin. His eyes were full of excitement as he advanced through the series of movements. He was clearly enjoying the lesson and she could see that he had a quicker blade than she did. The sword was a blur as he sliced the air and danced around the room.

"I believe you are ready for a more fitting challenge," Agnar said. He jumped and twirled so that he landed on the edge of a platform jetting from the complex next to them. Using a sword, he waved at the surrounding equipment. "Try your hand here."

She nodded and jumped onto the first level. She tried out

some of the moves Agnar taught them, but mostly she couldn't help but watch Bain.

It seemed that for him the jungle gym had become a formidable playground. He traversed its levels while slashing his sword at invisible enemies, and Erin couldn't help but notice that Bain fought like a lion as he drilled the defenses with his blade. He proved himself equal to the imaginary counter attacks Agnar explained. There was a certain power that handling the sword gave him. He looked invincible as he climbed higher and higher.

He took a few steps and flipped high into the air, landing on the other side and facing his same imaginary opponent. Where he came up with this stuff, she couldn't imagine. She tried a few moves with the sword while purposely keeping up with the levels he had covered.

She gasped as he landed a back flip from the floor above only to find Agnar suddenly waiting in front of him, sword at the ready. Now Bain had a real sword to defend against as they sparred. Erin was sure Agnar was going easy on him. He gave instruction as they went, and before long Bain was learning counter attacks.

It felt unnerving to see her twin fighting with a sword. She watched as the sparring intensified and Agnar increased his speed and tactics. It finally happened, though, that Bain was overtaken.

In a last-ditch attempt, Bain rolled off the level and dropped three flights, landing on his feet like a cat. He grabbed his ankle and fell to his side.

"Very good," Agnar said as caught up to Bain. "But you can't expect to land that quite yet. Maybe after a while you could pull that off, but for now you might think about having some sense about your tactics."

"Right," Bain muttered, holding his ankle. Already it was beginning to swell.

"Here," Agnar said, pulling something from his pouch. He placed a leaf over Bain's ankle and held it there. "It is an exarionne leaf. If you keep that on it for a while, you should find yourself as good as new in no time."

"Thanks," Bain answered, grimacing.

Agnar began to pace in front of the jungle gym. "You will be expected to practice swordplay until you have mastered basic skills in attack and defense. You must also learn how to disarm your opponent." He stopped pacing and winked at Erin. "It is considered a bit underhanded but can come in handy at surprising moments."

He walked around the weapons as if inspecting them. "I had forgotten how crude these training swords are. I shall have to bring my own personal blade next time for you to see. You will never wish to use these hunks of steel after that."

"Who are we preparing to fight?" Erin asked. She still felt queasy about attacking anything real and alive, and she wasn't very excited about Bain's injury either.

"Your future is not mine to predict. But learning to use a blade is considered as much etiquette as properly dining with a knife and fork. It is a necessary skill in your transformation."

Then he turned to Bain. "It should not surprise me that you have embraced swordplay with such valiance. It will bring me great pleasure to teach you all I know. It is up to you, however, to determine how you will use each skill, and ultimately, that is what determines your ability." He twirled a sword in the air and landed it back on the rack. "How is the ankle?"

Bain stood up and tested his foot experimentally. "It's better. Really better." He walked a few paces. "I need to get a stash of those leaves. They could really come in handy."

Agnar nodded. "I shall take my leave for now. We are always aware of your presence in this hall, so don't be too surprised when I drop in on you again." With that he bowed gracefully and darted through the room and out the steel door, leaving the twins staring.

"I don't know about you, but I'm starving," Bain said. He raced to the door before Erin could respond.

Chapter Seven

RULES

"I THINK HE'S ALL RIGHT," Bain said with confidence. "He has a really cool magic glow. It's this sage green or something. I wonder if he even knows that."

"Well, he is amazing with the sword. I don't think I would want to be on the wrong side of him." Erin pulled the last bits of crusts apart from her sandwich. It still bothered her that she was required to learn to use a sword. Why did she need to know how to fight? If they were learning something like karate, she would understand. Self-defense is smart. But swords can leave permanent marks. They were forged with the purpose of fighting to the death. She really didn't think she wanted to be part of something that ugly.

But then Bain looked almost powerful as he fought Agnar, and she could see the light in his eyes. He was enjoying it. It seemed he had been waiting his whole life to use one.

"That is what we are going to become," Bain said, interrupting her thoughts.

She looked up. She still hadn't committed to believing this yet, and the comment made the knot in her stomach appear again.

"Whatever he is, that's what we will be. He can run like us. He's stronger and faster though, and has skills that we lack."

"How do you do that?" she asked. The knot in her stomach

tightened, but a new sensation had overruled. It felt as though a warm rush of water flowed over her and echoed his words in her head. The feeling was stronger than it had ever been before, as if it was somehow compensating for the sinking feeling in her stomach.

"Easy, you just have to eat faster," he said as he sat down with the bag of cookies.

"No, I mean, you're right again. You've been doing that a lot today." She took a cookie and dunked it in her milk. "So we are becoming like him. Is that the same as the Fairy Godmother?"

"You rang?" Ella was suddenly in the doorway of the kitchen.

Bain blew milk out of his nose from the shock of her sudden appearance. Erin tried not to laugh at him. It was bad enough to look stupid, but to do it in front of this goddess was beyond humiliating.

"Please sit down," Erin started as she offered a chair at the table.

"I was in the neighborhood," Ella said. "I must admit I was able to overhear your conversation. I believe your question was whether Agnar was like me." She looked at the them and continued. "We are alike in many ways. We are of the same *kind*, as I explained before. He is an älv as I am an älva." She smoothed her gown over her lap. "Yet we are all different, just as all humans are different. No two are exactly the same. Not even twins." She winked at Erin.

"How long will it take to become what you are? And why us?" Erin asked. Even though she knew she had asked before, she wasn't satisfied. The questions bounded around in her head. She felt so ordinary. Couldn't they have found a more talented person to offer this amazing cottage to? Things still refused to add up in her head. And yet, none of it seemed like it could be real. No matter what her eyes saw or what her hands touched, this all seemed too impossible to be real.

"You were pure enough. Our world sensed your arrival fifteen years ago. It may seem like chance that you discovered this cottage, but it was always meant to be. You both had the disposition to explore your surroundings enough that it was only a matter of time before you found this hall. You are not the first to train, but it has been many years since a human has entered here.

"Then you passed the test of the door and became officially qualified to continue on the path to our world. You are not ordinary youth, you are chosen leaders. The potential that waits inside of you is only beginning to be discovered. The new abilities given to you are tools to enhance the gifts you have always had. These are the real gifts that we cannot give you. It is who you were before you entered here that makes this training so significant.

"And you asked how long," she continued, her hands folded delicately in her lap. "I expect you have already discovered that you can not measure time here. This training hall has been given a great many complicated spells and wards. One of them allows the inhabitants endless time while under its roof. It is a way for you to get the most out of your training without arousing suspicion.

"But for the two of you there is a catch. The spell was originally designed so that time only stopped for the one in training. There are two of you. You must consider that if one of you stopped training, time would move forward for the one outside of this cottage. Within these walls one will never grow even a minute older."

"So you are saying that it could take a really long time?" Bain asked.

"And yet, no time at all," she answered.

The conversation felt like an internal war to Erin. The knot in her stomach was competing with the compelling rush of warmth that would not stop trying to convince her that it was true. Didn't logic have a reasonable place in all of this?

"What if we don't want to become anything?" Erin asked.

"You have your choice. If you choose to end your training, you will lose your new abilities and forget everything associated with this place. But once you make the decision, it is irreversible.

You can never come back." She looked deeply into Erin's eyes, as though she could read her thoughts.

Erin felt the gravity of her choice. It could all be undone and it would be like the last two days had never happened. She was almost sure that would be better. Why they had taken it this far was beyond her. She should have talked Bain into staying home. Maybe he would have listened to her. What would Grandpa Jessie say if he knew what they were doing? She shuddered at the thought. He trusted them completely. And now they were talking to strangers and spending time in someone else's place. Not to mention the fairies.

"I will leave the two of you for now." Ella stepped out the door and was gone.

"Do you wonder what will happen to us if we just keep doing all of this?" Erin asked. "Are we doing the right thing, or are we going to end up regretting this?"

He was looking at the table deep in thought. "Well, I like it here. What's the worst thing that could happen?"

"You mean, besides breaking your leg or accidentally getting stabbed? Bain, do we even know what it means to become one of them?"

"If it means summer forever, I guess I don't really care. What are you afraid of?"

"You don't care? How can you not care about your whole future? And, yes, I guess I am afraid. What am I going to tell Grandpa Jessie when you come home mangled? We don't even know exactly what it is we're supposedly becoming. And what happens after we give up life as we know it?" Erin tried not to let the stinging tears give her away.

"Look, I'll be fine. This stuff is easy. You just need to get a grip. Maybe if you loosen up a little, you'll see the bigger picture."

"As if you have *ever* seen the bigger picture. How can you even say that? If you want the bigger picture, you're going to have to show me why any of this makes sense. The bigger picture is that somehow we have allowed ourselves to be vulnerable and naïve. How can we be sure that this is the right thing for us to do? You like the speed and the swords, but they're talking about life changes here. Are you ready to commit to something you don't even understand?"

His silence was infuriating. He wouldn't even look at her. "You choose, Bain. What's it going to be? Me or them?" She stood, waiting for any sign of reaction. Nothing. How could he be so mean? She shoved her chair and ran out the front door. Maybe she could make up those ten minutes after all.

Chapter Eight

SAYING GOOD–BYE

HE COULDN'T HELP IT. HE had rushed out the door of the cottage almost immediately after she did. There was no way he was going to let her grow even a minute older without him. Bain leaned against the trunk of a towering oak tree as he sat on the grass.

He didn't know if she was going to forgive him, and he wasn't ready to say sorry yet. He loved this place. It felt so good to be here. And he loved the älvor. He looked up to see their glowing light surrounding him like stars. He would have a hard time giving that up forever.

And the speed was so fantastic, the sword practice amazing, and there was still more to come. How could they just turn their backs on it now? The thought struck him like a dagger.

He was so preoccupied that he didn't even notice Adarae until she was sitting directly in front of him. He looked at her perfect deep blue wings. It seemed like a part of him might die if he could never see an älvor again.

"You are troubled, youngling," Adarae began. She settled herself on the grass. "Ultimately you will decide not only your fate, but many others. We have been waiting for you for many years. The way may be hard, but it will be worth much in the end."

"I don't know if Erin is ready for this," he began. He wasn't sure why he was feeling choked up. He knew that he would feel a deep regret if they turned their backs on this. Something about this place made him feel whole, like the self inside of him that had been waiting all his life to be found. Would anything else in his life ever bring him this feeling? He doubted it.

"Adarae, if this is the last time I can see you, I want you to know that it has been great knowing you. Even if I am forced to forget we ever met, I am sure a part of you will live in some corner of my mind forever." He looked back down at the grass. It was hard saying good-bye. But if they left the cottage today and never returned, he might not have another chance. He just wished it wouldn't be so.

"Bain," Adarae said in a soft, beautiful voice, "things will work out as they should. Let your heart lead you. That is how the right path will be found. It is a rare gift to have a twin. There are very precious few in our world." She fluttered to his hand and kissed it before darting into the sky.

He watched her fly away and marveled at the älvor's presence. Had they always been here in the woods just a little ways from his home? Was it possible that the butterflies he had seen in his yard were perhaps not always butterflies?

They had probably watched over the two of them all these years. He had only ever seen them from a distance, and without the magical glow around them, he suspected they looked like ordinary butterflies.

A memory flashed through his mind of being very young and racing around the yard with Erin, chasing butterflies high over their heads. It had probably always been the älvor. He just couldn't believe that he could have gone all these years without realizing what they really were. But all his life, he could never get very close to a butterfly. They were always flying out of reach and just far enough away that all he saw was their colorful wings.

He thought of Ella and her words. *Chosen leaders.* The idea escaped him. He couldn't imagine what he would ever lead. And yet, this place felt right. It was strange and new, but still comfortable and good.

But it was more than that. He felt like his life had suddenly begun, and he was thirsty for the knowledge and experiences that were sure to come. He had never felt so alive and so himself at the same time. It was all there inside of him, and he knew there was more, he just needed this place to help bring it out.

He looked over at Erin sleeping peacefully on the grass. Somehow, she had managed to fall asleep after giving him the silent treatment for most of the afternoon. He was pretty sure she was still mad at him. She was probably waiting for the apology he wasn't going to give.

He had never had to choose between her and anything else before. He always did what he wanted, and it worked out. But the feeling started tugging at him. It would come down to her. He would give his life for her, so giving this up should be no different.

Chapter Nine

JUST A DREAM

ERIN FOUND HERSELF IN A city with masses of beings. The älvor were there, but there were also so many people. As far as she could see, buildings and people filled the land. She walked around observing.

These people seemed to dance instead of walk. Everything they did was graceful. She realized that she had been so distracted by their elegance that she hadn't paid much attention to what any one was really doing.

People gathered around a little shop and it seemed like a perfect place to observe the intriguing community. She found a place across the street so she would be out of the way and unnoticed by the people passing by.

A little girl, who looked to be about eight years old, skipped along in front of her. Her blond curls bounced lightly behind her as she seemed to float along the road. Then she noticed something while she admired the girl's gleaming hair. As the curls bounced high and away, they exposed her ears. She watched carefully to see if she had been mistaken. The curls bounced again, and Erin was sure.

Unlike the rounded tops of the ears of everyone she had ever known, this little girl's ears were pointed. Erin knew she was staring, but the charming little girl continued to skip down the road as though she had noticed nothing at all.

Now she was trying to see everyone else's ears. How could she have missed such an obvious thing? Most everyone had longer hair that fell over their shoulders, men and women alike. She just thought that since they had such exceptional hair, it must bring them satisfaction to wear it long. Once in a while, a shopper would pause and tuck a lock of hair behind his ear, and she was able to confirm the truth.

To see this up close was incredible. All her life she had known of these people through stories. They were elves.

Then the realization crashed through her entire being. It was like the warm rushing water had turned into a turbulent waterfall and was crushing her with its weight. This is what she and her twin were in training for: to become one of them. The possibility opened her eyes in a whole new way. The ultimate truth she had been searching for was right here in front of her.

And yet, it felt impossible to be that incredibly beautiful and coordinated at the same time. She imagined it could take hundreds of years to accomplish that kind of magic on her. They were so gorgeous. Any one of them could be fantastically wealthy by doing movies or photos. There wasn't a bad looking person to be found. She noticed there were no overweight ones either, not that she worried about that for herself. A whole town full of supermodels. How could she ever fit in?

It all ended when she awoke to a soft brush against her cheek.

As she blinked her eyes in the sunlight, she remembered where she was. She gasped softly. Three älvor stood in the grass in front of her. They were a small rainbow as their wings bore colors of black, pink, green, and yellow. Each had a pattern and color variation that differentiated them from one another. They studied her with their large almond eyes. She waited for them to speak.

"Adarae has watched over you and Bain since you were very young. She has waited patiently all your lives for you to discover our world, and now she extends to you her blessing." It was a black and white fairy who addressed her.

"Thank you, but I don't really understand."

"Our *kind* does not generally associate with humans. They do not even see us for what we are. But the two of you are different. Adarae's blessing is her way of welcoming you into our colony."

Erin was still confused by the message but watched as the sky began to fill with a rainbow of wings. Many came, introducing themselves in tiny musical voices. Their jubilation carried them into the air again, and they danced around as Erin stood and circled with them. Soon the sky seemed to fill with hundreds of fairies, all of them flying around and welcoming her into their domain.

She reached her arms out with her palms toward the heavens. It was as if the sky was painted with proof of their reality. She laughed, twirling with the älvor flying all around her. The swirling colors made her feel like she was in the air. The fairies soared in every direction, laughing like bells on Christmas morning.

The sound that filled the air was so touching that she felt like laughing and crying at the same time. It felt as though her feelings had been put into a melody. Everything that had ever been in her heart was now floating around in a glorious rainbow of music. This could be the happiest moment she had ever experienced.

There were so many of them that she would never remember the names of those who flitted down to welcome her. She chided herself for being surprised when she was welcomed by male älvor as well.

She reveled in the glorious moment of the confetti-filled sky and felt that the world had stopped turning around, that time did not exist.

· · · 🦋 · · ·

"I know what I need to do now," she said. They had been sitting in the enclosed patio watching the sunset through the windows. "It is the biggest truth of all that I was given today, and now, I have no doubt what I need to do."

Bain waited quietly, seeming anxious to hear her verdict.

"I just hope we look good with pointy ears," she said. It felt as though she was leaving the world as she knew it. It was hard to fight the constant raging feeling that this was what they were supposed to do. But her responsible, logical side refused to agree. And now she had to admit that Bain was right. That seemed impossible too.

"Maybe I should let my hair grow out a little," he responded with a charming smile. "What do you think?" He pushed his hair down around his forehead and ears. "Do I look good?"

"Just don't make me call you Fabio and you'll be fine," she answered. It was hard staying mad at him when he was this happy. "Do you think our eyes will change too? Have you noticed how Agnar and Ella's eyes have a different shape? They seem bigger too, but it's hard to be sure if they really are."

"I don't know."

She looked out the window and noticed the fireflies were coming out. They bounced over the lawn here and there. Ever since she could remember, they would come out on the patio on summer nights to watch the fireflies. She loved to watch their glow bounce aimlessly around. She remembered the first time she saw one up close. They were kind of ugly and cool at the same time. From a distance, they looked nothing like the insects that they really were. The image of the butterfly-filled sky flashed through her mind. All her life the butterflies in her yard had looked nothing like the intelligent beings that they were.

"Thank you." Bain's voice broke the comfortable silence.

"For what?" she asked, watching him carefully.

"For having courage, for taking a chance, and for doing what you know is right even though it is hard. You know, I don't think I could have gone on without you. So, thank you, little sister."

"Only by ten minutes," she answered. But she couldn't help but watch his expression. He rarely talked so seriously. She could see the sincerity in his eyes and the ever-present white glow around him. How lucky she was to have such a great brother.

"You're welcome," she murmured softly, trying not to let her voice expose her emotion.

"I think a banana split is in order," he said as he stood up.

She loved the master creations he made with all the toppings they had in the house. It took quite some time to get to the actual bananas, though, as they ate through the layers of whipped cream, nuts, fruit, fudge, cookies, and ice cream.

Chapter Ten

ETERNAL BLADE

ERIN WOKE UP EARLIER THAN she usually did without an alarm clock. Bain was the morning person; she was the night owl. But this morning was different. There was an excitement building in her that motivated her to hurry the customary morning routine. All she could think about was getting back to the cottage and moving forward with all they had to do. This time she wanted it. More than that though, it felt as if it were calling to her.

She pulled her curly tresses into a quick ponytail and smiled to herself in the mirror. She couldn't help but imagine pointed ears there someday instead of the ones she had seen every day of her life.

The phone rang. It was Grandpa Jessie.

"Just checking on the two of you. Is Bain staying out of trouble?" he asked with his usual cheerfulness.

"There isn't much trouble to get into, Grandpa." *If you only knew*, she thought.

"You know, love, you really need to find something to do with your time. Maybe join a club, or think about a summer camp. You're always home when I call. It can't be healthy."

"Bain has been taking me on hikes. We'll be fine."

"Just don't let your summer waste away. Sometimes I feel like it's such a shame we live so far away from people your age." The concern in his voice was so familiar.

"Don't worry about it, Grandpa. Things are good." She stared out the window and tried imagining what he would say if she explained their real activities to him. She shook her head. She wouldn't be able to explain it to anyone.

"Tell Bain hi for me, love. And keep an eye on that boy. If there is something to get into, he'll find it."

"Sure, Grandpa. Love you." She was anxious to get off the phone. If he asked the wrong question, there would be disaster on the horizon. She couldn't keep up a convincing lie to save her life.

She hung up the phone and tried to pretend that she had done the right thing. Of course she couldn't tell Grandpa Jessie about any of this. What would he think? And she was supposed to keep her eye on Bain—did watching him swordfight or sprain his ankle count? Grandpa Jessie would have a heart attack if he knew they were spending time in a strange cabin. Make that a strange magical cabin. She was supposed to be the responsible one. Was she being responsible now? She tried not to answer her own questions as she pulled the door open.

Agnar was waiting for them in the steel door room. He bowed before beginning. "The queen sends her encouragement in your training."

"Uh, okay. Well, what do you have for us today?" Bain picked up a sword and began drilling some of the tactics from the previous lesson.

Agnar unsheathed a blade from his side and took the opponent stance. With one quick move, he sliced the blade of Bain's sword through as if it had been made of paper.

"Whoa! What is that thing?" Bain asked.

"This, my friend, is an eternal blade." He laid the sword on the flat of his hands so they could inspect it. The grip of the bright silver hilt was covered in soft leather. Scrolls embellished the guard as did rubies, sapphires, and emeralds. The blade itself did not appear to be made of a familiar element; it was marbled with white silver and forest green. The overall appearance suggested a piece of art rather than a weapon.

"It's beautiful," Erin said.

"It cannot be dulled, scratched, or harmed in any way." Agnar's eyes gave away his passion for his sword as he continued. "Each one is crafted specifically for its master. The designs are so unique that no two have ever been duplicates.

"The sword tells of its owner by its color, size, design, and gems. It is known as a signature among our kind." He was turning the piece in his hand, admiring it like an old friend. "It is also customary to always have it with you. I did not want to unnecessarily frighten you yesterday, so I chose not to bring it, but from this point on, you shall not find us parted."

Agnar offered the hilt to Bain.

"It feels heavy." He glanced sideways at Agnar before slashing through the air.

Erin watched with curiosity. It really was a beautiful sword. It just seemed strange how comfortable Bain felt around weapons.

The lesson began as they chose their training swords and practiced skills from the day before. This time, Erin really concentrated and gave her best as the combinations became increasingly difficult. She was surprised to find that she was beginning to enjoy her new education, and she swung her sword in complicated patterns.

"You are ready to spar each other," Agnar announced, after what had felt like hours of instruction and corrections. They stared back at him with shocked expressions. He smiled, "Don't worry. I will place a *ward* over each of you; one we like to use especially for training. It allows contact with your swords, but if a blade were to hit you, it would not leave a mark."

Bain looked at Erin with a mischievous grin. "Do you want to have a pillow fight?" he asked with his sword in the air.

Erin smiled sweetly back at him as she waited for Agnar to complete the wards. "You're ready to begin," Agnar said, and stepped back.

She didn't expect sword fighting to be this much fun. Even with Agnar calling out advice to her and sometimes shaking his head, the sensation of using steel against steel felt empowering.

They had each received enough blows to know exactly how this was impacting the other. The *ward* afforded confidence to be creative, if not a little reckless, and Agnar was constantly calling out corrections while he followed the two easily through the equipment.

"Okay, you two. Go on up and have a decent meal. I would not have you faint on my watch. Upon your return we will explore the finer points of lunging. Off you go, then."

Bain and Erin wasted no time finding their way to the kitchen. They bantered playfully while they ate.

"You fall for it every time," Bain said through his mouthful of sandwich. "If I feint high, you always meet me there only to leave yourself wide open. You make it too easy."

"At least I try to fight straight on. I think you would rather spend your time as a gymnast and a sword swinger than really work on tactics," she countered.

"I'm afraid if we were up against a real foe, I would more likely still be standing at the end of the day than you."

"Thanks. Now I feel a whole lot better." Even worse was the feeling that he was right. "But can you really picture fighting someone? A real person? Could you even do it? I don't think I could."

"I don't know. I guess you just do what you do in the situation you're in. Kind of like war."

"We're not even old enough to be thinking like this Bain. I can't think of one reason we need to know how to fight."

He started rummaging through the ice chest for more food. "The ice hasn't melted at all. It looks exactly the same as it did when we put it in here yesterday. No wonder they don't need a refrigerator in here, it's like a forever cooler." He was drinking an ice cold birch beer soda. "I'm going to have to put some ice cream in here and see what happens."

Erin wasn't unaware of his change of subject. "So do you

Älvor

think we'll be able to have those spells over us every time we fight?"

"Well, I'll tell you one thing. I don't think I would even point my sword in your direction if I thought it could really hurt you. But you have to admit, that whole sparring thing was pretty cool. I think it even beats basketball."

"Well, coming from you, that is saying something."

"There's something else. You know that blade he showed to us? It glows the same color as him; like it has his magic or something. Even when I took it from him, it still glowed. And it felt strange, like there was more to it than just a hunk of metal and minerals."

"What do you mean?"

"I don't know. It just felt like there was some kind of power in it." He shook his head. "I guess the only way you could understand is if you touched it too."

Chapter Eleven

STRANGER IN THE WOODS

BAIN LOOKED FORWARD TO HIS morning runs. It was not uncommon for him to cover tens of miles as he explored the mountainsides out of the view of the public eye. Here he was free to run inhumanly fast, following the wind and conquering the deer and the eagles in their own races.

His love for the outdoors only increased since he was able to observe it without fear of the wild animals that called the forest their home. His speed alone allowed him to observe the beauty around him in its natural state, untouched by the awareness of his approach.

As he ran through a familiar route this morning though, he heard a sound that did not fit into the usual rhythm of the forest. For each step he took, something was keeping pace. He darted glances in the direction of the sound, expecting to see a magical aura. There wasn't an animal in these hills that could keep up with his run. If there was something out here as fast as he was, it had to be magical.

A low growl shot through the trees in the direction of the footfalls. "You think you're the only one who can run, boy?" The voice seemed like an extension of the animalistic growl he had heard before.

Bain tried to see through the trees as they rushed by. Something did start to brush past his view. But it did not glow with magic. Whatever it was looked like an overgrown mountain lion. It was running on all fours in an oversized lope.

"Who's there?" Bain called. Maybe he could spook the monster away. But how could any animal run as fast as him? He was still in denial that it could have spoken.

A cat-like growl ripped through the woods again.

Bain wondered what it would feel like to be eaten by a mountain lion. He really wished he had a sword on him. Why learn to use a weapon and then not have one when he really needed it? He kept running. He thought about turning back home. But would the creature follow him there?

That would be a nightmare. He estimated he was about forty miles from home. Whatever was following him would have to end it here in the woods. He couldn't bring anyone else into danger. He could feel the bile rise in his throat as he considered an unarmed confrontation. This wasn't going to have a good ending.

Before he could decide how to face the overgrown mountain lion, a strange sight greeted him. Sitting on a fallen tree trunk was a tall, young looking man with black hair that hung around his shoulders. He was concentrating on the giant piece of wood in front of him.

The sound of the large beast's footfalls faded into the distance. It was leaving. Bain tried to slow his racing heart. He couldn't help but feel grateful for the company of this stranger. He was sure this man was the reason the animal was spooked away. What was that thing? He wasn't even sure there were cougars in Pennsylvania. It had been a rumor that some still roamed the hills, some even said they had seen them in the middle of the night. But that still wasn't going to explain its size. And how could it speak?

Bain tried to compose himself as he took in the scene before him. The stranger appeared to be carving a canoe from a fallen tree. He was dressed like any other typical man, with a T-shirt, cargo shorts, and hiking boots. His appearance would not seem unusual if it were not for the deep plum-colored glow that surrounded him, his magic.

Bain decided on a direct approach. "Hello," he greeted, trying to keep his voice level in spite of the moment of panic he had just overcome.

The stranger looked up at him and smiled. "I've heard a lot about you," he began. He stood and walked over to Bain and stretched out his hand. "I'm Carbonell," he said as he shook Bain's hand. "It's nice to finally meet you in person." He sat back down and resumed chiseling at the timber.

Bain watched him work. "My name is Bain," he started. He sat down on a stump facing Carbonell. "What exactly have you heard about me?" He closely watched the stranger chisel at his canoe.

"Just this and that," he said and set down his tool. "You're not exactly a secret." Carbonell fixed his penetrating blue eyes on Bain. "Why did you stop to talk to me in the first place?"

Now Bain lowered his eyes to the ground. Should he tell the stranger about his gift or the oversized cat? He suddenly realized how odd it probably seemed for him to walk right up to someone he had never met before. But what did this elf know about him?

"Your gift of sight has led you straight to me," Carbonell answered for him. "You can see magic. There are no others of our kind that can." He was chiseling again and seemed to wait for the news to sink in.

Bain decided on a different approach. "So, do you live around here?"

"I just came to your area recently," he answered. "Beautiful place to live, isn't it?" His canoe was already taking on a perfect shape.

"I've been here all my life," Bain answered. He was amazed at Carbonell's skill of crafting the wood. "I guess it's all I have ever known, but I still agree that it's beautiful."

He watched the canoe coming to life as the details were masterfully etched in. "Where did you learn to do that?" he asked without really thinking.

"It's something I picked up along the way. It can come in terribly handy when you need a watercraft." Carbonell answered without interrupting his work. "You want to learn?"

"Okay."

Bain was too fascinated by his handiwork to turn him down. Carbonell handed him the tools and instructed him on the finer points of woodcraft. Having never worked with wood before, Bain was captivated by the new skill. He was sure his speed and strength enhanced his abilities, as well. Carbonell guided him through various skills offering compliments along the way. He was surprised to find the satisfaction this new trade offered. The feel of the wood changing under his hands was almost hypnotic as each stroke of the tools brought the canoe new life.

However, he had also become so accustomed to not noticing the passage of time. When his thoughts wandered to Erin, he was startled to see that hours had already passed.

"I better get going," he said. "Thanks for the lesson."

"Now that you know where to find me, feel free to stop by again," Carbonell answered. "I am sure there are more things I could teach you."

Bain took a direct path home. He didn't feel the need to tell Erin of his new friend just yet. And she would definitely freak out if she knew there was a huge beast in the forest that could run as fast as him. There were some things that were better left unsaid.

Chapter Twelve

DOOR OF VINES

THE *BOOK OF KNOWLEDGE* WAITED alone in the center of the empty room. The pages once again appeared as aged parchment and still sat opened to the page they had seen last. It had been Agnar's suggestion that they try the book again. Erin approached with fascination and anticipation.

She carefully lifted the corner and turned the page.

> *There is much to discover in the life that*
> *surrounds you.*
>
> *Choose the door that is living, and inside*
> *you shall find new life.*
>
> *The more you give of yourself in the Door of Vines,*
> *the more you will receive.*

"What do you think it means?" Erin asked.

"Only one way to find out," Bain answered and raced out of the room.

The hallway maze was not intimidating anymore. The ability to run incredible speeds diminished the formidable feeling the endless maze formerly created. Although she knew the way to the Steel Door now, they had not taken time to explore the other long hallways that lay in the underground labyrinth.

It seemed as if they had come full circle a couple of times. She tried to estimate the miles they were running as they searched the halls, but it was too difficult to tell. At least they weren't running out of breath. She wondered how any basement could be so enormous.

They rounded another corner where a wall of green greeted them. It was as if part of the outdoors itself lay hidden underground in this mysterious cabin cellar. There did not appear to be a door, but a wall of green leaves, vines, and bright flowers colored pink, white, orange, and yellow. The natural mural stood high as a tall tree and spread as wide as a house.

Completely unsure of how to enter the room, she walked slowly up to it, admiring the magnificent work of nature. As she neared the center of the enormous vine, the plants began to shift and grow before her eyes. She watched with amazement as an opening formed in front of her large enough for them to walk through side by side.

Unexpectedly, the intensity of the colors seemed to overwhelm her. Amid the disorienting feeling, she began to realize that they were no longer indoors. Above them a perfect blue sky spread as far as she could see, while trees, plants, flowers and bushes of endless variety grew for miles. And she could see more than she could have imagined possible.

She had watched a television show once about the eyesight of eagles. They could spot a mouse running on the ground a mile away. She wasn't sure how scientists ever figured that out, or if it was really true, but now she was starting to understand. She had never seen so much at the same time in her life. It felt as though someone had just cured her of a blindness she didn't even known she had.

Then sounds filled her mind. She could hear running water as though they were standing near a brook. Birds called, and strange insect noises became more obvious. She couldn't understand how she had missed it before.

Before she had a chance to focus her attention on the source of each sound, a myriad of aromas ignited her senses. She was aware of the combination of familiar mountain air and foreign sweet flowers.

And she realized that there was simply more to absorb than her eyes, ears, and nose could keep up with. The majesty of the strange place had completely overwhelmed her sensory system. She felt herself tremble and thought she might pass out. Too much information bombarded her for her to think straight.

She looked around for a place to sit when she noticed that she had somehow missed the presence of an älva who was standing just before them. Her long blonde curly hair fell past her elbows and seemed to shine as brilliant as the sun.

Her white aura was a welcome sight. Maybe it was due to the recently sharpened eyesight, but the lady seemed impossibly striking with her tall slim frame and her bright green eyes. It even seemed she tried to understate her appearance by wearing a pale blue gown with a simple design.

The stranger curtsied ever so slightly, acknowledging each of them individually. "Welcome to the Door of Vines," she said, her voice hinting a new accent that they had not picked up on with the other elves. Her voice fit her appearance perfectly—it was soothing yet firm as though endless years had given her wisdom and temperance. "My name is Aelflaed," she continued. "I will be your instructor here. There is much to learn, so we will begin now. First, please close your eyes. I want you to choose a smell and find its source. Focus on just one and concentrate until you can distinguish it alone." She waited for a few moments.

The exercise brought Erin to a vine climbing through a tree with flowers boasting a deep purple that opened up with petals as big as her hands. Each was delicately lined with white and had a center that darkened until the purple color seemed almost black. As she approached the unusual plant, she knew at once that she had correctly found the source she had been searching for.

She couldn't help it. She reached up and picked one of the large blossoms. As she did, a shower of light coruscated from the petals like a miniature fireworks show. The flower she had been holding disappeared into shimmering light and was gone.

She almost picked another flower but stopped just before her hands touched the stem. Already lightning streaked up the stalk and lit the entire plant with a vibrating electric surge.

She could hear Bain talking to Aelflaed in the distance and followed the sound to find him sitting on the ground near a tree inspecting a piece of bark.

"It is used as a spice and has healing agents as well," Aelflaed explained, looking up at the tall tree fondly.

"It smells kind of familiar, like clove or something. But it's not the same. There's like a lime or lemon smell too," Bain said, turning the piece of bark in his hand.

"Go on then, put a piece on your tongue, like this." Aelflaed demonstrated pulling the stringy bark apart and putting the end to her lips.

Erin watched warily as Bain pulled a piece of the bark off and popped it in his mouth.

"You should try this," he said, and handed her the piece of bark.

She pulled a piece off as he had done and put it in her mouth. It reminded her of the flavored toothpicks she used to suck on at school when she was young. Her friends would soak the sticks in cinnamon, orange, cherry, or any other flavoring their moms' had around the house. During recess they would try the flavor of the day.

"We have grown this tree for hundreds of years," Aelflaed explained. "We have found many uses for it, and many are fond of the flavor it produces."

"What's it called?" Erin asked.

"It is the Exarionne. For centuries, we have cultivated this plant." Aelflaed was looking up at the tall tree with admiration. "The leaves have unparalleled healing ability. It is thought that the magic of the tree is produced in the chloroform."

Aelflaed paused for a moment and her expression changed. "You two need to understand, the sensations you experienced as you came here will stay with you from now on. Everywhere you go, you will experience the same heightened abilities to hear, smell, see, and taste; it is one of the purposes of entering this room."

Erin tried to imagine how it would be to always sense so

many things. Now she wouldn't even have to open the fridge to know that something was molding inside. She wasn't sure just how much she would enjoy this new ability.

··· 🦋 ···

Erin sat at the table and stared into her glass of milk. She hadn't expected to feel so overwhelmed. Everything smelled different. Even her milk tasted strange. She wondered if her world was permanently altered.

"What else do you think is in there?" Bain asked, as he crunched his apple. "The plants are cool, but I bet you anything there's even better stuff hiding in that place."

She watched him, wondering if he felt the same overwhelming feelings she did. If he did, it wasn't slowing him down. "What do you mean? What kind of things do you think we'll see?" She couldn't help being surprised as she bit into her apple. It was more crisp, juicy, and tart somehow. She watched the juice drip down the open white flesh of the apple.

"There is a lot of magic in there. The air has different glows in the distance. I can't see exactly where it is coming from, but the lights glowing in the horizon mean there has to be magical things waiting to be discovered." He was almost finished with his apple and was now gulping down a whole glass of milk. "Personally, I think we should explore the place. I can't wait to find out what's hiding in that huge forest."

"Are you sure you want to know?"

He just gave her a quick smile and cleaned up the table.

"Bain, Grandpa Jessie calls almost every day. He thinks I've spent the summer sitting around the house and keeping an eye on you."

"So?"

"So, it isn't true. It's been so hard pretending that we aren't waist deep into something so strange that I can't even begin to tell him about it. I've never had to lie. I don't like it. I don't know what to do." She wasn't sure why she was even telling him this, except that it only seemed fair for him to carry some of the weight.

"What do you want to do?"

"I don't know. I just want to stop feeling guilty. I want to stop telling lies. I want to say you're not getting into any trouble and know that it's true."

"That part's easy. I'm not getting into any trouble."

She didn't know what she expected. Bain really wasn't the type to take responsibility. But it was so hard carrying the weight on her own. "Bain, what's Grandpa going to think when he finds out what we've been doing?"

"He's not going to find out." He was standing with his hands folded in front of him. He looked so sure of himself as he leaned against the sink.

"It's not going to be easy keeping everything a secret forever," she said. She knew one of these days something would slip. Maybe it would be an accidental mention of the fairies, or she would comment on someone's aura. She wondered if Grandpa would notice that they both now had extraordinary sight and hearing. Would it be obvious? Would she and Bain seem different now that they could smell a rose from a block away? Maybe Grandpa Jessie would figure things out on his own.

Bain lifted up the floorboard. "Don't you think it would be even harder to try to explain it to him."

She sighed. "That's the problem."

Chapter Thirteen

INTO THE SKY

"Do you see that? It's like headlights. What is it?" Bain asked.

Erin wasn't surprised she couldn't see anything. He had been pointing at magical glows all day. Somehow Aelflaed was more interested in teaching them about the plants than finding the sources of magic.

But Aelflaed smiled. "Do you want to go and see?" she asked.

Erin followed the two of them. She supposed Bain had finally worn Aelflaed down. Instead of asking "are we there yet?" he would call out the colors of the glows and ask what it was. It was a little irritating, but Erin wasn't really into plants anyway. A diversion was a good thing.

Bain and Aelflaed slowed their steps, and Erin suddenly noticed what was in the clearing ahead. Standing in front of an enormous crystal blue lake was a herd of white horses. Their movement was distinctly more delicate than the horses she was accustomed to. She gasped when one of them stepped around so that its side was facing them. White feathers covered wings that were tucked in at the side of the majestic horse.

"A pegasus!" Erin cried, surprised at her own loud voice cutting through the peaceful scene.

Aelflaed was already petting the face and neck of one of the incredible creatures. She talked to them as though they understood her. She introduced them to Bain and Erin and continued her dialogue with the pegasi. Erin was not sure how to proceed; surely the horses were not responding to Aelflaed's conversation. But Aelflaed continued to stroke each one, talking softly as she went.

Aelflaed turned to them. "It is a more subtle gift, but if you open your minds to it, you will hear their voices." Aelflaed looked at the white winged horses lovingly. "Talk to them as you would anyone else, and they will tell you their thoughts. You must focus to hear what they are saying, but it is possible if you are willing to really try."

She stretched her hand out as if inviting them to meet the pegasi personally.

Erin approached the tall muscular horses cautiously. She could see the intelligence in the eyes of the one she now stood before. "Hi, I'm Erin," she began, feeling very self-conscious. She didn't know if it could understand her, and it seemed even crazier if it could. "Does anyone ever ride you?" she asked as she admired the large white wings at its sides.

The wings snapped open exposing its tall back, as if in answer to her question. Without thinking much about it, she jumped on. It bounded forward suddenly, and she instinctively tightened her legs around its middle. Seconds later, the wings began flapping and the ground sank from below them.

Even though she had never been on an airplane, Erin felt no fear as they glided through the air. Somehow she knew she could completely trust this flying being. They descended over the brilliant blue lake where their reflection was visible from her unusual seat. She realized she was laughing out loud as they rushed over the mirroring water below. She leaned over and watched the water under them now even closer. The pegasus let its hoof skim the water. With another lurch they lifted higher into the sky and she could see the hills and mountains that lay beyond.

There was no visible end to the land. Trees camouflaged the terrain that lay below them until everything from this height appeared different shades of green. Even though time was not measured here, she would want to stay in the air forever. The world below seemed to stop turning, and the only thing that really existed was this white winged horse and her.

At long last the pegasus did return her to the ground. She let herself down and felt the familiar solid feeling under her feet. Already she wished she could spend more time in the air.

Bain was staring at her.

"You were flying!" he accused. "I can't believe you just took off. What were you thinking?"

She couldn't think of an answer. "Sorry, I just—"

"Just what? You thought you would just fly over the country-side bareback?"

"I'm sorry. I wasn't thinking. I guess I probably shouldn't have done that." It was odd having him take the role of worrier. He must have been pretty shaken up by her flight.

"What if you fell off?" Bain continued. "You don't even have a parachute. Grandpa Jessie would have my skin if you died falling off a flying horse."

Erin's head came up hearing her grandpa's name. Somehow she had slipped and allowed herself to live in both worlds separately. And she was supposed to be the one to keep Bain out of trouble. She felt like she was failing.

"Do you think it will let me try?" Bain asked.

"What?"

He walked over and looked the white horse in the eyes. "I would be honored to ride with you," he said.

The pegasus seemed to nod and once again spread its majestic wings. Bain jumped on as he had watched Erin do. He nearly lost his balance as they abruptly took off.

She watched them fly into the sky. "But it's okay for you to do it?"

It was considerably more unnerving to watch him on the back of the flying horse than it was to ride one herself. Maybe that was why he had been so upset. But she wasn't going to let him off that easy.

She walked around the herd of horses letting her fingers drift over the soft white coats. "I must know your name," she said to a tall muscular stallion.

She stood there silently, allowing all of her senses to focus. She touched his face and closed her eyes. Willing her mind to allow his thoughts to reach hers, she waited patiently for his name, her hand still on the soft hair of the towering face.

In a deep voice she heard, *I am Eakann, Lord of the Pegasi.*

He stretched out his great wings, and she did not hesitate to climb on his back. Eakann's strength and speed were noticeably superior as he caught up easily with Bain and his flying mount.

Bain was holding tightly to the mane of the horse with his eyes squeezed shut.

"You don't have to do this," Erin called. "Let's just go back down."

"Yes. Go down," Bain said. He looked like he was going to be sick.

They landed, and he quickly slid off the side of the horse. She stayed on Eakann, hesitant to dismount the flying horse.

"Oh, go on then," Bain said to her, and then sat on the grass in front of the lake.

Eakann took off even faster than before and rushed through the air with inconceivable speed. She could feel the strength unmatched by the other pegasus. Now the trees became distant, and the clouds were equal to their height. The cool misty sensation increased as Eakann dove in and out of the white billows of clouds.

Eakann whinnied loudly and shot forward to the looming hills.

"Hey! Wait! Where are you going?" Her voice was lost in the wind that rushed past. Eakann didn't slow, but whinnied again and headed so far from Bain that she couldn't see him anymore.

"Great. Now I'm going to get lost on a flying horse. Bain's never going to let me fly after this."

Chapter Fourteen

PULSAR

A DISTANT SOUND PIERCED THE FOREST. The meaning was unmistakable. Something out there was snarling and something else had clearly been its prey. Erin leaned forward as Eakann approached the hill.

Through the trees she could see a pack of leopardlike beasts with shoulders that reached as high as her chest. One of them growled, baring its saber teeth that shone red with blood. There were six orange and black cats, but only the one in front was tense and ready to pounce. The others stood motionless with glazed eyes.

Erin held her breath as Eakann landed face to face with the monstrous cat. She slid off his back and ran for the trees. Eakann used his hooves to attack the large creature, whinnying loud enough to be heard for miles. The cat batted the air trying to catch the flying horse, but none from the rest of the pack moved. It was as if they had been paralyzed.

Erin watched from the border of trees, hoping to escape the danger. For once she wished she had a sword. As she backed deeper into the woods, she nearly tripped on a golden mound. It was moving.

Instinctively, she froze. She watched as the golden-scaled creature stretched its wings. It rose to its full height and she could now recognize the small dragon that stood only as tall as her waist. It didn't match what she would have imagined a dragon to be, dreadful and terrifying. This one was small and shone a brilliant gold that reflected the light with each movement.

Her attention flickered to the sound of the battle. The monstrous cat jumped up at Eakann, its large paws coming dangerously close. At least the beast hadn't seemed to notice her. She would have been such an easy target. The sound of beating wings filled the air as more pegasi arrived. With their deadly hooves kicking at the cat, they drove it into the woods. Methodically, the other five cats followed their leader into the trees.

The dragon collapsed at her feet. She reached out and touched its head. It felt like warm metal against her hand.

A low voice came into her head. *You are the youngling awaiting your destiny.*

"I am Erin," she said.

I am Pulsar.

The small dragon seemed to be sleeping. She sat on the ground next to its warm body. The words rebounded in her mind. *Awaiting your destiny.*

The forest was silent. All of the pegasi seemed to have gone. She watched the golden scales reflect the sunlight. Even though she should have been terrified of being lost in the woods, something here felt safe.

"Why do you say I am awaiting a destiny?" she asked the sleeping dragon. She wondered if she had imagined their conversation.

But then, his mind reached hers. *There is more to you than you know right now. The world has much in it that you are only now beginning to realize. There is a destiny that lies beyond. It is yours to find.*

"But I am nothing like the elves. They have gifts and talents I have never been able to even dream of. Am I really the right one for this?"

Worry not for your future, youngling. It will take care enough for itself. You can only change each moment. Each breath you take is another step into your future and another opportunity to choose. It is each choice you make that takes you to the end. There is nothing that is beyond your abilities if you choose it.

She reached her hand out to the metallic scales. The warmth of the dragon surprised her. He was much hotter than before.

His mind reached into hers once again. *Why did you stay, Fireborn?*

"What else could I do? You feel really hot." She wondered if the dragon was sick with some kind of fever. Maybe that's why it had collapsed.

Magic is stored in my heat. Dragons can build heat in such great strength that we can breathe flames. I have yet to, but someday I will.

While he spoke, she could see images of his words. She could see the magic building in him and understood the meaning.

"Why did you call me Fireborn?"

It is a title you have now earned through the magic you share with me.

She could see the magic he granted her flowing over her just moments before. It was as if she were seeing it through his eyes. "Why did you give me your magic?"

It was more common thousands of years ago for dragons to choose a human to share their magic with. We can give our magic to only one, and it must be someone who doesn't already have magic of their own.

She watched dragons of the past sharing their magic with humans. All of the dragons shared his diminutive size. "Can you teach me how to use it?"

You are not a dragon, so your manipulations will be much different than ours. The fundamentals are similar, though. First, you must be able to recognize the magic inside you.

"How do I do that?"

Start by closing down every thought in your head. Magic is inside every particle of your being. It will be easy to sense once you recognize what it feels like.

She tried to do as he said. She emptied her mind of the events of the day. It was hard not to let a stray picture or thought creep onto the blank stage of her mind. She waited, trying not to hear the forest or smell the plants. It was more difficult than she had imagined.

She relaxed all of her muscles to see if that helped. That is when the new sensation finally had her attention. She felt a warmness that filled her from her head to her toes. It was a warm, electric buzz of energy that was comfortable, almost soothing.

She experimented with the feeling, allowing a surge to go through her fingers as she willed the magic to her hand. "I found it!"

Being able to direct and manipulate magic is the next task. This is where another master will be much more helpful.

"What do you do with it?"

Dragons probably have it easier than you; our bodies are designed for it. We also keep our magic to more practical purposes, like hunting and breathing fire. But today I found myself unprepared. The Saepards ambushed me and went immediately for my wings. Unable to fly, I tried to subdue them with mind control. That was reckless, considering my inferior age, but it was do-or-die at the time. I have never before attempted to control creatures of their size or strength. I feared it would be the last thing I would ever do.

She could see his fight with the hulking Saepards. She was surprised at the power he had over them in spite of his lesser size. She now understood the strange behavior of the other five cats. He had been controlling them.

"So when do you get to breathe fire?"

It shall be soon. I have been practicing, but am not yet strong enough.

She smiled as she watched his countless efforts to direct enough magic into flames.

She curled up next to him and let the warmth of his scales radiate through her. As she let her thoughts drift through the pictures in her head, she stopped at an idea. "Pulsar, how big will you grow?"

For you, it will seem as if I grow before your eyes. I should hope to someday be as large as a cloud, and as I surely wish to live as many as a thousand years, I could someday realize that size.

The vision of him growing to that enormity was incredible. He seemed much less intimidating at the size he was now. "Will I ever have the chance to ride you?" He was a dragon after all.

Fireborn, there shall come a day when that possibility will be the only transportation you desire.

She could already see them soaring through the air, fast and high. The warmth of his scales repelled the cold air rushing through his wings. The thrill of the ride was much more intense and sensational than that of riding the pegasi.

I appreciate your vigilance, but I at last can make flight. I need you to go to the Door of Vines as quickly as you can. I will fly above so you can follow.

"Your wing, I thought you hurt it."

Dragons heal quickly.

She ran through the hills and forest floor using the dragon as a guide. Even as he flew she could hear his words in her head. It wasn't until they had reached the training area near the door that she remembered Aelflaed's words. Although no other creatures were allowed in this restricted area, it seemed the rule did not apply to him. She watched as he landed on the grass.

"I don't think you were supposed to be able to do that. I thought only people could come here. Shouldn't you have bounced off of some invisible bubble?"

"You have brought a dragon!" Aelflaed exclaimed.

"Is that really a dragon?" Bain chimed in.

She turned to face them, feeling guilty. "I found him in the forest. He followed me here. Well, I actually followed him."

"Excellent!" Bain said, and gave her a wink.

She breathed out. At least he wasn't mad at her.

Chapter Fifteen

LIVING GARDEN

"WHAT IS THE LIVING GARDEN?" Erin asked. She was sitting on the grass across from Adarae and Bain, who was quickly devouring a bag of chips. The training had become a daily ritual, but the hours were grueling, and leaving the cottage was the only way to ensure the day would ever pass.

"The only way you could even begin to understand is to see it for yourself," Adarae replied. "Do you wish to go?"

"Sure," Erin said and stood up. "Is it close?"

"Yes, but first you must both solemnly promise to keep the garden in strict confidence. You may share this with no one else," she said as she fluttered up eye level with Bain.

"You have my word," he replied, looking straight back into her eyes.

"I promise, too," Erin said. "Are you really going to take us?"

Instantly every älvor in the area was in flight, and the sky was filled with hundreds of colored wings. It seemed that the whole colony wanted to be there when the twins entered the garden. They followed the masses of fairies through the thick trees. Their speed was unexpected as they raced through the forest floor and the älvor seemed to disappear.

Adarae and Elir were the only two who stayed with Erin and Bain. They flew to the trees directly in front of them and each pressed a knot. The earth seemed to spread before them into an opening just wide enough for the twins to enter single file. Erin immediately recognized many of the plants from the Vine Door room. Aelflaed had instructed them on so many of their names and uses, but she felt surprised that she could remember any of it as they walked around the garden.

"This is our home," Elir said. She danced around their heads through the air. Sure enough, many branches in the trees held large lantern shaped dwellings that the älvor were now lighting up with their magic. In the center of the grand garden a large fountain flowed of clear sparkling water.

"This is our natural spring of popping water," she continued as they looked around.

"What is popping water?" Bain asked, watching the fountain spray water into a pool below.

Elir handed him a small orange flower that was shaped much like a cup. "Try some," she instructed as she handed Erin a similar pink flower.

They scooped the water and drank from the unusual cups. Erin was astonished to taste the carbonated cherry liquid. It was better than any soda she had ever had. She scooped another cup and drank some more. Bain was refilling his flower as well.

"Orange cream soda!" he said after finishing his third cup. "This is great!"

"We grow the flowers that produce nectar that can be joined with the fountain water to create a great variety of flavors." She then produced a smaller purple flower and filled it with the bubbling water. After draining her cup she hiccupped and zoomed into the air singing an unfamiliar melody. Moments later she returned and toured them through the garden, allowing them to sample the fruit that grew abundantly.

"This is our Blossom Peach," she told them.

As Erin picked the small orange fruit, the wonderful smell reached her nose and made her mouth water. Although the size was small, the taste of the peach was finer, somehow sweeter, and yet more perfectly tart than any she had ever had.

If the food here could be so wonderful, she wondered if everything else she knew would seem plain. Maybe they grew plants that satisfied the acute senses that the elves and fairies all seemed to share. She couldn't help but wonder what they would think of the food that waited for her in the kitchen at home after tasting something so divine.

Erin sat on the ground and watched the fairies flit in and out of their tiny homes, collecting fruit and socializing. It was strange seeing them in their own environment. She had only ever seen them flitting around the forest trees. It never felt connected. But here, there was a sense of community, of family.

"So do the älvor have children?" Erin asked Elir as she flitted about them. She hadn't noticed any extra small fairies yet.

"We do, but they are rare. Our lives extend beyond the realm of years humans enjoy. Centuries pass before our eyes and even our children grow up."

"Then, do your kind *marry?*" Erin was trying to imagine the miniature sized ceremony.

"Yes, of course! We have only one that we call our partner for life. It is a very joyous occasion when one of our young couples wed. Their lives will be then intertwined for hundreds of years."

Erin couldn't help feeling a sting of jealousy. Here these tiny angels could keep their family close to them for hundreds of years, and yet she had lost her parents while she was still a baby. It wasn't fair. And the dream had come back again. Hearing the woman scream her father's name echoed in her mind.

It had to have been her mother on the plane. Who else would have Erin's red curls and be reaching out calling her father's name? As much as Erin hated the dream, she treasured the glimpse of the woman she had decided was her mother.

"It's time to go. We can't keep Mrs. Hammel waiting any longer. I think we're pushing it today." Bain pulled her off the ground.

Mrs. Hammel was waiting for them in their front yard. "You two need to keep track of time a little better. I don't want you getting stuck out there in the woods in the dark."

Erin just nodded.

Mrs. Hammel didn't seem to take a breath. "Someone came to your house today while you were out. I haven't seen him around here, and he seemed kind of old to be one of your school friends."

"What did he look like?" Bain asked.

"He had long black hair, all the way to his shoulders. He really could use a hair cut. He seemed like a hiker. I was actually wondering if he was someone you take on your mountain explorations. You two do like to get out into the woods a lot."

"Carbonell," Bain answered. "But I wonder how he knew where I lived."

"He acted kind of strange. He kept trying to see into the windows, but I don't think he ever came to your door. I keep my eye on your place, you know. We wouldn't want some trouble-maker poking around."

Erin waited until Mrs. Hammel was nearly to her house. "Who is Carbonell?"

"Just someone I met." Bain didn't offer anything else as he went inside.

She wondered why Bain wouldn't talk to her about it, especially if this guy was looking into their windows. The thought made her shudder. Being home alone with Bain was fine most of the time, but she'd never had to worry about strangers before.

Chapter Sixteen

CARBONELL

MORNING CAME AND BAIN TIGHTENED the laces on his running shoes. His curiosity about Carbonell was incessant. He chose a direct route to the last place they had met, hoping that the monster-sized cougar had found another place to roam.

A skillfully crafted canoe sat in the same spot as before. He couldn't help but admire the handiwork of the wood.

"I was hoping to see you again," a voice said, cutting into the forest sounds.

Bain spun around in surprise. He hadn't even heard Carbonell approach.

"Do you like it?" Carbonell was looking at the canoe with a satisfied smile.

"Did you come to my house yesterday?" he asked, trying to gauge Carbonell's response.

"Yes. I was hoping to find you. There are some things I wanted to talk to you about."

"Like what?"

"You are in training now, and you have much to do still before you are ready, but have you even considered what you are going to do when you are done?"

Bain watched him, unsure how to respond. "No, I guess that hasn't really come up."

"I have friends, powerful friends. You would be welcomed

into our clan with open arms. We could use a man like you. There are many where I come from who are anxiously waiting for your training to end so that you might join us."

"Where do you come from?"

"We have our own city. It is a secret, even among the älvin races. No one has ever found it uninvited. You would be welcomed though. Your future would be secure, and you would be put in a great position of leadership, if you chose."

Bain listened as he watched Carbonell talk. Bain had been told before that he was a chosen leader. Perhaps this was what it referred to.

Carbonell smiled back at him, his teeth perfectly white. "Think about it. You need to finish your training before you can come, though. We can only use your skills once you have completed your transformation. You realize that if you quit early, you lose all your gifts, every last one. You have time to consider the possibilities." He suddenly hoisted the canoe up and over his head. "You want to come with me for a ride?"

"Sure," he answered.

He followed the canoe through the trees to the nearby lake. Carbonell produced paddles that had gone unnoticed tucked under the seats. Bain was pleased to once again be reminded of his super human strength as the water sliced easily under each stroke. His arms never tired as they paddled through the water.

They remained silent for the most part. Bain felt like he was seeing the familiar lake for the first time. His new abilities to sense allowed him to see the fish swimming under the water and more clearly observe the birds in flight. The smell of the water was very strong, but the trees surrounding the lake balanced it out. The calls of birds were more pronounced, as was the chatter of the squirrels. He was surprised to realize the enormous amounts of life that surrounded the body of water.

Today he was wearing his watch. He did not let time get away from him and too soon the hours had passed. As he ran towards his home, the sound of the large cougar echoed in his head. He wasn't sure if it was the nearly soundless padding of the cat's run or a low rumbling growl that made him look around.

"It's only a matter of time now," the growling voice seemed to say from a distance.

Mountain lions can't talk, he told himself. They can't talk and they can't be that big. He hoped he had been imagining the shadow that followed him for a few miles before fading into the forest.

Chapter Seventeen

ROOM OF MAGIC

THE BALL FELL ONCE AGAIN to the stone floor. It bounced once before suspending motionless in the air. Sweat trickled down Bain's forehead as he concentrated on the ball.

Basketball had always come easy; he had been playing on the school teams since junior high. The coach always drilled it into their heads to keep an eye on the ball. It was all about the ball. He thought that the years of drills and games would have taught him all he would ever need to know about controlling the ball.

But here it was completely different. His hands were not allowed to touch it. Keep the ball in the air for as long as he could without touching it—that was the task.

He couldn't help glancing over at his sister. Her ball floated directly in front of her face, which, incidentally, did not look pained with concentration. She watched the ball as if it were a fascinating bug.

Again his ball bounced on the floor, forcing him to return his attention to his work.

"Let the magic do the work, Bain," Master Ulric reminded him. "Find the force inside you and let it do your will."

Bain had been so excited to enter this room. Of all the new gifts they had received, he was sure this would be the most fun. Now he was thinking that the running and swordplay probably beat this out easily. Even though he had to train for endless hours with the sword, he found the concept natural. Running, to him, was a lot like eating or sleeping. He loved doing it, and to have incredible speed without effort was really a dream come true.

Since entering the room of magic, however, nothing felt natural. His ability to see magic in other things did not have much effect on his own personal control over it.

Master Ulric informed him that they would begin with the most fundamental concepts, and move on from there. So here he was, trying out material manipulation with a basketball. He thought he might be progressing a little, though. At least now he could sense the magic inside of him enough to summon it.

He let his mind wander, and the ball dropped to the floor again.

Master Ulric put his hands in the air. "I think it is time for a new exercise," he said. "One of the most practical skills you must learn is warding. There are many levels of warding, some requiring a practiced hand, while others even the two of you might be able to handle soon."

He raised his arms and Bain watched a flash of his deep, warm blue aura spread out around him. Although Master Ulric's lips were moving, no sound penetrated the blue barrier. Master Ulric lowered his arms. "The touch and sound ward not only protects against contact, but allows no sound to escape. There are many other kinds."

Presently Master Ulric disappeared entirely. Bain watched the air where he had been as if willing the elf to reappear. Instead of seeing the form of a man, Bain watched the deep blue glow keeping the place of his presence.

Erin gasped. "He's gone!" She turned to look around the room.

"Uh, Erin, he's still there. I can still see his magic." The blue light gave away Master Ulric's position even if Bain couldn't see his form.

"It takes time to decipher the different qualities of the wards you wish to execute," Master Ulric continued after flickering into view. "Begin by calling the magic energy inside of you and forcing it to surround the air around you. This is the most basic style, known as the bubble ward."

Bain tried to imagine a bubble around him. He couldn't decide if the magic should come from his hands and then somehow surround him, or if it needed to leak out of his whole frame to surround him. Either way, it didn't seem possible.

He tried holding out his hands and forcing the magic out like a shower. He stepped forward, trying to walk intentionally into a table. Something was working because he could not walk into the table. Even as he leaned into it, the edge would not contact him.

Proud of his quick work, he spun around to show Erin. But the bubble did not make it all the way around him. He caught the edge of the table and ended up on his back.

He got back up and smiled at his audience. At least there were only two. Erin was looking at him shocked, and Master Ulric just smiled.

"The sound ward, however, is not only less complex, but can be especially helpful when used with the invisibility ward," Master Ulric explained. "To produce this ward you will need to focus on canceling the sound waves around you. It is as if you are holding the air around you still. Your magic will do the work, you only need to direct it. Think about the sound waves as if they were visible fields surrounding you. By directing your magic, you will be able to cancel all waves emanating from your being."

Bain tried to imagine every noise creating waves around him. It would be so much easier if he could see them the same way Master Ulric seemed to.

"You will be working with the sound ward until no noise escapes," Master Ulric continued. "This spell should have significant meaning to you, since you will be required to master it, as well as the touch ward before you will be allowed back into the Door of Vines. Aelflaed insists the two of you must be able to protect yourselves before you go gallivanting all over the hills." He gave Erin a meaningful look.

She dropped her eyes to the floor.

They started practicing. Bain couldn't help but gloat just a little that Erin was responsible for their restrictions. He wondered if she had ever been the one in trouble before. This time he was off the hook while her cheeks burned red every time someone mentioned the dragon.

"Can you still hear me?" Erin asked as they practiced. Master Ulric had taken to pacing the floor and muttering unintelligible things as if he were in a deep conversation with someone they couldn't see.

Bain smiled and nodded his head. "Clear as a bell. My turn." He began whistling a tune.

"You did it!" Erin clapped.

"It's not that easy. Try whistling, and I'll let you know when I can't hear you anymore."

Making noise and concentrating on the magic at the same time was not very easy. They practiced until they were able to turn on the ward at will, but they still needed each other to know if it was really working. Inside the ward, they could hear everything around them just as before.

"Do you think we'll know if this works without anyone there to listen?" Erin asked.

Bain just shrugged his shoulders and started whistling again.

Chapter Eighteen

Small World

Erin was relieved to spend time outside the cottage. Working with magic was exhausting, and without being able to measure time, it felt like they were in the cottage forever. Her school teachers had nothing on Master Ulric. Maybe he thought that since they were stronger now, their minds needed to be too. He worked them so hard she could hardly think straight by the end of the lesson. The Living Garden was an oasis as she let her mind unwind. And the best of part of all was the sun moving through the sky, proving that another day was actually passing.

Erin watched as a black and white winged fairy floated down to them. It was common now to see patterns of astonishing complexity on their wings, and yet, she still marveled at their intricate beauty. Even before she was very close, Erin recognized Skyla.

"There has been an invitation extended to you. Adarae wishes to meet both of you at our wall. Please, follow me." Skyla had short spiked black hair with large chocolate brown eyes. She spoke to them with authority as if her position was one of importance and she was used to being obeyed.

Erin glanced over at Bain. He seemed a little surprised. She gave him her hand, and they pulled each other off the ground.

They had not yet explored the deepest reaches of the älvor's haven. As of yet, they had remained in the areas shown to them by the fairies. It didn't seem respectful to just wander around their home uninvited. The size of the garden seemed more than sufficient for the tiny fairies, and yet the area they were now hiking through bore resemblance to the plant variety in the Door of Vines. It seemed there was still much of the garden yet to be seen.

Adarae greeted them when they entered a clearing in the vegetation. Before them a rock wall rose as high as the trees. The cliff side jetted upward majestically causing them to catch their breath.

"Welcome to the Wall," Adarae began. "As you have been privileged to witness our sanctuary as well as the Door of Vines, we feel you are ready to share with us one of our treasures."

She darted up to the mouth of a small opening in the wall. Singing in an exquisite voice, she beckoned something from within the small cave.

They watched the dark hole above them with expectation. Adarae kept singing in her lulling voice as if to encourage while she waited with her hands open to the cave. Something bright purple glinted through the hole and was lost again in the darkness. Erin waited, her eyes trained on the opening, now eager to see the source of the color.

Slowly, the same purple came into view, revealing a head just smaller than the size of her fist. Its large dark eyes blinked in the sunlight. Without warning, the creature sprang forward into the air, clearing the wall completely and leaving nothing under its feet.

The purple scales were familiar to her, but the creature's wings would never have entered her imagination. Flying in circles above her head was a dragon the size of a falcon with wide purple, black, and white butterfly wings.

With Adarae riding on its back, it was truly an astonishing sight to behold. They lifted higher until they were a speck in the distance, like watching a helium balloon float away.

Skyla was at their side again. "It is a Faerie Dragon. We are honored to have a few in our colony. They eat only the fruits and nuts we grow in our garden."

"You ride them, even though you can fly?" Erin asked, then wondered to herself if she had been impolite. Her cheeks began to flush in embarrassment, and she waited to see the fairy's reaction.

"As accomplished as we are in flight, the Faerie Dragons can travel long distances with greater speed. When the need arrives for us to travel over vast amounts of land, we ask the dragons. They love the excuse to spread their wings and let the ground disappear under them, so they are most accommodating." The tiny älvor spoke with an air of dignity.

Erin was surprised at how young and small she felt next to this exquisite fairy. "Do they speak to you through their minds?" she couldn't help but ask. They only way she was familiar with was how she and Pulsar communicated.

"They do love our songs. We can understand their language, and it is not necessary to communicate in such an intimate fashion. Some believe the Faerie Dragons only stay with the älvor because they love the music, while others believe it is their special diet that ties them to us."

They watched as the speck in the sky grew, and now the outline of the dragon was clearer. Its fantastic speed was easy to appreciate, and it seemed to be in a full dive falling out of the sky.

It was Bain's turn to show amazement, and he whistled at the speeding dragon. It landed lightly on the ground as if it was weightless. Adarae floated up to them, seeming breathless from the ride.

"He is my favorite. His name is Riken and he has been a dear friend for many ages. I do think he is the fastest of the dragons that live here, albeit, the most shy."

The purple dragon had already gone into its hold where its wide eyes watched them from a safe distance.

"I think he is really something," Bain offered. "I just don't know how you stay on when he falls straight out of the sky like that. I'm pretty sure I couldn't. Then again, I wouldn't want to try."

Erin listened, knowing that their differences were as stark as night and day in this area. She had been imagining Pulsar and herself someday jetting through the air at such speeds. To her it felt like freedom, not impending doom. She was already missing the contact that was ever-present with the golden dragon while in the cottage.

She hadn't told Bain about that. It didn't seem fair that she had a personal tutor while he was forced to struggle. Pulsar was always there in her head, guiding her along. Sometimes it didn't really help, but other times she picked up on the spells because of something he suggested. But Bain had it pretty hard. She couldn't bring herself to admit that the dragon had been helping her all along. Help that she couldn't share with Bain.

And Pulsar had become a familiar voice in her head. She could only hear him when she was in the cottage. Maybe they were just too far apart when she stepped outside of the cottage doors, but his voice would disappear, leaving her alone. It was hard losing that friend every time she left the cottage. His voice was becoming so familiar. It was the only thing that made Master Ulric's lessons bearable.

She watched the cave where the purple dragon hid. Another thing the fairies could have that she couldn't; a home with not only their families, but also with dragons. Why did she have to live so divided? When would her world start coming together? Would there be a place where Pulsar could always be with her? She knew with a stab in her heart that it was already too late for her family. Grandpa Jessie and Bain were all she had. Not that she was complaining. But she still couldn't see a world where all of them could be together. Grandpa Jessie with a dragon living in the backyard? Somehow she couldn't see Pulsar sleeping next to the blueberry patch.

There were so many things she still didn't know. Even though she spent hours, endless gut-wrenching hours, with at least one elf everyday, they had failed to explain how she and Bain would finally become elves. Or when. It was such a big unknown. The reality of actually changing into an elf was so foreign. It clashed

with her logic so much that she spent most of her time in complete denial that it would ever happen. She really couldn't see
herself becoming one of them. No matter how much she trained,
they would never be able to teach her that.

Chapter Nineteen

MAGIC BASKETBALL

BAIN FOUND HIMSELF PRACTICING SPELLS everywhere he went, sometimes absent-mindedly. Master Ulric was patient, but unyielding. He required them to succeed and would wait infinitely for them to perform each task to a satisfactory level.

They had worked mostly on wards and material manipulation so far. Bain realized that it would take several lifetimes to learn how to do everything possible with magic. It overwhelmed him when he stopped to think about it, so he rarely did.

"Basketball," Bain called. The sun had set and the lights illuminated the court behind their house.

"Okay. If you insist on being beat again," Erin answered.

"We could play with hands if you want."

"I don't think so. This is the first summer of my life I have ever beat you in a one-on-one."

He smiled and threw the ball out to the center of the court.

Even as the game began, he felt like they had stepped back in time. All the summers before this one there had been endless hours to fill, and not much to do. He could see why the cottage was set up to train one person at a time. Even though they were there together, it felt solitary as they worked. The opportunities for interaction in the cottage now arose in the kitchen over a cold soda more often than in the Room of Magic.

"Two points!" Erin called as she did a victory dance. "It's

four to six. Should we stop while I'm ahead?"

"You wish." Bain focused his magic energy on the ball, this time reaching both hands out towards it as if willing it to fly through the hoop. He watched with amazement as the ball flew across the span of the court and through the hoop touching only the net. Usually his aim was reckless, but this was clean and extremely precise. And it felt different this time.

He tried to figure out exactly what he had done different. How was he ever going to get better at this if he couldn't figure out how to replicate his success? It wasn't easy watching Erin beat him at everything magical. Sure, she was always getting better grades, but grades were nothing compared to magic. Anyone could get grades, but how many people could do magic?

"You scored three points!" she yelled and started another wiggly dance.

He couldn't help but laugh. "Did you see that?" he asked, watching the ball bounce off the court. "I might just have to go out for the elf team."

"That was amazing. But I'm not sure if they play basketball."

"It's just like Master Ulric always says." Bain lowered his voice in a weak attempt to mimic the rich sound of Master Ulric's bass voice. " 'Let go of every thought except what you are trying to accomplish, then reach within the very cells of your being and call out the magic to do your will.' I think I usually let my mind wander, 'which is a direct enemy to controlling magic.' "

Erin laughed at his imitation. "Yeah, but we might have to stop playing if you keep beating me. I was just getting the hang of creaming you."

"Hopefully that wasn't a one-time kind of thing," he answered. But he was still a little awed by his own performance. "Actually, I think I learned something."

He lifted his hands towards the door. "Open Sesame."

Nothing happened.

He yanked the door knob.

She laughed again and followed him into the house.

· · · 🦋 · · ·

Erin burst into the Door of Vines. "You're almost as tall as me!" It had been too long since she had seen Pulsar.

Master Ulric had kept them for hours again today working on wards. After Erin gushed about Bain's perfect shot the night before, Master Ulric told him he would probably do well with a wand. He finally passed them off on their wards and sent the two of them off to the Door of Vines. He may as well have announced that it was Spring Break.

Pulsar welcomed her with a low grumbling purr.

She came nearer and was startled to already feel his magic reaching her. The urge to touch his golden scales was irresistible. As she reached his neck she felt a surge of hot electricity that made her legs tremble. Visions of him breathing fire for the first time filled her mind. His joy and power of emotions ran through her, as though they were her own.

"I can't believe how hot you are! I can barely touch you now."

It is so good to see you, too, Fireborn. Would you like to take to the sky?

"I don't think you're that big yet."

No, but we could try the winged horses. You seemed to get along with them well enough.

"Do I sense a bit of jealousy?"

He didn't respond.

It was true that she couldn't help but miss flying. It was an incredible sensation riding the pegasi. And with the dragon's help, it wasn't hard to find them. It didn't take long for the herd to launch skyward. The dragon kept his distance, but her mind never left his link.

Do you have to stay here, or can you leave the cottage? Her thoughts reached out to him easily. She was used to talking to him in her mind, but it was still strange seeing him so far away and hearing him so close at the same time.

It is not known whether I could return to the cottage once I leave. The spell would likely repel my ability to enter. For now, it is wiser for me to stay here.

She was watching the blue water below reflect their flight. It should have been impossible, yet nothing felt more natural or right. She had never feared heights, and although she had only flown upon winged horses, she was happy in the sky. It was as if this was what she had always missed and never realized.

Are we ever going to be able to stay together? Her mind flowed like water to his.

Even though we may be separated by distance, part of me lives in you, just as part of you lives in me.

His answer was not what she was hoping for. But what should she expect? She was turning her back on the human world and becoming fast friends with a dragon. She didn't know what would happen to Grandpa Jessie. It didn't seem like they could live at home and be elves at the same time. And Pulsar would never be able to blend in.

Pulsar, maybe you could live in the forest near my home.

It would be hard, little one.

Bain made it to the lake quickly. He knew exactly where to go. The water lay before him in grand crystal blue making him wish for the canoe Carbonell carved.

He watched the lights glowing from the trees exactly the same as the älvor's outside the cottage. He easily climbed the nearest tree with the agility of a squirrel. Finding the älvor was the easy part. The fairy he was approaching shone a lavender glow. He found all of the fairies to be exotic, but this one was especially foreign. Her hair was white and fell around her face in a jagged cut. Her bright purple eyes watched him carefully as he settled on the branch.

"I bring the friendship of Adarae," he began. "It is an honor to meet you." As always, the words that came out of his mouth seemed to come of their own accord. He could never figure out why it worked that way. He would never talk to anyone else like this. But when he looked at the mystical tiny face, the words seemed to invent themselves.

"You are privileged, indeed, to have a trust of friendship," she said with a voice that sang in an unfamiliar accent. "What do you offer?"

He looked at her with confusion. "I offer my word that is true and my ears that can listen." At least some part of him knew what to do while his mind caught up. Sometimes he wondered why the fairies didn't look at him like he was some kind of nut job. His friends at school would have.

"You have learned well from the älvor. What do you seek from me?"

"Can you communicate with Adarae? Does she know what we do here?"

"Our communication is throughout every colony in the world. All älvor have a connection if they choose to use it." Her bright purple eyes looked at him in amusement.

"Then, can you tell me what you know of Carbonell?" He felt that it was a stab in the dark, but worth a try.

"Carbonell has been in the kingdom for many years. He has an independent streak that has led him to diverse places in the world. Many elves choose to live their entire lives within the boundaries of the kingdom. It is for each to choose." She began to float from leaf to leaf with her lavender and deep green wings.

"So do the elves dislike him for his desire to see the world?"

"The älvin world does not give in to quick judgment. Carbonell has been accused of having some questionable friends as a result of his explorations. Perhaps it is a subject you will choose to raise with him." She darted into the air high above him and the conversation was at a close.

He felt as though there was still much to discover about this älv that waited for him outside the cottage. He had been weighing the offer to go with Carbonell to his city after completing his training. It would be incredible to see the world.

His mind wandered to the strange encounters with the over-sized mountain lion. He still hadn't mentioned it to anyone, not even the älvor. Something made him want to protect everyone he knew from it. It still seemed impossible that a monster of that size could exist. And talk. That couldn't be possible. But it haunted him. Sometimes the words would repeat in his mind when he wasn't expecting it. "It's only a matter of time now."

He shook his head. Maybe the cottage was getting inside his head too much. Maybe he was imagining this, just like a scary monster under the bed.

He stayed in his perch on the branch and watched the water sparkle before him. Out of the sky there suddenly appeared several pegasi flying over the water. In the distance, hardly visible, he recognized the golden dragon keeping a distance from the flying horses. He wasn't even surprised to see Erin hugging the back of a pegasus with her legs. She seemed as comfortable in the air as he did running on the ground.

As breathtaking as the enormous wings were, he did not feel even a tinge of jealousy while he watched the herd fly up and down, playing in the sky. He could almost feel his stomach turn as he imagined himself on one of their backs. No, he was much happier on the ground. She could have the flying horses.

Chapter Twenty

ELLA'S WAND

BAIN CRAVED THE PEACE THAT the Living Garden could offer. And since the garden was not a part of the training hall, he was sure that it would be okay for him to go there alone. He was out again, for his usual morning run, but his thoughts were racing faster than his feet.

When he realized that the door to the garden lay just before him, he let himself in. He sat in his usual place in front of the popping fountain and let the sound of running water fill his mind. Somehow this place offered a sense of peace that he rarely reached anywhere else.

It shouldn't have surprised him when Adarae floated down to greet him. She had a way of sensing his feelings. But something kept him from telling her about the mountain lion or asking questions. He wondered how much she already knew.

"I can't do magic now without picturing a wand in my hand. I just know that if I had one, I would do so much better." The idea of a wand had grown in his mind until he could no longer stand it. He knew he needed one, and he was sure he knew how to use one.

She watched him. "There is a way. When is the last time you asked for Ella?"

"I don't know. I guess we haven't given her much thought lately. We've been pretty busy." He twisted a blade of grass around his finger. "Do you think she would be able to find me a wand?"

"It would be right of you to ask her. She is your Fairy Godmother."

"About that, she said she was given a gift from the älvor, something that gave her the title of Fairy Godmother. Can you tell me what it is?"

Adarae's laugh tinkled like tiny bells. "Bain, I forget how much you still have to learn. Is there not anything you can think of that sets her apart from the other elves you have met thus far?"

"Unless you mean suddenly arriving unexpectedly, I have no idea."

"Well, you are getting closer. Perhaps this would be as good a time as any. Why don't you ask for her?"

"How do I do that?"

"Just speak. Call her name, you will see."

He felt his face flush self-consciously as he readied himself. "Fairy Godmother Ella, I wish for your presence," he called out to the empty air.

He watched the path leading into the garden, expecting her to enter in through the gate. A small breeze and a whisper of movement lifted his eyes in time to see Ella float down to the grass before him.

If he had ever felt conspicuous in his life, he definitely felt it now. He thought he should have been prepared for her exquisite face and tall slim frame, but without his sister here, he was overwhelmed by Ella's presence.

He scrambled to his feet quickly and bowed clumsily to her. He looked up to see her smiling sweetly back.

"Uh, I hope it's okay that I called for you," he stuttered.

"Most certainly, Bain. How can I be of assistance?"

Ella's eyes were mesmerizing, and he looked away to organize his thoughts. "Master Ulric has suggested that I could do well with a wand." He looked back into her bright eyes and briefly marveled at her beauty. He looked at the ground and plunged forward with his request. "Is there a way I could have a wand before I am allowed into the kingdom. I just know I could do better if I had one. I really want to learn all I can, and I've really been practicing hard, but it's like something's missing. I can't get it out of my head, and I'm pretty sure the answer is a wand." He knew he had rushed his words together in his nervousness. He glanced up to see her expression.

"Bain, you have but to ask." She reached her hand out and touched his shoulder.

He waited, unsure of what was expected of him, his eyes never straying from hers. She seemed to be assessing something as she rested her hand on his shoulder, as if calculating and deciding. When she seemed to find a resolution, she turned and lifted into the air and floated out of the garden.

"She can fly." He stated to Adarae. "That was her gift, wasn't it?"

"Ella has gained favor in ways seldom seen in our world. She once risked her very life to save a single älvor from certain death. Ella was young and didn't know the status of the älvor she was protecting.

"She put herself in harm's way selflessly to save the colony's leader. To thank Ella for her willingness to sacrifice, our leader bestowed her with the gift of instant flight. It allows her to come and go wherever she pleases.

"It was a natural role for her to become a godmother. She could choose to watch over humans and älvin kind alike since she could come and go so quickly. The queen commissioned her to take you and your sister in her charge at the cottage, but she usually chooses for herself." Adarae flitted about while she spoke.

He considered her words and imagined Ella turning up unexpectedly all over the world. It was an incredible gift, and she used it selflessly. He remembered Erin telling him of her white aura and realized that she probably was more angel than elf. He couldn't help but wonder at her stark beauty paired with her endless compassion. He was sure he would never get used to her presence.

"Where will she go to find a wand?" he asked Adarae, who now rested on a thin branch of a tree.

"If there ever was an expert in that area, it would be Ella." She flitted to a nearby bush and picked a bright pink berry.

He wandered through the garden too, picking fruits as he walked. He was careful now to wear a watch and pay attention to the time; it was never what it seemed it should be since the cottage.

Ella waited inside on the same chair as she had been the first time they met. Erin greeted her while Bain beamed expectantly. He was sure his longing was about to be realized. He was so thrilled with the possibility, he simply could not suppress his growing smile.

Ella stood, allowing her red and gold gown to flow around her reminding him of her unnatural elegance. "I have brought you a gift," she said.

Although her hands had been empty moments before, now she suddenly held a package wrapped in paper and a red and gold ribbon. His hands trembled when he lifted the package. It felt heavier than he had expected. The bow and paper came off to expose a bright silver stick. He found where the wand fit perfectly into his grip and was pleased at the perfect balance.

"It is of platinum, with a diamond core. It suites you with its strength and purity and cannot be tarnished, marred, or broken while in your care," she explained. "Go on and test it, Bain."

It seemed that the wand was waiting anxiously to do his bidding. The metal under his hand was comfortable and powerful, and he had no trouble choosing a spell. Pointing to the chair beside him, he used his wand to command it to lift high into the air and rotate slowly around.

His wand easily concentrated his magic and felt weightless as he directed the chair's aerial performance. Carefully, he set the chair back down and inspected the wand. Its sleek exterior reflected the light with its bright silver metal. He would have expected it to feel cold, but the temperature was almost as warm as his own hand. The grip was formed to fit exactly into his hand, as though he would be the only one whose hand could hold it.

Reflecting a prism on the wall before him was a diamond tip. How this detail had escaped him thus far was indeed a mystery. As he examined the diamond tip he marveled at the size of the barely protruding rounded gem. Although his knowledge did not extend to the cost value of jewels, he was sure that this unblemished clear rock was worth a lot of money.

"Thank you, Ella. This is really amazing. Where did you find it?"

"Years ago I decided to try something new. A wand made out of the purest minerals in the earth: pure, and yet equally strong. Metal and mineral craft was an entirely different art form and required much training. In the end, though, a new kind of magical artifact was born. Your wand has been in the creative process for over a hundred years. It was not until now that its full purpose was made clear to me, and I was finally able to not only finish it, but find its rightful owner."

"I don't know what to say. How will I ever pay you for this?" He watched her carefully.

Her exquisite eyes rested on his with perfect ease. "Money has no value to me. If you feel a sense of gratitude, pay it with goodness. I should think you are ready for today's lessons. I believe Master Ulric is waiting for you." With that she turned and was out the door, or maybe she had suddenly vanished. It was difficult to tell as he watched the empty space she had just occupied.

Bain was eager to try his wand in the Room of Magic. Adrenaline seemed to rush through him as they raced through the halls. This time he would be really good. He just knew it. The wand would fix everything.

Master Ulric showed no surprise at his new wand and set them to work immediately on wards and manipulations. Bain was pleased to realize that his wand responded to his wishes effortlessly. Previously difficult spells were now coming together easily. He had now finally achieved invisibility and could match Erin trick for trick as they practiced their wards. It felt good to finally do magic as well as her. He was sure that with just a little more practice, he would be ahead of her. The wand could do no wrong.

Master Ulric presented each with a basin of water. "Thermal control, or changing the temperature of objects, lies within the particles, the very elements that make it up. To make something warmer, you must speed up the molecules' movement, to cool, slow them down." He emphasized his words with an aerial display that appeared as a hologram.

"We will begin with water, as it is the most responsive and safest to experiment on. Start by focusing your magic on slowing the molecules down to lower the temperature. You may begin."

All of his confidence had not helped as he now stared blankly into the basin of water. Pointing his wand at it, he imagined the water slowing and cooling. He could feel the magic flowing from the wand. Dipping his other hand in the water, he felt more bold as there was a cool edge to it. Now closing his eyes, he summoned his store of magic and forced it through the wand, willing it to slow the hydrogen and oxygen molecules until they became a solid wall. The sense of magic leaving him was surprising and he felt nearly out of breath when he opened his eyes. Incredibly enough, the basin of water had frozen just as he had commanded.

He looked over to see Erin's progress. She seemed a bit dazed, but her water was frozen solid just as his. She winked at him, and they shared a triumph in succeeding so quickly.

"And now, you shall bring your water to a full boil. It is the same principle in reverse. Please begin." Master Ulric paced the room, his white hair flowing over his shoulders.

The process of speeding up the molecules was something that escaped Bain completely. He looked at his basin of ice and thought of his days at home boiling water in a pan, and how it seemed to take forever even while it sat on a hot stove.

He placed the tip of the wand on the ice. If he could make

his wand into the burner, he would be able to melt the ice and warm it eventually into a boil. Instead of focusing on the water itself, he concentrated his efforts into making his wand tip fire-hot. It seemed less overwhelming to only have to warm his wand, and the ice below was dipping where it touched.

Pleased with the results, he surged more magic into the wand, commanding the platinum and diamond to hold the heat together and create a surrounding wave of fiery magic. The ice gave way and soon oblong blocks floated in the water. Boiling ice water was not going to be easy.

More magic and more focus he thought as he watched the water grow and the ice pieces dissolve. He closed his eyes and reached to every available source of magic he could find in himself. Forcing the magic to flood into his white silver wand, he felt the response and control he had hoped for.

Upon opening his eyes, he discovered a ball of clear light surrounding his wand while it continued to fuse heat into the water. He had become so accustomed to the magic auras of those he often saw that it had become a normal part of his sight. But now he realized that he, himself, had an aura as well—a colorless light.

He was certain that the glowing wand was showing the magic he had conjured and the strange light was only visible because of its concentrated quality. He supposed he had seen it since the first day in the Room of Magic but had not ever realized it. Even now, he wondered if he would still be able to see it if he removed the wand from the warming water.

He jolted to the realization that if he allowed his mind to wander, the magic would dissipate, and his work would begin anew. Experience had taught him that much over and over again. Carefully focusing on the light itself, he willed the white hot mass to heat. Although it seemed tedious to heat water at home, here he was sure that his metal wand could withstand temperatures that could melt rock. Intensifying the magical torch, he felt the water moving in response, evaporating upon contact with the clear flame. Impossibly soon his basin of water spewed into a cloud of steam leaving the dish hot and empty.

 · · · 🦋 · · ·

Erin shrieked as she watched her brother disappear into a cloud of steam. Immediately, she *directed* the steam to cool, and the air turned into a misty fog. A little dazed, he gazed back at her with a ridiculous grin. His face was a little red, probably from the steam. His hair was dripping wet, as though he had been caught in a cloud-burst.

"Are you okay? What happened?" she cried.

"I guess I got a little carried away. I turned my wand into a Jersey torch and evaporated all the water." He was looking at his wand which showed no sign of the magic fire ball. "Pretty cool, huh?"

She just looked at him, trying in vain to seem stern, but it wasn't working and a small smile escaped. "I just barely melted my ice into water. Maybe I should try out your wand."

"I don't think so. You have dragon power, after all. We wouldn't want to tip the scales too far in your favor."

She was at his side in an instant, giving him a light slug in the arm.

Chapter Twenty-one

ON THE RUN

"Bain!" Carbonell called. "How's Master Ulric treating you?"

"Hey, Carbonell. Have you taken to morning runs now too?" Bain answered. He was disappointed to have his peaceful run interrupted. He shook off the feeling and tried to tell himself not to be rude. He had been avoiding the hill where they had met before. He hadn't seen the mountain lion since he changed his route.

They ran in silence for a few miles in the densely wooded hills. It seemed as though sweat should have been dripping by now, but even this sonic speed running didn't make him pant for air. He hadn't actually tested himself against a speedometer, but he estimated he traveled roughly forty miles per hour. Naturally, Carbonell had no trouble keeping up with him.

"It doesn't hurt to fit in some exercise," Carbonell interjected to the sound of their feet padding through the forest floor. "So how are the magic lessons going?"

"I think I'm getting the hang of it. It's just a matter of technique mostly."

"So, do you want to practice with me? I bet there are some things an old hand like me could teach you."

"I don't know. I usually practice with Erin, you know, give her a shot at beating me."

"Well, how are you with material manipulations? Show me something."

Bain stopped his run instantly and pulled out his wand. Without thinking too hard, he directed a fallen dead tree trunk to lift off the ground and then set it back in its place.

Carbonell watched with a masked expression. "Can you blow it up? You just force the magical energy to pull in several directions at once."

He shot a ray of deep plum colored magic to a nearby log and it blasted pieces in every direction. Bain instinctively put up a ward to protect himself from the flying debris.

"Why would I want to do that?" he asked as the pieces settled back onto the forest floor.

"It's fun, and I bet Master Ulric won't even think to show it to you."

"How about I start with something smaller then," he said, pointing to a small twig.

Pointing his wand at it he concentrated on *directing* the magical forces against the branch. At first the slender branch hung helplessly in the air, but as Bain's strength increased, a crack was heard and the twig gave way to the magical energy.

"Wow! Don't ask me to start blowing things up though. That felt really weird, almost wrong." He looked at the slivers remaining of his intended branch. "I don't know if I'm supposed to do that."

"What do you mean? There really aren't rules about that kind of thing. You'll get used to it."

They continued their run, but Bain was intent on not changing from his course back to his home. Their conversation became sparse and finally Carbonell bid him farewell.

He was only a few miles from home when the familiar growl cut through the silence. He stopped and pulled his wand out, facing the direction of the noise. He gripped his wand, holding it in front of him like a sword.

"Not here. Not this close to my home. I will show no mercy if you come near me!" he shouted. He knew he was bluffing, but then, he was threatening a wild animal that could talk.

Another growl ripped through the trees, this time nearer than before. "Brave words, boy. Maybe someday I shall test them out." Another growl rang through the forest as the cat's retreat sounded on the forest floor.

As Bain ran the short distance to his house, he contemplated the animal. He wished he could ask Grandpa Jessie about cougars. He shook his head. He could only imagine his grandpa's response to him suggesting there was an oversized talking mountain lion in the hills near their home. There was no way Grandpa would believe him.

Chapter Twenty-two

GRADUATION

ERIN HAD FOUND THE SKY beneath her again today as she rode a brilliant white steed. Pulsar was a generous distance away but his mind was speaking in her ear as if he flew close enough to warm her with his golden scales. He had already grown taller than the Pegasi, and it surely was only a matter of time now before he would allow her to ride his back. She wished to feel the strength of the dragon's large wings and muscular back while he jetted through the air.

Her thoughts had been straying to the dragon a lot lately. She didn't want the sound of his voice to leave her head. And yet, what kind of world could she live in with a dragon? Part of her had decided that as long as she had both Bain and the dragon, she could live anywhere and be happy. And yet, if they found a place like that, life as she knew it would be over.

Do you know how much training is required before I am allowed into the kingdom? Her thoughts reached easily to the golden dragon glinting in the sunlight.

This is not an area where I can help you. The rules established in the kingdom over such things are not part of the world I know. I can help you focus your magic, but not navigate such rules.

Do you think I am ready? I mean, to ride you, do you think I can do it?

You look as though you were born riding the backs of flying creatures, but we shall see.

The battle continued in her mind. She knew that they were supposed to become elves. But what was that going to mean for her future? Was she going to change so much that she couldn't live with people anymore? She didn't think she could leave Grandpa Jessie forever. There were just too many unknowns. No one would tell them exactly what would happen when they became elves, or even how they were going to do it. It felt like stepping off a cliff.

Erin knew that she and Bain had already crossed a threshold that they could never turn back. Already they had changed too much. The world in which she was born would never be the same, and yet the unknown world of the elves seemed beyond her reach as well. Her stomach tied in knots as she considered officially leaving the world she knew and entering a new one.

Be still, Fireborn. You are greater than you think, and you can do this. You are enough, and when you need help, I will be there.

I know, but I think I am going to be sick about this until it's over.

She watched the trees rush by underneath them. The forest floor looked small from this distance, and from this height, she began to finally believe that her problems might be smaller than she thought, if she could just look at them differently too.

Without realizing, she closed her eyes, watching the view through Pulsar's eyes, while she let the air stream through her hair. If peace and happiness had a place, then it must be somewhere in the sky, she was sure. At least now she knew what she needed to do.

$$\cdots \maltese \cdots$$

"Bain, we need to find Ella. We have to find out how we graduate from here. I have to know, and you have to help me." Erin had found Bain working on his magic by the lake.

He looked up from his spell he had been practicing. "I'll let you call her this time. Just ask for her and see what happens."

It was Erin's turn to feel self-conscious when she spoke to the air asking for her Fairy Godmother. A red blur shot in front of them and settled into a tall, elegant Ella.

Erin faced her with resolution. "Ella, we wish to know what is required of us to be allowed to enter the kingdom." She kept her eyes trained on Ella's and felt her dragon's confidence backing her own.

Ella smiled another soft, warm, knowing smile that she seemed to have anytime they saw her. Erin noticed a sparkle in her eye, as if something had changed that she didn't understand.

Ella turned to Bain now, looking into his perfect blue eyes and asked, "Do you share this request?"

"Yes," he answered.

Now Ella's eyes were unexpectedly sparkling with tears as she smiled at them. "Then you are ready. The both of you will be allowed to enter our kingdom now, only you must let me arrange for the ceremony. The queen herself must be present, and the others will wish to prepare for your arrival."

With that, she kissed Bain and then Erin on the forehead. Erin felt it was much the way her own mother would have, had she still lived. Before she could ask any questions, Ella was gone in a blur of red.

"Are you ready for this?" Bain asked her.

"I don't know."

"I know what you mean. It is like we've been going along for such a long time, not knowing when the next step would come, and bang—we're suddenly here."

"How long do you think it will take?" Erin wondered just how long she would have to accept the truth. She wondered if she would ever be ready to change her life forever.

"I can't even guess. Do you think they have the same food there? I bet they don't wear jeans. I'm wearing jeans no matter what, though."

Food and jeans. She supposed that was all Bain needed. She wondered how he could take this so easily. Moving on was the only way she could think of solving this. She knew they needed to take the final steps, but if they waited much longer, she was sure her rational side would take over. She was tired of the constant war in her head.

Chapter Twenty-three

MEMORIES

"ADARAE, YOU HAVE TO COME!" Erin persisted. "All of you, you all have to be there."

The blue fairy flitted at eye level, clearly enjoying the moment of suspense. "It would be an honor."

Erin felt like the pieces of her new world were finally fitting together. The thought of Pulsar always at her side made her feel that her heart was somehow becoming whole. She watched as the other älvor danced in the sky.

She felt guilty for being excited to take the irreversible plunge. Once again the battle took over, her logical side sparring with what she knew in her heart. If she was going to become an älva, she wanted to get it over with. Maybe once she changed, she would no longer question the wisdom of her choice.

Bain looked at her with an intense expression. "You know where we're going; you were there in your dream. Tell me everything you can remember." He sat down on the grass with a cup of popping water.

It was easy for her to recite the scene from her dream. It felt more like she had walked the streets with her feet than dreamed them. The memory came in a rush as she told of the small part of the world she had seen. The älvor seemed to gather closer as she spoke, as if even the memory of the kingdom drew them in to her.

She finished with the little älva that skipped along the road with her gleaming blond curls and the ears she had finally discovered. As she looked up from the grass she had been staring at, she found a sea of almond shaped eyes watching her from many levels. They had landed on the grass, bushes, and branches to hear her story.

Although Erin had grown accustomed to their presence, she had never held the attention of so many at a time. Usually they came in and out of conversations, staying here and there as they went along. It felt unnerving to have all these eyes, watching her as though she were inescapably captivating.

Adarae landed on her lap. "It is impossible to visit the kingdom without the knowledge of our kind. We have kin in every part of the kingdom, and therefore have knowledge of everyone that has ever been there. You are the first exception. It seems you have walked the streets in your dream, and your description fits accurately with the land we know and love. Forgive us if we marvel at your words, youngling."

"So, it really is like my dream? Everything?" she asked, looking into the piercing deep blue eyes.

"The girl that you describe, her name is Bella. Look for her in the kingdom, and tell her your story." Adarae darted into the sky, signaling the entire colony to fly as well.

Bain and Erin were left alone on the grass once more, watching the air filled with a rainbow of wings. Even in large numbers, the whisper of their wings sounded so faint, she could almost not hear them.

As she watched them go, Grandpa's reminders came into her head. It was up to her to keep Bain out of trouble, and leaving the world as she knew it probably wasn't what Grandpa had in mind. How were they going to really leave? Grandpa was gone most of the time, but he called often. He was still convinced that she had been sitting around the house all summer. She felt a stab of guilt at the charade she had kept up for him.

It was almost like lying. The knot in her stomach twisted. It was exactly like lying. Not telling him the truth was the same as lying. But it seemed like the only way. She was suddenly glad that she was the only one who could see whether someone was telling the truth.

For a moment she allowed herself to consider laying the cards on the table and telling Grandpa everything. It would be better than deceiving him. She shook her head. It was impossible. The violently cold lump in her stomach that crept up to her chest was impossible to ignore. It would be wrong to tell him any of this. It would be even worse than lying.

Chapter Twenty-four

ICELAND

As they walked home, she pondered the future. Even if she was terrified of what they were getting into, she was so attached to Pulsar now that being able to stay with him somehow balanced her fear. And she wouldn't be alone. Bain would be there every step of the way. If he could do this with her, she would make it through.

"I think it's time we thought about Grandpa Jessie," Bain said. "I don't suppose time is going to stop in the kingdom."

"Can you believe that school is going to start in three weeks? What are we going to do?" Erin thought it was ironic that they were walking slowly home. Now that they had committed to leaving, they were dragging their feet.

"Have you ever considered being a foreign exchange student?" Bain asked.

"What do you mean?"

"We can tell Grandpa Jessie that we've been accepted to study abroad this year. It's true, after all. I bet we can get Ella or someone to come up with some documents. It will buy us some time to stay in the kingdom."

"Do you think he'll go for it?" She thought of everything she had told Grandpa Jessie this summer. If he believed she was sitting on the sofa all day, he was going to fall for this too.

"There's only one way to find out." Bain sprinted off towards home.

. . . 🦋 . . .

Erin was surprised how easy the whole thing was coming together. Ella was impressed by Bain's plan and accommodated his request for papers. According to the documents, they had been accepted to an elite program in Iceland and would be given food and lodging for both their junior and senior years of high school, which would include the summer. The program would begin in three weeks. The same day as school.

"The two of you still seem so young to me. It's so hard for me to watch you head out into the big world. How will I ever get along without you?" Grandpa Jessie said as they sat across the dinner table.

He had taken the news well enough, but he still mulled it over with them constantly.

"I know, Grandpa, but if we don't go, we'll miss out on something we'll never have the chance at again." Bain was working hard at the story.

Grandpa Jessie leaned on his elbows beside his empty plate. "It's not that I want to keep you from such an adventure, it's just that I'm going to miss the two of you like a squirrel without a nut. I didn't see this coming. Well, maybe with Erin's grades, but for the both of you, that's extraordinary."

"Well, I have been doing a lot of extra homework this summer. I guess that has to count for something." Bain pitched as he leaned back in his chair.

"I thought I'd never see the day you took to your schoolwork seriously. I suppose it was only a matter of time. And a full ride scholarship besides. If your parents were alive they would probably have a heart attack."

Erin smiled. She knew how much Grandpa Jessie loved her parents. She wished her memory of them included something besides the haunting dream of their final moments. But she only ever heard sweet things about them, like how they would go on a walk together every single night. Even after Bain and she were born, the ritual had not been broken. Maybe that's why Erin loved to be outdoors. It made her feel close to her parents somehow.

Grandpa broke into her thoughts. "And the two of you are nearly sixteen! I suppose I should be grateful you will be here for that occasion. At least I will get to have the rite of passage talk with the two of you about dating. Not that you don't already know everything I am going to say, again."

"I wonder if we can take driver's ed in Iceland. That was pretty much the only thing I was really looking forward to this school year," Bain said, clearly trying to steer Grandpa into another direction in the conversation.

Their birthday was bittersweet. Grandpa Jessie seemed to beam with pride as they opened their gifts. He gave them matching luggage, Bain's was blue and Erin's purple, which included all the different sized bags that fit together with straps. In the smallest bag, folded neatly into a pocket, was a considerable sum of cash.

"If you're old enough to spend two years across the ocean, you're old enough to decide how to spend money wisely," Grandpa Jessie offered.

Mrs. Hammel brought gifts too. In addition to the travel-sized necessities and candy, she bought Bain a gold rimmed watch that showed the time on two different faces. She explained it was so he would always know what time it was in both his homes. For Erin, she had an ornately sculpted hand mirror with a matching ivory comb and brush.

"It's for the beautiful red locks I will miss seeing." Mrs. Hammel had too many tears in her eyes to continue.

Erin crossed the room and gave her a hug. "Thank you."

Erin couldn't believe she was crying. But of all the things she felt she was, beautiful was not ever one of them. Smart, maybe, but Mrs. Hammel's comment hit her to the core.

The charade included packing clothes and necessities for the big trip. To Erin's surprise, Grandpa Jessie took them into town one Saturday to get passports. Apparently the visas were being processed for their stay in Iceland.

Putting clothes in their suitcases solidified the reality of the move. It was hard imagining leaving the only home she knew. Erin considered what she should bring. She felt that part of this was pretending, and yet leaving was real, all the same.

She sat staring at her purple suitcase, packed and ready to go. Bain stood in the doorway watching her, his hands tucked into his jean pockets. "You all ready?" he asked her.

"Are you?" she countered.

"What do people need to go to school in Iceland anyway?" .

"No clue."

"Well, then I guess I'm ready." He walked into the room and sat on the floor in front of her. "I told Grandpa Jessie that we arranged a ride to the airport. We're leaving tomorrow after he goes to work, so we'll have to say our goodbyes in the morning."

"Can you believe this?" her hands spread to the suitcase.

"It's going to be hard leaving, but I can't wait, all the same. We have never been anywhere farther than two hours away from here our whole life. If we don't die of culture shock, I think we're going to have a blast."

"It feels weird deceiving Grandpa Jessie. He's so proud of us for the full-ride scholarship. He must think we're geniuses or something." She was staring at her hands in her lap.

"I think it's the first time we've ever tried to trick him."

"Well, if you don't count the pet snake you tried to hide in your room, or the tadpole collection you tried to keep in the refrigerator. Then again, I don't think he really believed those were pickles in the first place." She glanced up and caught his grin.

"I almost forgot about that. In that case, this really isn't such a far stretch after all."

"Going to Iceland, we don't even know what language they speak. Good thing Grandpa Jessie didn't think to ask us about that. Seriously, he's probably going to want us to send pictures and letters. How are we going to manage that?"

"That will be Ella's job. She's the one who made us Icelanders in the first place."

He walked over and sat on the bed. "Don't worry. Everything is going to work out. You'll be fine, and I'll be there with you." He picked up her pillow and tossed it in the air. "Enjoy your last night in your own bed for a while." He faced her with his best innocent smile. "Tomorrow at this time we'll be in a whole new world. Better bring your pillow."

Chapter Twenty-five

DRAGON RIDER

SAYING GOOD-BYE TO GRANDPA JESSIE didn't require any acting on Erin's part. Her tears were real as she hugged him and told him how much she loved him. She watched Bain hug Grandpa Jessie and realized how much he had grown over the summer. Already his height matched their grandpa's. They slapped each other on the back.

As Grandpa Jessie finally drove away, she felt her tears ebb and a new excitement fill her. Now that it was official, and they were leaving, she couldn't help but look forward to the kingdom.

They had been playing at the charade for so long now, that the real plan escaped her. Erin knew they were packing their luggage to the cottage, but other than that, she had no idea how things would play out.

As they walked down the road with their suitcases she tried to memorize the land. She wanted to remember the hot humid air, the birds singing, the bunnies zipping across the road, the green trees and bushes, and the smell that she knew as home.

The cabin came into view, and it seemed the whole colony of älvor was waiting to greet them. Adarae came and announced that they would join them in their journey to the kingdom. While the cabin filled with fairies, they met Ella in her usual chair. She came and touched their suitcases, which disappeared in a flash of light. Erin looked at her with surprise, but she simply turned and began to descend the stairs.

Erin looked at the smooth stone walls. She was transported in her mind to the first time they had been in this staircase. It seemed they had rushed past it every time since their first visit, and the memories of early summer filled her. She couldn't resist the urge, and reached up to the cold smooth stone just as she had their first day. She thought of the strange book and how mystified she felt the first time she saw the letters move and the pages turn to stone.

Fireborn, she heard in her mind. *At last we shall be dragon and rider.*

His thoughts rushed through, and she saw his words coming to life. She was scarcely aware of the steps as she followed the procession, her mind wrapped in the images Pulsar was sharing with her.

She allowed her mind to focus on the procession once again. They had already made it into the Door of Vines. Aelflaed stood waiting for them, radiant as ever, with her blonde curly tresses draping over her pale blue dress. Agnar, too, was there, looking such a stark contrast from the lady, with a spark in his eye and a quick smile for Bain. Master Ulric stood on the other side of Aelflaed with a knowing smile that crinkled around his vivid blue eyes.

But the three elves were not what held Erin's attention. Standing behind them all was her magnificent dragon. It seemed he had transformed since she had seen him last. His height was more intimidating as he towered over the elves before him, his face more formidable, but his deep topaz eyes shone with his excitement and happiness. He had grown up somehow in the short time they were apart.

His golden scales were the same familiar color and his suede wings were as she remembered, but there was still something different about his build. Maybe it was his height, which was noticeably greater, but it seemed his muscles bulged ever so slightly, creating angles where softer lines had been.

Ella was the one to break her reverie when she announced that they would be flying to the kingdom. The group stepped further into the vegetation while Erin looked back up to the towering dragon.

You knew about this, didn't you? Flying to the kingdom?

Of course, Fireborn. His answer was soft, yet she felt an underlying surge of excitement.

She followed the others through the tall trees and into a clearing where they were met by five pegasi. She knew their names because she had ridden them all in her other visits here. It was not difficult greeting them on a personal level and hearing their response even before the short distance between them was closed. Although she had spent considerable time with these beings, she still stood in awe of the majesty and beauty they possessed.

Ella was directing Bain to one of the winged horses and explaining that they would need to fly to span the distance quickly. Erin watched his mouth drop a little, and then a look of determination replaced his momentary reaction. He mounted the pegasi, trying his best to look confident. The others were already on the backs of the brilliant white horses when Ella turned to her.

"It is time," she began, and waved her hand through the air. Before her a large gold toned leather-looking mass appeared.

Confusion swept over Erin's face.

"This is for you," Ella told her with a happy smile.

Erin continued to eye the piece with a puzzled expression. "Um, thanks Ella," she answered.

"It is a saddle. It will make your ride much more comfortable." Ella looked up at the dragon. "May I?" she asked.

Erin heard his response and watched as Ella directed the saddle through the air and onto his back. The straps and buckles found their places and the contraption began to make sense to her as the pieces found their way across his chest. Where the stirrups should be, wide bands hung down with straps crisscrossing to a foot hold.

Pulsar met her with his liquid gold eyes. *It is time, Fireborn.*

She approached almost cautiously, and then remembering herself, bounded the last distance. He held still as she made her way to the saddle and tightened the straps around her legs. She noticed that the saddle provided not only a form of cushion, but insulation from the immense heat that now radiated from his body; his scales reminded her of burning vinyl car seats in the summertime.

The others were already lifted above the tree tops when she finished adjusting the straps around her legs.

Show me what you've got, Erin told Pulsar, bracing for his powerful jump into the air. His wings spread out wide and began to pump the air as he lifted. She was amazed at how smooth his take-off was.

Hearing her thoughts, he answered *I have been working on that just for you.*

It was even better than she had imagined, riding on his back. His size, alone, outstripped the pegasi, but there was an unexpected smoothness as well, as if each movement was deliberate and controlled.

They didn't communicate other than to simply revel in the novelty of flying as dragon and rider. The wind rushed by, but was warmed by his fiery scales so that it felt like a summer breeze.

She noticed that he chose to fly well above the altitude the pegasi settled into. Their load seemed suddenly unfair compared to the massive bulk of the dragon with his small rider. He flew as though he carried no extra weight at all.

So, you can get to the kingdom through this room? she asked as they flew.

The mountains that had always loomed in the distance now rushed by beneath them, and still, the land stretched beyond as far as she could see.

It should not surprise you that you have always been close, relatively speaking.

She could do no more than wonder at his words and how far it would be until they reached the land of the elves. The journey continued, stretching out into hours. She was thankful that she did not need to hold on with her legs, and grimaced at how Bain must be taking this extended flight.

She had plenty of time to examine the saddle where she sat.

The dark butterscotch leather was as soft as butter under her hands. In front of the seat were handles, side by side, for her hands to hold. Unlike the familiar horn on the horse saddles she knew, these hand-holds were positioned at waist height, allowing her to feel secure as they glided through the air. Though Erin should have felts cramps in her legs from the long ride, her legs felt the luxury of the padded fenders with their leather laces securing them in place. The whole thing was molded so skillfully that it fit her contours, absorbing the impact of their subtle movement changes in flight.

She began to wish she could reach Bain with her thoughts the way she did with Pulsar. Watching Bain below, it was impossible to tell how he was faring. Perhaps his unnatural strength would make the journey bearable, even if it did not curb his motion sickness. The others flanked him and seemed to encourage with their glances in his direction.

She felt a twinge of regret that she was not flying directly with them. But it had felt like an eternity waiting to ride Pulsar.

Below, the landscape was finally changing. The thick forest gave way gradually to a valley where the trees spread far enough apart to see grass. She could feel the change in air pressure even before they began their descent as involuntary yawns overwhelmed her, and her ears popped. It was clear that they were finally landing, and the butterflies that had once inhabited her stomach were now in full force. She was nearly shaking when they touched ground, and she no longer had the excuse to hold to the firm saddle handles.

As she dismounted, she tried not to visibly tremble from her nervousness. She had almost forgotten Bain's plight, but now looked around for him. Just as she feared, he was sitting on the ground with his head between his knees. She approached him carefully and rested her hand on his shoulder.

"Are you okay?" she asked, guessing the answer.

"Just give me a minute, or an hour," he said through his arms that wrapped around his bent legs. She couldn't see his face at all.

She found Ella easily, hoping there was something that

could be done. "Do you have anything for motion-sickness—Dramamine or something?"

Ella disappeared before her eyes.

Erin walked over to Bain, and sat by him as he tried to breathe steadily. He never dared to lift his head from his position. She talked to him about the dragon, the soft saddle and the smooth flight. She knew she was babbling on, but it gave him something to think about other than his nauseated condition.

Ella was back in a few minutes with some pills and a bottle of water. Bain accepted both without question and downed the pills.

They continued to sit on the grass, and Erin slowly became aware of the surroundings. A soft breeze blew and the air seemed cool, yet comfortable. The smell was different here, with a hint of salt somehow. She had never smelled the ocean, but she wondered if it was somewhere nearby. The grass seemed ordinary enough, and as she looked around, she found trees and plants that were familiar. It was not as green and humid as her home, but the air felt calm without the repressing heat and humidity.

Bain looked up at her with his ocean blue eyes. There was an unmistakable sparkle there, and she knew he had recovered from his flight enough to feel the inescapable excitement of being this close to the end of their journey.

She stood and offered her hand to pull him off the ground.

"We are nearly there," Ella announced.

The group followed her through the grass towards a gathering of trees. Now it felt much like the mysterious cottage as a set of large double doors appeared where air had been moments before. She looked at the others, but realized that the surprise was only for Bain and her.

The towering doors resembled the first door they had found in the enormous basement of the cottage. The scrolling and embellishments were curious, and she found herself trying to decipher the patterns.

It should not have surprised her to have the doors open on their own accord, but she gasped and stood back as they revealed a previously invisible city.

Chapter Twenty-six

ĀLFHEIM

LINED UP ON BOTH SIDES of the entrance road were countless faces. Some were smiling, some unreadable, all had their eyes trained on the newcomers. Erin had not considered what exactly would await them here. She looked out at the sea of faces on either side, the road ahead completely clear.

In the small village she lived in, parades were not uncommon; it was as if holidays were particularly honored. Memorial Day, Independence Day and, of course, Christmas, brought out the whole population. As she looked out to the crowd around them, she realized just how small the village she lived in was.

Although it was clear that this was a parade of sorts, she felt no inclination at all to smile and wave. In fact, she was considering an invisibility ward, but was sure she would not be able to maintain it in such a distracted state.

At least all eyes were not on her alone; Bain was scrutinized by the onlookers just as carefully. She noticed the different look coming from those who met Pulsar's omnipresent gaze.

She could hear some of the thoughts that passed through his mind as they walked with a measured pace down the street. He had blocked her out of his mind enough that the phrases and expressions she intercepted were fragmented, but clearly he was enjoying their attention much more thoroughly than she was. She couldn't help but steal a glance up to his topaz eyes, not sure if she should risk glaring at him just a little. His eyes never met hers, though, so she turned her stare back to the road.

She sighed and decided to try to enjoy the moment, as strange and foreign as it was. There was no familiar face in the throng of onlookers, so she focused on the building ahead.

The white building hovering in the distance was difficult to compare. It was not quite the same as a castle, but it exuded an ancient elegance that did not seem European or American. Although it sprawled across a vast lawn, it did not intimidate, but seemed to be welcoming her to it.

Large windows looked out from the front, framed in curving lines. There were columns bracing the entrance, but unlike those that graced southern plantations or capital buildings, these were wrapped in vines and flowers that seemed to be as much a part of the building as the walls. She was eager to have a better look at the tall, majestic structure, and hoped that their path would lead directly there as the crowded street seemed to indicate.

She made a sideways glance in Bain's direction. He had a forced look of determination set on his face while his eyes jotted out to the people and back to the road. He seemed to feel her staring at him and turned to her with a meaningful look.

How many times had she seen that look in his eyes before . . . their first day of junior high school, his first dance, the first time a girl called him on the phone, registering for high school . . . She knew she was daydreaming to keep her mind off of the gazing crowd.

Suddenly, she felt a warm touch on her hand. She didn't even have to look to know that it was Bain reaching for her hand. Somehow, she did not feel embarrassed, or childish. Here, in this world of strangers, it seemed comforting and acceptable. They walked on in silence, but the simple gesture gave her confidence, filling her with gratitude for her life-long friend.

She ventured more glimpses at the crowd, realizing that the procession was relatively quiet—no music or loud speakers announcing their arrival. She could hear the low buzz of conversations, but the unusual quiet was disconcerting.

It was a relief to finally proceed through the plush green grass that hemmed the beautiful building. The trees dotting the yard held älvor, and as they crossed the emerald lawn a sweet song filled the air. The bell-like voices rang in harmony, creating a soft, yet exuberant melody.

She was transported in her mind to the Living Garden and the afternoons spent in the small paradise of her tiny exquisite friends. It occurred to her that she had lost track of Adarae's colony just shortly after they had arrived in the Door of Vines, but here, among the perfectly spaced trees, they were impossible for her to find.

The seven of them reached the front steps of the building where the doorway greeted them in a two-story height, allowing the dragon to follow unimpeded. The music continued even as they entered the great hall. It was much larger than the exterior suggested. The space was open, and above, where a ceiling should have been, the sky greeted them. The floor shined white with marbling veins of silver, while plush, thick carpets nestled under sofas settled about the room.

But it was the trees that seemed to grow straight out of the floor and reach the heavens that drew her attention. The branches were filled with the brightly colored butterfly wings of the älvor.

Ella guided them to a sofa, and they all sat in a large semi-circle around the room. From here, it was easier to admire the trees and sky that the walls had somehow captured.

She was aware of Pulsar since he had finally brought his attention back to her. Now that the parade through town was over, he was allowing her back into his thoughts. She could sense his present giddiness, and it made her smile.

Bain still held her hand as they sat on the soft furniture. He seemed more at ease since entering the grand building and leaving the crowd behind. They gauged each other in glances but remained silent while they waited.

With her eyes, Erin traced the bark on the trees all the way to the branches. The colored wings of the älvor were visible, thanks to her new extreme eyesight, but their faces were still too small to see clearly from this distance. From here it was easy to imagine Adarae, Elir, and all the others in the trees above. The calming, happy music continued softly in the background, making her feel strangely at home. If she closed her eyes, she could easily imagine herself sitting in the garden absorbing the sunshine.

It startled her when a tall, handsome, dark chocolate-skinned älv entered the room. His deep coffee eyes rested on her and Bain, and he approached them with a steady gait. He was dressed strikingly, with a dark purple tunic that set off his stunning colored skin, black pants, and tall shiny boots. His thick, curly hair was long and pulled at the nape of his neck with a leather band so that it half covered the tips of his ears.

She couldn't help but gape at him with his striking presence.

I doubt it is custom to stare, Pulsar interrupted her trance.

She could only hope that her cheeks were not turning crimson and giving her embarrassment away.

The elf stood before them, tall and lean, and smiled warmly with dazzling white teeth. "Welcome to Älfheim. My name is Anjasa. I will be escorting you to see the queen momentarily, but first, I will show you to your rooms to freshen up from your trip." His eyes flicked to the sweat marks on Bain's shirt. "If you will, please follow me." His deep voice was friendly, yet commanding. He turned on his heel and strode away while the twins tagged behind.

Erin looked back at the others still seated, noticing that their clothes did not even appear ruffled from the flight.

Go on, Fireborn. There is nowhere they can take you that I won't be able to speak to your mind.

She followed Anjasa through a series of halls and levels before they finally came to their separate rooms that adjoined with a center wall.

"You will be meeting with the queen shortly. You should find everything you need in your rooms. Please consider the clothes in your wardrobes your own. It would be most appropriate for the two of you to look your best." With that, Anjasa bowed and turned to descend the stairs.

The suite that she was assigned to was open and bright. A large balcony jetted out with wide double doors leading out to it. She made sure to tell Pulsar that he would be able to visit her room after all.

As she explored the spacious accommodations, she found a wardrobe filled with clothes and a big bathroom, complete with a free-standing bath tub and a large framed mirror over the dainty sink. On one wall sat an ornate desk with a chair that held her familiar purple suitcase.

Taking her bathroom things along, she washed her face and tried to tame the unruly red curls that chose their own course. It was a hopeless cause to try to look the part of an elf if she relied on her own suitcase. The reality was catching up with her. She was finally going to do it. It was too late to turn back. It would be so much easier if she didn't have so many unanswered questions.

How was she going to change? What would that mean to her future and the people she loved? The teachers at the cottage had been most unwilling to reveal details. All of Erin's questions had been deflected, leaving her guessing at the answers.

But she was here. She opened the wardrobe and shifted through the dresses that hung there. She settled on a forest green gown that was surprisingly light and elegant without too many embellishments. A subtle floral design cut through the fabric at a slant in a deeper tone of green, ending at the shoulder.

It felt foreign to wear something so exquisite. Jeans and T-shirts ruled her wardrobe year round. She turned almost unwillingly to the mirror. She didn't want to be reminded of all of her shortcomings, especially when compared to the overly beautiful elves.

She stared at the transformation the dress created. Her eyes seemed to be the same color of the dress, and her fair skin, that she had always felt self-conscious about, somehow did not seem out of place. And, if it were possible, her independent auburn curls seemed to complete the ensemble in spite of their unruliness.

She admitted that she looked better than when she left home, but it wasn't going to make this any less difficult. Maybe the dress would hide the churning she still felt in her stomach. The war wasn't over yet.

She knocked on Bain's door, surprised that he wasn't already in the hall waiting for her. He opened the door a little ways, and with a relieved smile, let her in. His hair was wet from washing, and he was wearing jeans. She laughed when she saw the variety of shirts displayed all over his bed.

"I don't know what I'm supposed to wear," he began.

She inspected the selection and chose a white cotton long sleeve shirt. It did not have much detail to it, and Bain always looked brilliant in white. She sat on a chair and waited as he shrugged the top on over his head, and ruffled his wet blond hair. It had grown out a little in the three months he had avoided haircuts.

"I think I'm going to try these boots out," he said as he sat down with a soft brown pair.

She wasn't sure how the jeans were working with the outfit, but decided against giving advice.

"Are you nervous?" he asked as he pulled his second boot on.

"Yeah, kind of," she said. But she thought "kind of" as in being kind of dead or kind of falling off a cliff.

"This place is so big! Do you have a balcony too?"

"Yes. I bet you can see mine from here." She walked to the tall doors and out to the landing. "It looks like you can visit me from the front door or the back."

He was behind her suddenly taking in the view. "I wonder who all lives here, in this enormous place. Do you think we'll actually get to stay here?"

"Who knows," she said, then turned to see her tall twin, looking handsome in his new outfit. The shirt was longer than he usually wore, but worked somehow, even with his jeans. "Did your boots fit?"

"Perfectly, and they're comfortable too." He walked back

into the room. "Are you ready to see what happens next?"

The excitement in his eyes was impossible to miss. But the twisting knots in her stomach were in full force now. Erin thought about the unknown event looming in the near future.

"Ready or not . . ." Her voice wasn't as steady as she hoped.

He came over and squeezed her hand. "We're in this together, you know. Don't worry—if you trip, I'll say it was my fault."

She smiled meekly and let him lead her to the door.

Chapter Twenty-seven

THE BRIDGE

Anjasa led them into a large assembly hall. At least that's what Erin decided it was. A flowing river separated the room down the center so that they stood on one side of the bank of the rushing water. Seated across the river, in a semi-circle, were a few dozen elves.

Erin felt like her butterflies had turned into birds beating in her stomach and throat. She hadn't expected such a large audience of strangers for her life-altering event. It was terrifying.

Erin recognized her teachers sitting on the left side of the throne, waiting patiently. It was odd to see them here, outside the cottage rooms. It was hard to imagine that this city was their real home.

Relief flooded her as Pulsar entered and made himself comfortable behind the row of teachers. She realized that they had not spoken much since she last saw him, and that it was as much her doing as his.

You look magnificent, Fireborn.

She flushed involuntarily at his words. It didn't seem like anyone had the right to compliment her looks, especially here among the overly beautiful elves. At least she was the only one who could hear him. She was so nervous. She wasn't even sure what they would be expected to do. Were they going to have to prove their skills right here in front of the queen? What if she messed everything up?

His deep voice was back in her head, *Don't worry, this too shall pass.*

Ella was suddenly in front of them as well as a familiar pedestal holding a large magical book. It was the same book that they had been reading in the cabin. It seemed like years ago now.

"It is time for you to turn the page," Ella said to them, and then vanished from sight.

They both stepped closer as Erin turned the yellowing parchment and watched the pages become stone again. She peered together at the words inscribed.

THE BRIDGE OF ETERNITY

Should you choose to cross, be warned that there is no turning back.

*You shall be transformed forevermore,
owning a new life,*

one that will require your whole heart and much work.

Now begins the second part of your journey.

Erin looked up and gasped at a wooden bridge gently arching over the gaping river that separated them from the waiting elves. The shiny deep-toned structure showed no indication of its sudden materialization.

She took a deep breath. In a sudden rush, images flashed through her mind. Grandpa Jessie, Mrs. Hammel, the patio at home in the summer, the green mountains with misty haze—all of the things she was leaving behind.

Pulsar saw them too. *Fireborn, this is what you were born to do,* his voice filled her mind.

The truth of his words crashed through her unexpectedly, overtaking the gnawing in her stomach. He was right. The truth made her whole body tremble. It was trying to push every possible doubt aside. She didn't understand why it was true, but she looked across the vast river to her beloved friend. His liquid gold eyes were clear even from this distance.

Thank you, Pulsar. I will try to not disappoint you.

She glanced up at Bain. He nodded back at her and took her hand. Together they made their way over the intimidating, polished bridge, watching the water currents rush beneath them.

She couldn't help but marvel that such a large river could flow so fiercely through a building. The sound of rushing water drowned out any other noise. The glossy bridge was incredible as well. The wood seemed to be a deep cherry, and it was polished to the point of showing their reflection. She was aware of each step they took over the masterpiece and couldn't help but wonder if they would feel different when they reached the other side.

Though the river was impressively large, she felt like the other side greeted them too quickly. The row of chairs stood neatly in a row before them filled with dignified faces. Erin stood before the queen and felt an air of nobility that compelled her to bow for the first time in her life.

"Rise," the queen commanded. Her face was timeless, outside of the vast wisdom that emanated from her pale blue eyes.

"Welcome to Álfheim. I am Queen Áldera."

Erin tried to breathe normally, but her nervousness was still overpowering. Her eyes wandered almost involuntarily to the rows of elves on either side. Everyone she knew was there, and so many she didn't. She couldn't be sure how Anjasa managed to find his seat without her noticing.

"Will the masters please rise," Queen Áldera commanded. She took her throne once again and shifted her gaze to where their teachers stood. The twins responded by standing before the first one in the row.

Agnar had been their first trainer, so it seemed natural to have him greet them first. His eyes smiled at them in spite of his otherwise formal demeanor. "I am pleased to present you each with an eternal blade. This piece will become a permanent part of your magic as soon as you touch the hilt. It will serve you loyally and become your trusted friend. But be warned: if you commit an unjust death, it will strip you of your magic."

With this he brandished a long blade from behind him. The hilt was carefully wrapped in leather. The sword master bowed as he bestowed the eternal blade upon Bain.

Bain held the blade on its flat side inspecting the white and silver marbling. He stole a glance at Agnar, who gave a slight nod. Bain smiled as he unwound the leather from the hilt.

Bright silver shone out as the covering came off, revealing a bright grip and pommel. His right hand closed on the grip and he tested the perfectly balanced weight, the bright metal hilt reflecting the same color as his wand. Light glinted off the handle and cast prisms on the floor. Diamonds studded the hilt while small sapphires were embedded modestly in a swirling pattern around the large glittering precious stones. As perfect as his wand was, the sword was its equal in every way.

Agnar presented him with a sheath, and secured it to Bain. He bowed one final time to Bain and stepped towards Erin.

"Your eternal blade," he said, with a slight bow.

His hands were swift, and she almost didn't catch the blur of his arm while he reached from somewhere behind him and was suddenly holding another blade.

She smiled as she saw it, as if it were already familiar to her. The blade was much shorter than Bain's. Swirls of deep green and jade mixed with white to create a beautiful marbled blade. She lifted it carefully from Agnar's hands and, following Bain's example, unwound the leather around the hilt.

The soft gold hilt surprised her, as did the taupe suede leather on the grip. She was surprised to find diamonds and emeralds crested on the handle, so skillfully cut that they seemed to be producing their own light. It seemed more a piece of jewelry than a weapon of destruction.

Her right hand found the grip, and as she closed her hand around the supple leather, a surge of magic seemed to bond between her and the sword. It wasn't the same sensation she felt when she forced her magic into a spell. This was involuntary, as if the blade was uniting its strength with hers, forming a companionship.

Agnar secured a sheath on her as well, with such practiced hands that it seemed as though he never even touched the fabric on her dress. She was surprised at how comfortable the blade felt at her side; it seemed to have always belonged there.

Bowing slightly once more, Agnar stepped back and took his place in the row.

Aelflaed was the next teacher in the line. The twins stood before the beautiful elf and waited.

She looked at them and spoke with her soft, yet firm voice, "I now present you with a token of the land in which you studied." Her hands were swift and from behind her she produced a bow and quiver of arrows for each of them. "The wood is of the bara-clond tree. It will not break under your care."

Erin held the bow and quiver, wondering how to carry it when Aelflaed presented them with a sling that fit over their backs. Aelflaed curtsied ever so gracefully and stepped back to join the others.

Next in line was Master Ulric, one of the few elves that showed wrinkles around his knowing eyes. "Magic is a lifelong study. To aid you in your conquest, I give you these Changing Brooches. The metal has been infused with spells, and as you learn to use it, it will transform into innumerable things." With that he handed them small metal pins and bowed before returning to his place.

Erin admired the small pin, but wondered at its significance. Hers was shaped like a leaf on a stem, while Bain's resembled a sword and shield. She decided that it was probably customary to wear them and turned to Bain to pin his to his shirt before he could protest. He returned the favor, pinning hers carefully to her dress.

The queen stood once again, making it clear that they should return their attention. She spoke with a warm voice, "Come."

Erin felt the nervous knot twist in her stomach as she approached the throne.

The queen continued, "There is one final piece I give you."

Instantly, a thin silver band was in her hands and she placed it onto Bain's brow. Even as she stood back, she held another swirling band of gold and placed it on Erin's head.

As soon as the metal touched her hair, Erin felt a warm wave of heat flow like water down her head and neck and continue to reach her whole being. The feeling was that of standing under a warm waterfall, but impossibly, not getting wet. It was so unexpected that she could only stand like a statue, cemented to her spot with the strange magic.

Eventually the sensation subsided enough for her to remember where she was, and once again to look into the goddess eyes of the queen.

Queen Āldera raised her hands to the seated elves. "I now present älv Bain and älva Erin Fireborn."

Chapter Twenty-eight

CHANGE IS GOOD

ERIN AND BAIN SAT ON the floor in his room. Now that the ceremony had ended, along with the unbelievable feast, she was happy to find a moment out of the spotlight.

"It is going to be hard getting used to your new look," Erin said, watching Bain's face.

She had seen him gradually change over the last few hours. His ears, which were still visible in spite of his attempt to grow out his hair, pointed at the tips. She supposed that they should feel more like they fit in here, but instead it enhanced the foreign feeling of the kingdom.

It wasn't only his ears. She was sure he had somehow grown a couple inches taller, and she couldn't be sure, but he even seemed to have a leaner, more muscular build. *Is that even possible?* she mused to herself. No one could really grow taller and stronger in a couple hours, could they? There was something different about his face too. It was as if an artist had taken his features and added subtle angles making him look slightly more grown up. Or maybe that was her imagination too.

She had avoided looking into the mirror when they got to Bain's room. She had felt her own pointed ears with her fingers but was nervous about seeing them with her own eyes. It was easier to pretend that she wasn't really that different now, but the golden circlet on her head was a constant reminder of the warm energy that still buzzed inside of her like a lingering medication. No, she didn't really want to know how her life had changed, yet.

"Well, I like it on you," Bain said, snapping her out of her wandering thoughts.

"What do you mean?"

"Your ears are adorable."

"How do you know? You can't even see them." She couldn't believe she was flushing in embarrassment from *his* words, of all people.

"You tucked your hair behind one ear, and it is very cute."

"You better watch it. I'll be calling your ears cute." Even as she spoke, she heard the wrong notes in her voice, weaker than she meant them to be. Unexpectedly, she felt his fingers on her chin as he lifted her face to face him.

"Erin, you are an älva now. You are going to have to accept that at some point. And I might as well be the first one to tell you that you are beautiful." He sighed and let go of her chin. "In the last few hours you have grown a little taller. Your walk is more graceful. Even your hair shines more, and don't even ask me about that. The only thing that could make becoming an elf good for me is to have you like the change as well. So please try to accept it." He sat back and leaned on his palms. "Besides, it will help me not to feel like a freak if you at least pretend to like it."

He stared at the blue suitcase sitting in the corner. "Do you think Master Ulric will teach me how to make my pants longer? I am going to have to wear boots forever to hide my high-waters."

She laughed at him, and at the same time realized that she had been right about his sudden growth spurt.

"You look good in boots," she answered, and he tried in vain to glare at her.

"I feel like we're staying at a fancy hotel, with no key and no locks. We're not even sure who's in charge of us," Bain said. He looked out the window. "I say we go explore this place. We couldn't see anything really as we came in. There were too many people."

She could hear the excitement growing in his voice and it sounded more like he was talking about taking a hike back home than meeting a world of strange elves.

"Okay," she answered, and she really did mean it.

The best part of going outdoors was having Pulsar join them. With Bain and Pulsar, she didn't feel alone, but they couldn't help but be conspicuous. Bain decided that he really was looking for some jeans, so they set out on the premise of denim shopping.

The streets were quaint, lined with perfectly level bricks. The shops were close together in the town center, with houses dotting the vast countryside. The buildings were medium sized, and each with such individual character that they scarcely needed signs to indicate what goods waited inside.

There was a blacksmith selling all sorts of metal works, and Bain insisted on perusing through the store, examining the metal pieces carefully. Erin couldn't be sure what most of the goods in the store were really for, but waited patiently, watching her twin with amusement.

There were plenty of clothing shops. The fabrics and styles were so foreign to the clothing she owned. They did find some trousers made of denim, but the cut and style were so strange Bain wouldn't even try them on.

It didn't take long for them to realize that their money was not the currency used in this place. If they were intent on purchasing something, they would have to find a way to exchange some of their cash for the paper money they used here. They decided to keep looking around for now, but made a note to ask someone when they returned to the castle.

As they strolled along the brick road, she smelled the bakery, smokehouses, and many other food shops. They almost had to make a run to the castle for some money as Bain's stomach grumbled.

A boy elf, about ten years old, met them suddenly on the

street. "Can I touch the dragon?" he asked them.

Erin looked up at her towering friend.

I will handle this, Pulsar answered.

"Uh, sure, stand right here," Erin directed.

The boy reached up to Pulsar, and the dragon lowered himself, spreading his wings to cover the side where the boy stood. He carefully stroked the suede soft wings, taking glances at his large topaz eyes.

"He understands me, doesn't he?" the boy asked, his hands still moving slowly over the velvety wings.

Erin nodded.

"What is his name?" he asked.

"Pulsar."

"Welcome to our city, Pulsar. You are the most beautiful dragon I have ever seen." He looked again into Pulsar's eyes.

Pulsar nodded his head in appreciation to the child elf.

"Oh, I almost forgot! My mum told me to invite you into our shop for something to eat." He looked at them conspiratorially. "Actually, I think she just wants to meet you. She's been gushing about you since you came to the city. If you don't come, she'll never stop."

They followed the boy into the store. The baked goods filled the store with a warm, welcoming, delicious smell. Behind the counter stood an älva with straight, brown hair and light brown eyes.

"Welcome to Álfheim! My name's Meg. I am so pleased to make your acquaintance. I've been telling Andy here that it's about time the two of you came to our kingdom. What, with all the work you've been doing, and goodness knows how much time it's taken you. You simply must try some of my cherry pastries."

She hurried around the counter and pulled two chairs out for them in front of a small round table. "I've never met twins before. It must be simply marvelous to have a twin, isn't it?"

She had already set the pastries out for them on little plates and was looking at them as though they were her own children. Erin nodded dumbly and realized a little late that the lady expected them to answer.

"You two simply must come to my shop as often as you can. Free of charge, of course. You two like chocolate milk?"

Again they nodded as she fussed over them. They didn't have to speak much as Meg filled the silence. Somehow, Erin began to feel at home—like there was another Mrs. Hammel wanting nothing more than to dote over them and keep them stocked with plenty of goodies. Meg even offered her baked goods to Pulsar, who had to kindly refuse. Erin smiled at his answer. He couldn't even imagine eating bread.

Eventually they made their way out of the shop, but not without baskets of rolls and pastries and the promise to return often. The afternoon stretched on, feeling more like a strange parade than a casual stroll. Even when the elves did not stop to chat with them, it was hard to simply walk by without attracting attention. Erin watched Pulsar, who was glowing like a lighthouse, and decided that it was he who was responsible for catching every eye. His scales were almost blindingly gold in the bright sunlight. It was easy to pretend that he was the only one anyone was really interested in.

Even so, she had never been greeted by so many strangers; beautiful, graceful, incredibly intimidating strangers. She grew steadily quieter as the day stretched on, hoping that she would become somewhat invisible next to the conspicuous dragon.

"We haven't seen much of the palace," Bain said as they made their way down the cobbled street.

"What are you saying?" she asked. "Are you giving up on the jeans?"

"I think I'm going to have to wait on those for now. I really can't see wearing fifteenth century trousers. Whatever those things were, they weren't jeans."

"I guess that means we have to figure out where our rooms are. You should have brought the red twine. I could have tied it around a few trees and maybe the banister."

Bain just smiled and took off in a run towards the grand white building.

Chapter Twenty-nine

GONE

THE SUN STRETCHED ACROSS THE downy ivory quilt, finally touching Erin's eyelids, encouraging them to open. Her first day in the kingdom was a surreal fairy tale that stretched into her dreams. Now that the warm sun brushed her face, and her dreams were finally put away, she tried to place the events in order in her mind; riding on Pulsar, meeting the queen, becoming an älva, all impossible things to the real world she had lived in her whole life.

She opened her eyes to see the elegant room, reminding her of the reality of the day before. She reached up and touched her ears. Sure enough, they came to points at the tops where roundness once was. She realized that today she would finally have to look in the mirror.

Yesterday, it was easy to stay busy with Bain. He had not been disappointed in their explorations; it would take days to see all that the castle had to offer. It was exactly the kind of distraction she needed to offset the unbelievable events.

She hurried to get ready, eager to see him. She was sure that their free time was about to be filled with training. There were so many questions filling her head that she didn't mind the thought of having a mentor guiding them along.

The previously avoided mirror now stood before her. Of course Bain had been right. She was a little taller, and her face somehow more grown up. It wasn't that she thought it was a stranger reflecting in the mirror, but she could not match the face with her feelings. Was it possible to look like an elf, and still not know how to be one? She tried to convince herself that she could pull this off. She could somehow be one of them, one of the overly beautiful creatures that seemed to not belong to the world, but in a world of their own where their gracefulness and dazzling features would be ordinary.

Maybe they didn't know how wonderful they looked. Maybe they couldn't see their own staggering beauty that would put any human to shame. She smiled at the idea. It was working. If she could make herself believe that, then there would be less to try to live up to—less to overcome.

Confident in her new outlook, she decided to sneak over the balcony to Bain's back door. It was too easy jumping the short distance between their balconies. Excitement filled her as she turned the knob. Today was going to be even better than yesterday. Anything would be better than having to be on display for a whole city of stunning strangers.

She was surprised to find his bed empty. She sat on a chair expecting that he was just in his bathroom. Looking around the room, she suddenly felt uneasy. The blue suitcase that had been in the corner was gone. His bed didn't even look slept in. Even if he had decided to go out for a morning run, why would he take his suitcase?

She knocked on the bathroom door. No answer. There was no one inside. Now she was searching the room. The wardrobe had been emptied; there were no clothes to be found anywhere. The room appeared to have never met her twin. The walls seemed to be moving in, or the room was beginning to spin. Panic reached icy hands around her chest. Nothing of his was left here, as if Bain had not existed.

She ran to the bathroom, the only place she hadn't searched. Maybe he left something, proof that he had been here. Something that could convince her that everything was all right.

And there on the counter was the proof. A small piece of

paper folded over with her name written on the outside. Her hands shook as she unfolded the note.

> *Erin,*
>
> *I'm sorry I had to leave so suddenly. I knew you would try to talk me out of it if I waited too long. It had to be this way. I wanted to see the world, and now I have the chance. You'll be fine; you have the dragon.*
> *I'm sorry.*
> *Bain*

She sunk to the floor as her legs refused to hold her. She couldn't believe that this could be possible. Her best friend, her life-long companion—he couldn't be gone. He could never be gone.

She wasn't sure when she had begun crying. She was vaguely aware of the carpet she had crumpled onto. Her mind refused to process the words on the paper.

He couldn't leave. How could she live without him? She lay there on the floor, oblivious to time passing. Without Bain, what could matter anymore? Her mind became numb, and she wished for unconsciousness. Couldn't she just faint like they did on old movies. Was there any escape from the crushing news?

Her sobs were now soundless, as if there were no more tears left in her eyes. But her chest still hiccupped from the long drawn out cry. It wasn't until she could hear her own breaths that she realized she was not alone.

It was more of a sense of someone else present than a sound. Her face was still turned to the empty bathroom. Out of obligation, she lifted her head to see the visitor. Standing silently on the balcony was Pulsar, his deep gold eyes looking on her with gentleness. Now that her eyes were focusing on him, she realized he wore the saddle.

Come, Fireborn.

It was as if his words released another dam of tears, and they streamed as she ran toward him. Remembering his burning heat, she jumped to his back onto the saddle. He covered her in his soft velvet wings as she clung to him, tears watering. She cried on his back, allowing his heat to comfort her. He waited until once again, the tears ebbed.

Hold on, he commanded, and lifted into the sky.

She didn't have to think about it, she hardly remembered strapping her legs into the plush fenders. Below her the landscape was sinking into a dollhouse-sized town. Ahead there were trees, reminding her of the Door of Vines. Maybe it really was the same place.

The warm wind whipped through her hair and sounded in her ears. She allowed Pulsar into her thoughts until she was sure he had the note memorized as well. Mostly her mind was numb, making every detail seem unreal—the clouds below them, the trees in the dense forest, and most of all, time passing.

They just kept flying, as though they never needed to land. The sun had cleared its path through the blue sky—the only indication of the day slipping easily away.

Pulsar had not offered advice, but kept a steady pace with the beating of his wings, listening to her thoughts and her emotions. She was grateful that he just knew what to do, that she didn't have to tell him what she needed. She wasn't even sure if *she* knew.

The mountains were finally under their shadow and Pulsar chose a clearing to land. Slowly she unlaced her legs from the saddle, and without thinking, slid her hands over the golden scales. Her mind caught up to her as she realized that she no longer felt a burning sensation from his heat. She could detect his temperature, but was somehow immune to the burning effect it had on her before.

You are an älva now, Fireborn, she heard him say to her mind.

"I didn't know it would change this too." She wrapped her arms around his warm smooth body, absorbing his heat, and letting it restore her magic.

She slid to the forest floor, resting her back against his

form. "I can't believe he would do this to me," she said again, wondering how many times that thought had crossed over and over in her mind. "Is it my fault? If he thought I would be more understanding would he have talked to me about it? Did I keep him from what he really wanted?"

Pulsar's thoughts were filled with compassion. *Little one, you cannot blame yourself for his choices. I have no doubt that he loves you, and it would seem impossible for him not to know you love him too.*

"I can't go back," Erin answered. "I am not going to live in a world of strangers alone."

You may stay here as long as you wish, until you are ready.

Her hands held her face, and she wondered vaguely why her head was not throbbing. For all of the crying she had done, she should be paying the consequences by now. "I guess it's just me. Bain can live without me; I just can't live without him. I don't even know where he is. I can't call, write, or reach him at all. He's just gone. Maybe if I just knew more, I could have let him go." She shook her head. Her own words felt like a lie to her. She knew she couldn't just let him go. She would have wanted to come too.

And maybe that is what hurt the most; knowing that she was probably the one to cause this kind of parting. She was the weak one. She was the one who couldn't let go.

The thoughts twisted like a knife in her chest. *Was he jealous of Pulsar?* "You'll be fine, you have the dragon." It echoed in her mind, like an accusing verdict. Did he really think that anyone could replace him? Wasn't she allowed to love more than just him?

Her thoughts tumbled around in her mind, never ceasing, never finding answers. It was a double-edged sword; her pain for his absence that was caused by her own need to have her brother near. The terrible truth of knowing that she couldn't have let him go just yet crushed her with its weight.

It helped that Pulsar was eternally patient. He tried in vain to comfort her, and in the end, just waited for her thoughts to slow.

The sun finished arching across the sky, and night had finally settled when Erin drifted into a fitful sleep, curled up into a ball. Pulsar spread his velvety wings over her and rested his own head on the forest floor.

Chapter Thirty

FIRE PRACTICE

Erin had been surprised when Pulsar arrived in the morning with her suitcase. He was a little evasive about how he had managed to acquire it, so she stopped asking about it and decided to enjoy the provisions. It was strange to suddenly call a forest her home, but the grief and anger boiling under the surface kept her from wanting to return.

Do you want to hunt with me? he asked, after she had brushed her teeth with the ice cold stream water.

"I guess. What do you hunt?" She decided that the sound of her voice eased the mood that seemed to have settled in the quiet forest.

Deer, mostly. It depends on what I'm in the mood for.

Not wanting to be left alone, she climbed on the saddle. They were in the air so suddenly that if she had not been securely in, she would have jerked back onto the ground.

Sorry, I wasn't thinking. I have never hunted with a passenger before.

Erin checked for her blade beside her and was pleased she hadn't lost it during take off. The familiar rush of air was comforting, and she tried to focus on the ground below instead of the day before. Instinctively, she reached her mind to his, trying to understand what he was thinking about.

Although he was skilled at blocking her thoughts, he did not try to keep her out. She closed her eyes and watched the hunt through his mind. She could see the small herd of deer below and could now understand the thought process Pulsar used.

It seemed less painful than she thought it would be. Part of her was squeamish as she anticipated the end point of the hunt. The deer he had singled out did not even run. He used his magic to close down its mind bringing instant unconsciousness, and then, with another wave of magic, stopped its heart. The hunt was over in seconds.

However humane his methods may have been, she did not feel like she had the stomach to watch him eat. She found a clearing after they landed and built a fire, with Pulsar's able help. After he had taken his prey to a new location, he returned to her with a skinned piece of venison.

Cook it over your fire. I will not have you waste away while you are with me, Fireborn. With that, he cleaned a spit for her out of a branch and left her to her work.

The meat popped and sizzled over the fire creating a tantalizing smell. She hadn't realized how hungry she was; it had been a whole day since she had eaten. As she watched the meat cook she mused that if it hadn't been for Pulsar, she may not have thought about eating for days.

She used her magic to slowly turn the meat over the fire, wondering vaguely how long they could live here in the mountains. Pulsar would have no trouble, of course, and she knew that Aelflaed had taught them enough about the plants for her to find edible vegetation.

Then the memories flooded in; Bain dripping purple juice down his chin as he bit into a new fruit. Aelflaed hadn't warned them, but encouraged them to take a bite, and then laughed as the spring of juice shot out. They had purple juice all over their shirts as well, not that it mattered much. Bain had been overly pleased that she had been just as messy with the strange spurting fruit as he was.

Bain. She couldn't let herself think of him yet. She was the one to push him away. She was the reason he left. And she was the only one who was suffering the consequences of her own weak need. The reason a black hole had taken over where her heart should be was because she needed him too much. She just couldn't exist without her twin. Without him, she didn't know who she was. And that was why he had left her. He must have wanted freedom from her suffocating need to be around him. She didn't know how she was ever going to find her way out of this dismal hole in her heart without the sunshine Bain filled her with.

But she couldn't think about it, or the cycle would start over, and she would spend another day crying. No, she needed to be strong. If nothing else, she had Pulsar to think about. Surely, no dragon ever dreamed of spending days upon days with a crying damsel in distress.

She focused purposefully on the cooking meat. Her years of experience in the kitchen at home were paying off now, as she could see that it was finally done. She allowed a small smile as she used *thermal control* to cool the piece down so that she could take a bite. It wasn't the same flavor as the meat she cooked at home, but it was perfectly tender, and filled her empty stomach with its warm sustenance.

Are you feeling better? His words brought her eyes up to meet his as he sat just across from her. He already knew where her mind was, though. *I think it is time we learn some of the tricks of the trade,* he continued. *There are a few things we need to work on.*

It wasn't hard to talk her out of sitting alone. The sky was as much a home to her as any with its welcoming freedom. She let the rushing wind clear her mind. When they reached an exhilarating altitude, the training began.

You must become familiar with flight maneuvers. This will aid in evasion and defensive as well as offensive tactics.

She didn't feel like questioning his planned activity and decided it would be a good distraction from her daunting thoughts.

You should tighten the straps on your legs, and tuck your head in. We are going to start with a straight dive, pulling out just over the treetops. Don't let go.

She strangely felt no nervousness in freefalling out of the sky. Instead she welcomed the experience, trusting him easily with her life. As soon as she had secured her legs snugly and pulled her body close to his, he flipped upside down and set his wings against the streaming air. Instinctively, she closed her eyes and watched their fall through his mind.

She was surprised at the complete control he felt over the rocketing flight to the ground. A long scream of raw exhilaration followed their streaking form to the earth as she let the moment release her inhibition. The fall continued as if time no longer existed, the sound of the rushing air filling her ears and the clear view of the approaching land becoming her only reality.

When he did pull out of the dive, it was breathtaking. His graceful curve found air currents that buoyed them easily above the trees. More maneuvers followed, and soon most of the day had been spent.

She watched the roaring campfire from her seat on the fallen tree. Even with the ink black night filling the trees, she did not feel tired. Now that her mind was not filled with flight training, it was making room for other thoughts. She knew she still wasn't ready to face the kingdom yet. Sleeping on the ground in a forest was easy compared to the loneliness she would face without Bain in a foreign crowd.

It wasn't hard letting Pulsar into her thoughts while she weaved through her situation in her head. He was lying on the ground beside her, radiating almost as much heat as the fire. She had been talking out loud to him since they landed; hearing her own voice filled some of the void of the silent forest. "So am I breaking any rules by being here instead of there?"

You are free to live and do as you please. No one owns your time but you.

"So Bain can just pick up and leave, and no one has a problem with that?"

He has just as much freedom as any other there.

"Do you think anyone is worried about where we are?"

Aelflaed knows of the situation. They are aware of Bain's leaving, and, of course, they know that you are with me.

"I guess I am just so used to us keeping track of each other. It feels so weird to be out here on our own. And Bain—I try to picture where he is. On an airplane, a train, I don't know. I would have never guessed he would just leave. Not in a million years. "Maybe I don't know him as well as I thought. I could have only seen the side he is when he is with me. I know we're not the same. Not even close. But I can't stand being so far apart with no cell phone, no e-mail, just nothing." She let her head drop to her hands again. She wasn't going to cry again. She couldn't spend every evening crying.

Pulsar interrupted her thoughts. *You are in need of a distraction. I think it's time you tried out your blade.*

She looked up in surprise.

The fire is your foe. Let's see what you can remember from your training, Fireborn.

She stood up slowly, not sure if his therapy was what she was in the mood for. She unsheathed the sword realizing that she hadn't looked carefully at it since the ceremony. The metal twisted into an elegant, yet bold pattern until it seamlessly met the jade marbled blade. Holding it felt almost as energizing as touching the dragon's scales as a surge of magic flowed into her, warming her with its buzzing energy.

"But how is sparring thin air going to help me? Don't I need an opponent?"

I won't have you forgetting all of your lessons. Practicing without a partner is more noble than allowing your training to go unused.

She faced the bright flames and whipped her blade in a trial move. It seemed to respond not only to her physical direction, but to her very thoughts, as if it could read her mind. Then suddenly a blade of fire rose from the flames and struck her sword.

"Pulsar!" she yelled.

She could only feel his determination in return.

Again the fire advanced with a low swing of an orange-tipped blade. She didn't have time to marvel over how Pulsar was able to control the fire as another blow came from the side.

She crossed her blade and deflected the flame.

Her blade became a blur as she struck it through the air, increasing her tactics and maneuvers. She really hadn't forgotten Agnar's lessons, and somehow, even here in the black forest, she could hear his advice and commands and she battled the flaming sword. The firelight glinted off the blade as she danced around it with her deadly play. It had worked its magic, allowing her mind to be completely occupied once again.

The fire finally died down and the opponent disappeared into smoke.

I think you are getting faster, Pulsar offered.

She sheathed her blade and sat down.

Before her thoughts could drift, he continued, *Every day you will practice with your blade. If you have the need to defend yourself, you will find yourself not unequal to the challenge.*

She knew he was being careful not to remind her of Bain or the kingdom. But it didn't matter. Bain was in her heart no matter where he happened to be on the planet. No distraction could keep her from that.

"I'll make you a deal," she began, looking earnestly into his eyes. "I will train with you out here for as long as you want. I'll do anything you ask. I will practice diligently. And in return, I want you to help me find my brother."

We don't have to be out here. If you wish to go back to the kingdom, you may. You would be welcomed with open arms.

"Okay, a revised deal. I will work hard at anything you want me to learn, but I have to find Bain, and you have to help me."

So you want to remain exiled in this forest?

"For now," she said, almost smugly. She knew it was too hard to return just yet. "But will you help me?"

My every happiness rests with yours, Fireborn. But you should know, there are no leads to Bain's location. No one saw him leave, and he left no trace of his intentions.

"It's like finding a Bain in a haystack."

More or less.

Chapter Thirty-one

ON AN AIRPLANE

THE PINE NEEDLES ON THE ground made a soft enough mat, and with her sweatshirt folded under her head, it almost seemed comfortable. But when Pulsar stretched his large wing over her, like a velvet canopy, and the warmth filled the air like a summer night, she finally felt at home, only, a new home. Pulsar had filled part of the hole in her heart, left when Bain disappeared. *Oh well, she thought to herself, I guess a half a heart is better than a heart that is lost.*

The warm air helped her drift to sleep, and soon she found herself in a dream. Only, it didn't feel at all like a dream. She was sitting on a small plane with two seats on each aisle. The flight attendant stopped at a row in front of her and spoke something in a different language. The accent and flow of the words were completely foreign to her.

As the attendant moved on, she became aware of the people on the plane. It was not completely full. The seat beside her was empty, and just one portly man with olive skin and oily straight black hair sat sleeping across from her. She watched him snore for a moment, and wondered idly where they were going. Then a voice split the silence like thunder. It was Bain's voice. She frantically pulled the seatbelt off her lap and bounded into the aisle.

There, just a couple rows up from her seat, was Bain. She ran to see him, but stopped cold as she saw his face. He was sleeping, or it looked like he was. The peaceful countenance she had known all her life had been replaced by a haggard look. He must have muttered something in his sleep because he was clearly incoherent.

The only thing more disturbing than his condition was the aura coming off of the man seated beside him. A dark bruising aura surrounded this man, who seemed to also be sleeping. His black hair hung to his shoulders, reminding her of the other elves with their long hair. She chided herself for comparing a man with the elves. Surely there were countless men who wore their hair long. His clothes did not stand out, just an ordinary T-shirt and pants.

She couldn't help reaching out to Bain's face. Maybe she could wake him and ask where he was, where he was going. Even if all she could get from him was a warm smile, it might be enough. But as her hand closed the distance to his face, she was swallowed into darkness, and he was gone.

It took her a minute to remember where she was; the cover of Pulsar's wing allowed no light to penetrate. The night was all around her in the sounds of the forest. Pulsar was sleeping with steady long breaths, and, like always, she could not reach his mind while he slept.

She lay there looking at the dark air, thinking. Bain had never looked so worn, except when he had the flu, and he was rarely sick. The look about him was wrong for just being sick; like he was worn through in a different way, not just physically. He seemed to have purple shadows under his eyes. Maybe he was having a bad dream.

Just a dream, she reminded herself. She had only seen him in a dream. It couldn't really be just like seeing him. It was just another dream, like all the ones she'd ever had that didn't make sense. She wanted to see him so badly that she just dreamed of him.

The airplane had felt so real, though. She could hear the hum of the engine and feel the cool air in the passenger cabin. Then there was the flight attendant with her silky light brown skin.

How could she dream hearing a language she didn't know? That thought made her jolt. Was it really possible to dream someone speaking a language you have never even heard before? She replayed the details in her mind. If only she had been paying more attention to the plane, maybe there was something that would tell what airline it was. A clue to where the destination might be. But she had been careless. All she had paid attention to were the other people. So she locked the image of Bain into her memory and eventually fell into a dreamless sleep.

Chapter Thirty-two

CAMPING

MORNING FOUND HER ALONE. SHE assured herself that Pulsar was finding water or hunting. It would be easy enough to find him if she tried. She pulled some fresh clothes out of her suitcase and headed to a nearby stream. It was a lifesaver that Mrs. Hammel had insisted she bring a hand towel, shampoo, soap and everything she used daily. She had no idea she would end up relying on her suitcase so completely.

An image of the luxurious room at the castle crossed her thoughts, and she quickly pushed it aside. It looked exactly the same as the empty room next to it. The room Bain was no longer in. She splashed the icy water on her face, trying to wash her mood away. The freezing water was a welcome deterrent from the impending thoughts.

The forest was filled with the sounds and smells she had become so accustomed to during the training days. She ticked off the names of the plants: winter willows, canordill bushes, and lunaberries. She was pleased that she remembered so much from her lessons. It helped to find a rathabush filled with succulent plump berries where she filled her grumbling stomach. The morning air was positively glorious with the sun warming the ground, and the plants and animals filling the area with its splendor.

As she listened to the calls of birds and the chatter of the squirrels, she noticed a new sound enter the scene. Footsteps, breaking branches, and she even smelled something different. Instinctively, she surrounded herself with an invisibility ward and concentrated carefully on maintaining it.

Through the brush, just in front of her, a large brown furry beast entered. She watched with curiosity, keeping immaculate care to not let her ward falter. A mammoth sized head sniffed the air as the rest of its bulky body came into view. It lumbered to the berry bush and sat down to eat.

The creature put to shame every bear she had ever seen on television. The honey-colored fur seemed to indicate a grizzly, rather than a black bear. But she didn't think bears could grow to the size of an elephant. She had seen elephants before. The circus provided her with that much experience. Had they displayed hulking bears this size, they truly would have brought out a crowd.

The bear seemed oblivious to her presence as it cleaned the berries with its massive claws. The enormous paws had yellow-white claws the length of her hand. Its beady black eyes paid no attention to anything but the juicy berries it was stripping from the bush.

It was a combination of fascinating and horrible to watch the enormous bear clean the bush of every berry and leaf. The stench of the bear was almost overwhelming, but the teeth on the creature gave her no desire to try to relocate yet. She waited for the beast to lumber off before she released her ward and bolted through the trees towards camp.

Pulsar was waiting for her by the stream that ran through the clearing. She admired his size as she approached him. She realized that his face could seem formidable to a stranger, as well as his towering height. To her, it was Pulsar, but she imagined how terrifying he could be to an enemy.

He hummed a deep rumble of satisfaction as he read her thoughts. "Oh, come on. You must know how completely enormous you are." She couldn't help laugh at his purring response. "So, what have you planned for today?"

There is something I have been saving for you. Would you like me to show you?

"Sure." She couldn't penetrate his barricaded mind as she waited for his response. The glinting scales were reflecting the sunlight like an enormous disco ball, scattering shards of light in every direction. Even as her eyes adjusted to his brilliance, he disappeared.

"Where are you?" she asked, looking up to the sky as if he could have somehow taken flight instantly.

I am still here. Then, just as suddenly as before, he came into view.

"So you can do the invisibility ward too? I guess I never thought about you using it."

It is even better than that.

"What do you mean?"

I can make other things become invisible too.

"So, if I'm riding you, you can make us both invisible without me helping?"

Exactly. It is one of the advantages dragons have. The principle is somewhat the same as your ward, but demands much less concentration. It is more like breathing fire. I can produce a flame just by thinking of it. With that, he tilted his head and blew a fiery blaze into the sky that looked like a bomb had just exploded in his mouth. The orange flames held a steady violent stream as he spewed fire into the air.

His face lowered and he stopped the arsenal of flames. He leveled his eyes with hers. *You're not afraid?*

"Not even close. Just make sure you don't singe me when I'm sitting on your back."

The day was filled with invisibility and fire. Pulsar had justified the practice easily—he suggested trying it for the first time under serious pressure. She really didn't want to find out if she could turn into a crisp piece of bacon on his back during some kind of battle, so she was eager to let him practice while she rode.

The height they flew protected the trees from the scorching

heat, allowing them to maneuver tactic flight patterns while yawning fire. Pulsar was meticulous to practice every dive and pull out while switching their invisibility on and off. She never could be certain of their status as he was always visible to her while she was on his back. *Just like the ward,* she thought.

Once again, Pulsar successfully occupied another day, stealing her away from her thoughts. She was kept in check with his constant monitoring of where her mind wandered.

The bonfire was becoming a nightly ritual of sparring with the flaming foe. Erin slashed the night air with her glinting blade. Pulsar watched with an unwavering gaze as she performed each movement. The fire provided a target for her release of anger. As she gave herself to the raging emotions, the blade would fly faster and faster until only a green and gold blur was visible. When she fought with the sword, she could use her blade to attack the loss in her heart and the guilt of pushing her twin away.

It was while she threw her whole self into the fight that her mind was her own and not accessible to Pulsar's. The ability to block out the dragon from her mind was discovered quite by accident. Each night she would pick up her blade and begin the fight, only to find her thoughts uninterrupted and free to wander where they may. At first, she hadn't even noticed the absence of Pulsar's voice in her head. It wasn't until he asked her one night after a vicious battle with the bonfire that she realized what she had done.

Unexpectedly, he was pleased that she was learning to block him from her thoughts. He had always had the ability to block her, and to be on a more equal level, she needed to learn the same skill. So it became a mutual understanding; the bonfire was her distant island, a place where she could visit her thoughts and feelings alone. Some nights the battle wore on late into the night since her physical strength had increased with her relentless practice.

Chapter Thirty-three

TRUTH AND LIES

ONCE AGAIN, THE BLACK WARM air covered Erin. She pulled the folded sweatshirt under her head. Night sounds filled the living tent as she lay thinking. The days had passed, and she had lost track of how long they had been out here in the forest. Day after day, night after night, they ate, practiced, trained, and slept. Did it matter if she returned to the kingdom? What would she do there, and how could she not feel lost without Bain?

Pulsar's breaths were long and slow, indicating his sleep. This is when she was free to go to the darkest corners of her mind, the most painful. She knew she probably shouldn't. She had cried herself to sleep so many nights already. Her eyes closed against the memories; his sunshine hair, his ocean blue eyes, and his smile. It was Bain's easy smile that made her feel whole.

Absently, she pulled the folded note out from the pocket of the sweatshirt. She had kept it close, and even though in the black of the night she could not see it, she knew every word. She knew every curl of his letters, the way he wrote his name. She recited the words in her mind for the thousandth time, and let them float before her closed eyelids.

Although she knew she should sleep, she let her mind drift easily through the sentences, as though she were reading it from miles away. And that's when the words jerked her so abruptly that she gasped as if the wind had been knocked out of her.

"It had to be this way," she thought, as if testing the words again. Involuntarily, a shudder ripped through her whole being. Carefully, she let the other sentences march past her mind. Nothing happened. So she went back, "It had to be this way." Again the shudder, and this time she felt sick too.

She knew.

Never before had she tried to wake the sleeping dragon. His enormous wing covered her like a five man tent. She went for his exposed side and pushed with all her strength. He didn't even seem to notice her efforts.

Material manipulations, she thought, and forced his draping wing into the air. The gap between the wing and the ground grew wide enough for her to run through, and she let it drop to the ground. And yet the dragon slumbered on.

His ears were easily the size of her head, and she hoped he would hear her voice through the haze of his sleep. For safety measures, she surrounded herself with a touch ward to protect her from his spines if he woke too suddenly as she leaned in to his ear.

"Pulsar, wake up!" she shouted, right into his ear. She had not anticipated the swift reaction that would have easily gored her had she not been under the ward.

Fireborn, are you all right?

"I'm fine," she assured him, "but I found something tonight." She opened her thoughts to his, allowing her discovery to spill into his mind. "It's not true! It didn't have to be this way. I just don't understand." She was pacing the ground, oblivious to the quiet night. "It's true I would have tried to talk him out of it, he really did want to see the world, and he really is sorry. But it didn't have to be this way." Her frustrations streamed out in a muffled scream. "What is that supposed to mean, anyway?"

I am sorry, little one. I cannot be sure.

Her pacing continued as she fought to decipher the riddle. "He wanted to see the world, and now he had the chance, but it didn't have to be this way. What way? The way he left in the middle of the night without so much as telling me? Or was it not telling me where he was going and how to reach him? Or was it the way he promised he wouldn't leave me alone, and then he did?"

The familiar tears were threatening to come to her eyes as her emotions rushed through her. "How did I not see this before? I have read the note so many times, but never even once caught that phrase."

You were calm tonight; I saw it in your mind. Instead of feeling the consuming sadness or anger, you were at peace. Maybe if you let yourself calm down again, we will find more truth.

She knew he was right, but was not sure how to let go of the bubbling feelings that flooded her thoughts. Instinctively, she walked towards Pulsar and reached her arms around his chest. The familiar warmth of magical energy instantly filled her, helping to restore her frame of mind.

"Okay," she agreed. "But this might take me a while to figure out."

Go to sleep, Fireborn. We will talk more in the morning.

Glancing up at the full moon and the angelic stars reminded her of the late hour. Reluctantly, she settled back down to her makeshift bed and breathed in the warm night air.

Chapter Thirty-four

GOING BACK

THE HEARTACHE OF LOSING BAIN did not disappear with the morning light. Even though she was sure that her new discovery was significant, she was no closer to an answer, no closer to finding him. She let Pulsar wind her through another day of aerial training. He was so good at occupying her mind. The pain in her heart always seemed to lessen while they flew through the clear sky.

She couldn't help but notice that he was getting so much better at controlling his fire flow while flying complicated patterns, maneuvers he must have hidden somewhere in the recesses of his ancient mind. She often wondered where he came up with his next plan. Even the eagles did not dive out of the sky the same way he did.

While they flew, she worked on the riddle in her mind. It was as good a time as any. She was almost calm as she whipped through the air on his back, and although it took much of his concentration, it really did not require much from her own mind. By now she was used to the acrobatic flight.

So from the altitude of airplanes, she let her mind work on it. Over and over she repeated the wrong phrase. Now that she accepted the untruth of the statement, her body no longer physically responded to the words.

"It didn't have to be now," she tried out loud, feeling for the edge of truth. She was sure that sentence rang with some truth. Questions popped into her head more than answers. "He could have waited as long as he wanted. He didn't have to leave in the middle of the night. How did he leave, anyway? Where would he go by himself? He didn't know how to get to an airport anymore than I did." Something caught her attention in her ramblings. She tried it out again, "Where would he go by himself? He didn't go by himself."

She was getting so much closer; she could feel it. "He didn't go by himself," she tried again, and it felt that she had won the prize. It rang with such surety that she could bet her life on it.

Pulsar had been only half listening to her reasoning, letting her feel her way around the issue without much interruption. And she knew it. She was becoming much more aware of how in her mind he was. When he wasn't listening, she could feel the difference instinctively, as if she had always known, but only now was realizing it. Maybe it was a result of spending so much time alone with him, with no one else to talk to.

"Did you hear that?" she asked him. "He didn't go by him-self!"

Does that help?

"I know what you mean. Who do we know that would take off with him like that, with no warning?"

Is it who you know, or who he knows?

"That is such a weird question. We know all the same people, in the kingdom, anyway." She let her mind wander from person to person, all the people she could think of that they had met. None of the names she thought of made any sense in the story. Part of her mind was trying to tell her something; something that was just out of reach of her conscious mind. If she tried to look directly at it, the thought would disappear.

Instead, she began to picture Bain packing his clothes in the middle of the night. She tried to see him sitting at the desk writing the note to her. In her mind, the thoughts felt wrong. The pictures in her head were lies. It wasn't like that. He didn't just pack his clothes up and sit down to write a note, as if he were heading to a slumber party with his friends. It wasn't like that.

It all became more confusing. She tried to sort through the story, but she could only tell what didn't happen, and she was no closer to seeing what did. "Oh, help," she said to Pulsar, who followed her thread of thoughts.

I think you have uncovered some interesting things, Fireborn. The queen herself may be interested in your discovery.

"The queen? What does she have to do with any of this?"

She is very much a part of everything.

"Okay, you are going to explain, aren't you?"

He adjusted so they were now sailing fluidly through the air, abandoning his practice for the conversation. *You and Bain have been on her mind almost since you were born.*

"What are you talking about? She couldn't have even known us when we were babies."

She could feel his rumble of laughter under her while they flew.

"What could possibly be funny about that?" she demanded.

I thought by now you would have realized how possible it was for their kind to know as much as they wanted about humans. Of course she knew about you as a baby—both of you.

"So, you're trying to tell me that Queen Āldera has known Bain and me all of our lives?"

Yes, but you already knew that. I have seen that conversation in your mind. Ella told you that they had known of you for fifteen years.

"Ugh. I guess I didn't really catch that the first time."

Queen Āldera told the kingdom of your coming. She knew of your transformation long before you did. But she didn't know it would be twins at first. She can see glimpses of the future, and until you both were discovered, she only knew that her kingdom would see newness.

Once it was confirmed that it was twins destined to find their world, celebration broke out among the land. Twins are extremely rare, and legend spurs the notion that twins are more powerful than single individuals. Some think there is a synergy that combines the magical abilities, making them together more powerful.

"So, how do you know all this?"

I have seen it in Queen Āldera's mind.

"She let you see her thoughts?"

Some of them. Of course, she is so very skilled at deciding what she wants me to see. But, yes, she did show me her concern for you, in particular, as well as Bain.

"Okay, Pulsar. Tell me what I'm supposed to do."

Do you really want me to?

"I think so, but then, I think I already know what you're going to say." She felt him wait for her continue.

What will I tell you?

"You will say to go back to the kingdom and tell them what I know."

Anything else?

"Yeah, you probably will tell me that it won't be as bad as I think it will." Again, she felt him shake with a low rumble of laughter.

Fireborn, I shall never have a dull day in my life with you around.

"That's what Grandpa Jessie used to say to us when we were kids."

He was right.

Even though she had agreed to return to Ālfheim, it didn't make it easy. It wasn't like going home, but she wouldn't want to go there either. Anywhere without Bain would not feel like home. She had talked Pulsar into waiting until morning before taking their journey. She knew she was stalling, but he agreed without complaint.

The nightly ritual resumed as she battled the flame with her glinting blade, but this time, she fought her own fears. She tried to cut her loneliness into shredded ribbons and her heartache into slivers. If she could fight those emotions down, she might find more resolve and determination.

Then light flooded the darkness in her mind.

That is how she would go back. It wouldn't be for her, it

would be for him. Everything she did from here on out would be to find Bain. The blade blurred in her hands as she slashed through the air. *I will leave part of myself here in the forest. I will leave the sad heartbroken girl here and find Bain.* Her thoughts filled her with unexpected strength.

Chapter Thirty-five

THE EYES HAVE IT

She had not paid attention to the landscape on their trip to the isolated forest. Now, with resolve drowning out her fear, she watched the terrain below with new eyes.

The decision around the fire had proven itself this morning when she packed her things and strapped them to the saddle with a new sense of confidence. This was going to work. She still felt the fearless determination and held to it with a deep vengeance. She could be strong, for Bain.

The thought of finally finding him had etched into her mind until it felt like a real possibility. One thing was certain; she wasn't going to find him in the forest, wallowing in loneliness.

It surprised her that the trip had been so long. She couldn't remember riding him for hours, but half the day was already spent in the sky. Pulsar helped pass the time with conversation and a few fire throws, just to break up the long journey.

The sun had already arched across the sky when the kingdom finally came into view. From here, the sprawling landscape, dotted with buildings reminded her of the vast size of Álfheim. The white mansion rushed towards them, creating butterflies in her stomach involuntarily.

She braced herself. She would not be nervous, afraid, self-conscious, or worried. She laughed out loud at her own thoughts.

Of course! Be just like Bain! Who could be a better expert than herself? If anyone knew him, she did. But never once in her life had she tried to be like him.

The enormous balcony to her old room greeted them. Everything looked immaculate inside the elegant room. Even the wardrobe was filled with clothes. She allowed herself the luxury of a bath. This had been the longest campout of her life.

The soft clothes hanging in the wardrobe seemed more appropriate than the jeans and t-shirts she had been living in. Without a washing machine, all of her clothes lacked a crisp, fresh-smelling appeal. Mrs. Hammel hadn't even thought of packing laundry soap.

She stood before the full-length mirror gauging her own reflection. She wished she had paid better attention to how many days she had been away. It could have been a month or more. Even still, she couldn't remember seeing her own eyes looking like the ones gazing back from the mirror. There was a distinct almond shape that turned up just a little on the outer edges. It seemed familiar, and startled, she remembered Adarae, Aelflaed, Ella, and all the others she knew in the magical world. Her deep green eyes stared back at her somehow accentuated, or bigger than they had ever seemed before.

Like wearing a mask, she thought. *I don't really look like Erin anymore. It's like wearing a mask.* Her thoughts conveyed easily to Pulsar. *Maybe it won't be so hard acting like Bain when I don't really look like Erin.*

Pulsar interrupted her thoughts. *You look exactly like Erin, only an älva.*

Even so, this breakthrough still held possibilities in her mind. It was like wearing dark sunglasses, and even though everything looked the same through her eyes, the view was obscured to others looking back at her foreign face.

She thought of Grandpa Jessie. What would he think of her now? Not only had they lied to come here, but now Bain was gone, and it was her fault. She thought about writing Grandpa Jessie. What would she say? The truth, or more lies? It would be too hard. Maybe there would be a chance later for Bain and her to go back home to visit. At least that would save her from the pain of deceiving, or the torture of telling the truth. She still couldn't bring herself to tell Grandpa Jessie about the whole elf thing. Maybe he didn't need to know about any of this. They were half way around the world, after all, more or less.

It didn't take long for her to realize that she really had no idea what to do next. As she finished putting things away and cleaning up, the quest could no longer be delayed. She assured Pulsar that she would maintain contact with him as she searched the grounds for a familiar face.

The palace was enormous. At least it seemed to be something like a palace or castle. The walls felt more like a home than a stone castle, but the place was so big, she was sure she could get lost in it. She tried to retrace the steps to the room where the ceremony was, but she guessed she had missed a staircase or taken a wrong turn when she found herself in a large aviary.

It wasn't exactly like the first room they entered, but there were trees filling the endless room. Birds filled the air with their soft sweet calls. A beautiful fountain caught her attention, and she wandered over to it, pleased to discover the reason for its familiar sound.

Just like the Living Garden, a crop of teacup sized flowers waited beside the bubbling water. She filled a pink cuplike flower and drank the sweet carbonated water. It felt so much like home that she couldn't help but peek into the air, hoping to find butterfly wings.

"Oh, Adarae, I wish you were here." She said it as much to herself as anything. A movement caught her attention and she spun around to find herself face to face with a stranger.

She forced her jaw to shut after realizing that it gaped open. Before her stood an elf who looked around her age. He was taller than her with bronze hair that fell in subtle waves to his shoulders. His light brown eyes seemed to search her face before he bowed quickly and gracefully in one fluid motion.

"I'm sorry if I startled you."

"Uh, that's okay." She could feel her cheeks begin to burn and tried to force the blood away from them.

"My name is Joel." He looked around at the empty room. "I haven't seen you around here before."

"Well, I'm Erin. I haven't really been here very long."

"Erin? You mean Erin Fireborn?"

She nodded meekly, with a small smile.

"It is an exquisite pleasure to meet you, Erin Fireborn." He took a knee swiftly and kissed her hand.

She couldn't help but laugh nervously. No one had ever done *that* before. At least his aura suggested that he was being truthful.

"Well, as an officer of the queen, may I offer you a private tour of the grounds?"

Why did her cheeks have to burn again? She tried to look casual as she nodded her reply. He held out his arm for her to link her own arm, just as if he were leading her to the dance floor. She didn't know what else to do and could hear Pulsar laughing at her in her mind.

Go on, it isn't that bad, he chided.

So she tried to casually link her right hand over his arm, and he began his tour, clearly pleased with himself. He led her through the endless building, pointing out architecture and explaining the significance of certain rooms. She was sure she would require a map to ever see these places again. There had been more than one enormous room filled with as much nature as the outdoors themselves. It was as if the only way the elves could stand to be indoors was if they could bring the outdoors in with them.

"And this is my favorite room," he said, with a flourish of his hand. "I call it the thinking place." A waterfall jetted over a rock wall into a pool below. Flowers and vines tangled sporadically around the banks coloring the floor with a rainbow of petals and leaves. He led her to a rock where they sat watching the waterfall. She noticed the bright colored fish swimming in the pool, exhibiting unnatural colors of hot pink, lime green, orange, and white.

"So, Erin Fireborn," he turned to look at her, "what brings you to the thinking place today?"

"Wow, uh, I guess I have a lot of things I could think about."

"Anything you want to think out loud?"

"Okay, here's something. If you were looking for someone who took off to who knows where, where would you look?"

"You want to try to expound on that? That isn't much to go on."

She gave in and told him the story of Bain. She didn't know why she felt comfortable around Joel. He was practically a stranger, but he treated her like a queen, and seemed to want nothing more in life than to hear her every word.

"The world is a pretty big place," he offered. "I am guessing he is at least out of the country."

"What do you mean? What country?"

"Iceland. Ālfheim is in Iceland. Didn't they tell you?"

She couldn't help but laugh. "I thought we were just pretending to go to Iceland. I had no idea we really did." The thought bounced around in her head. "But Iceland is in the middle of the ocean. How did we get here without crossing it?"

"Now, there is an interesting question. The cottage has a few tricks, doesn't it?" He leaned back on his hands and stared out at the waterfall. "I've never been there, but everyone knows about it. It's a training arena, and it has a magical transport linking it directly to the kingdom." He turned casually to her. "Kind of a necessity if the masters are going to get in and out of there without an airplane."

"An airplane?" Her mind involuntarily leapt to the airplane in her dream. She stared into the water and let the silence lengthen.

He watched her carefully from the side as if trying not to infringe on her thoughts. After a few minutes passed, he finally interrupted. "What are you thinking about?"

"How many airports leave Iceland?"

"Keflavík International Airport is the largest airport in

Iceland, and it's not too far from here. If he was looking to leave the country, that is probably where he would go."

"So, do elves fly in planes?"

It was his turn to laugh. "It sure beats a slow boat. If we want to travel, we usually do it much the same way as the rest of the world."

"But I haven't seen any cars."

"Well, we can run just about as far and as fast as the people that live locally can drive. Almost no one here owns a car."

"So, you pack your suitcase and run to the airport?"

"Usually we leave the kingdom and call a cab in the nearest city. Helps us blend in a little better."

"I guess it wouldn't be that hard for Bain to figure out where the airport is. He could have brought all his money and bought a ticket." She watched the waterfall with its mesmerizing sounds. "But where did he go?"

"Well, there's Munich, Barcelona, Copenhagen, Madrid, New York, London, and that's just a start. There are a lot of possibilities."

"I don't think he's by himself. I have this feeling that someone helped him leave. I just can't think of anyone who would do that and not tell us where he went. Maybe whoever he went with is still with him." Her ramblings seemed to resonate. She tried to compute the factors. "I guess the question is, who do I know here that is missing? How do you find people in this huge place?"

"Most of the time, we just know where people live, and go from there."

"Do you guys have cell phones?"

"Some do."

A phone wouldn't help her. She didn't have anyone to call, and Bain didn't have a phone. "Do you think we could look up flights and trace where he went?"

"That might be possible, we do have connections with the human world."

"Have you ever been outside of the kingdom?"

He shrugged his shoulders. "No."

"Why not?"

"No reason to. Where would I go, and what would I do there? Here I don't have to pretend to have the handicaps of humans."

She couldn't help feeling a little pricked by his comment. After all, she had been one of them not too long ago. "So you could be happy living in this little place forever?"

"I don't know. I guess if I ever found a reason to leave, I might give it a go."

The conversation seemed to meet a dead-end. She didn't have anything in common with him, and he didn't have any helpful leads. They sat in silence, letting the waterfall drown their thoughts with its sound. Pulsar took advantage of the moment to remind her about the queen.

She cleared her throat and asked, "How do I visit the queen?"

"Usually, you need an appointment. Do you really want to see her?" He turned to face her.

She nodded, looking into his magnificent eyes.

"I think I could pull some strings and arrange that. Do you want to see her today?"

"I guess. Can I?"

He winked at her. "Wait right here, I'll go check on things." He presently disappeared in a sprint that would put a cheetah to shame.

She watched the bright fish swim in the crystal clear water. *What do you think, Pulsar?*

I think he likes you.

That's not what I mean. Her exasperation fumed. *If I do see the queen today, what would I tell her?*

Tell her the truth. Explain the note and your discovery.

Will she believe me? Does she even care?

You're going to have to trust her; she does rule the entire älvin race.

Are you just trying to make me nervous?

I don't believe you need any help doing that, he countered. *You'll be fine. But be honest, and don't try to downplay your part.*

You're talking about my dream, she thought, *and the note.* In the world she left not so long ago, she would be considered out of her mind to suggest that dreams and feelings were any sort of evidence. *Am I ever going to find Bain?* She knew he didn't have an answer, and that it probably wasn't fair to ask, but the task seemed impossible, even if it was completely necessary.

I believe you will.

His words felt right, and she could almost believe it too.

Chapter Thirty-six

ONE-ON-ONE

JOEL HAD APPARENTLY BEEN ABLE to work his magic and was now leading Erin through a corridor. She was almost becoming comfortable with the odd custom of being led by the arm. She wasn't entirely sure she would feel the same way in front of others, however, and especially the queen.

She knew that Pulsar was amused by her awkward feelings, and he seemed a little too pleased that she was spending the day with Joel. The tall double doors opened just as they arrived, with no indication of who was doing it. Material manipulations she reminded herself. She still was not accustomed to such casual use of magic.

At home they had to be so careful to not draw attention to their abilities, and even though they used their magic outside of the cottage, they restricted themselves considerably. Here it was simply ordinary. Like flipping on a lightswitch, it was a miracle that had little significance.

Her reverie was interupted by the sight before her. The room was warm and green, and felt more like a summer day in the jungle than a room in the palace. The vaulted ceiling and walls were glass, creating an enormous greenhouse. She could hear the chatter of monkeys and was sure she spotted a lemur in one of the trees before it leaped out of sight.

Before her stood Queen Āldera dressed unassumingly in a

simple azure gown of cotton. But her presence was not diminished by her apparel. Even as her pale blue eyes met Erin's, her majestic quality inspired Erin to bow in a small curtsy.

"Hello, Erin Fireborn. What can I do for you?" Her voice was warm and welcoming.

"I need to talk to you."

The queen beckoned her to sit on a wooden bench and chose a chair across the path from her. Joel excused himself, promising to return soon. The setting seemed too casual for a meeting with a queen, but it did put Erin at ease and their conversation began effortlessly.

She was surprised at how much Queen Āldera already knew. It seemed the only new information she had to add was her interpretation of the note and the dream.

"Erin Fireborn, I gather you see auras of good and evil, of truth and lies. That is your gift from the Room of Truth." Her clear blue eyes seemed impossible to look away from.

Erin did her best to recount the story of their first day in the cottage, and the auras she sensed since.

"But I thought everyone knew about that," she concluded.

"This is the first time you have shared this information with our kind. That fact may gain us unexpected advantages." She stood and began inspecting the greenery around them. "Is this the first time you have dreamed something that felt unusually real?"

Erin felt a sudden jolt of butterflies. "Um, not exactly." She found herself explaining the dream of the kingdom, and the day she told the story to the älvor, including their odd reaction. "They told me to find Bella and tell her the story. I completely forgot about that."

"You have a rare gift indeed. We have known of Bain's gift from almost the start and have tried to anticipate the effects he would have on our kingdom. But I hadn't imagined your gift would be equally profound."

"I don't understand. What do you mean? How is my gift profound?" She was sure she sounded foolish but was completely perplexed by the queen's response.

"By using your gifts, you will indeed be able to find Bain. And that is only the beginning. As you learn to use your gift, it will serve you in innumerable ways."

The words were bounding through her head with such velocity that she couldn't sit still. She followed the queen's lead and paced the floor. Her heart was racing at the words spoken. She knew it was true, she would find Bain by using her gifts, but how?

"Tell me what to do." She couldn't help the abrupt request. Everything inside of her was wound tight, waiting to spring. If she could find Bain, then she did not want to wait another minute. She caught her breath as she found herself directly facing the queen. She must have not been paying enough attention to where she was going.

The queen stared into her eyes for a long moment in silence. It was as if she were looking for something. "I think we could start by introducing you to our tech team. They are the computer geniuses of our city. They might be able to trace the airlines that Bain traveled on, for I am certain your dream was more than mere coincidence."

With that she was pressing a button on the wall that looked like an intercom system. "You will have an escort to their lab. They will assist you in any way they can." Clearly her comment was a dismissal as she seemed to instantly disappear into the lush foliage of the room.

The double doors opened, and Joel offered his arm once again. They strolled through the halls and she tried to catch up with the thought of tracing Bain's flight.

"Why don't any of the doors have locks?" She knew it was a random question, but she hadn't seen a lock in the entire city, and she was desperately out of casual conversation ideas. They had been walking in silence since she left the queen.

"It is the Changing Brooches, of course." He said it as if she had been particularly slow on the uptake.

"I must have missed that lesson," she answered.

"The Changing Brooch is fairly fundamental. Have you played with it at all yet?"

Now she truly felt embarrassed. It had been sitting in her suitcase every day while in the woods, and she had only remembered to pin it to her top just before she left the room. The same was true with her golden circlet. Even then, she was merely trying to avoid any insult that might result in leaving the gifts behind. She absently touched the small gold pin.

"Should I take that as a no?" He had somehow found his way directly in front of her and was now showing a lopsided smile. "May I?" he asked, nodding at the pin at her shoulder.

"Okay," she managed to say, but was too afraid to attempt a more coherent sentence with his dazzling smile beaming down on her.

His hands were quick while he unlatched the brooch and held it in front of him. "Beautiful," he murmured, as he let the light reflect off of the surface.

"So, what does that have to do with the locks?"

His smile returned instantly. "Hold out your hand," he commanded.

She obeyed, lifting her palm.

"I want you to imagine the lock on the front door of your house. Now, pretend you are standing outside the door, and you wished you had your key." He placed the pin on her outstretched palm.

The metal felt cool at first in her hand, but then she concentrated on her door at home, and it seemed to melt. A familiar buzz of magic crept through her hand igniting the brooch with warmth. The leaf shape disintegrated and molded itself into a perfect replica of her house key.

She looked up at him in amazement.

"See," he said. "We don't really need locks when everyone has the key."

"Amazing," she said in a hushed tone. She turned the key in her hand. It was the same silver key from her memory, even worn with scratches and not very shiny. The letters were even visible describing its brand name. "How do I turn it back?"

"Just think of your brooch in its former state."

She squeezed the key in her hand and focused on the leaf. The warm buzzing returned and she could feel the metal changing in her hand. The golden leaf sat in her hand once again. "That was so cool! What else can it do?"

"It is limited only by your imagination, and, to some degree, size."

"So, you're saying that if I imagined a silver Porsche, I would be out of luck."

"That would be taking it a bit far."

"What about money. Could I turn it into a million dollars?"

"Only if you never planned to spend it, you wouldn't want to give your brooch away."

"So it can look like something other than metal?"

"Why don't you give it a try?"

She imagined a driver's license with her picture and information on it. The metal leaf obeyed her wishes down to the small photograph of her in the corner. "I always wanted my very own driver's license."

"May I?" he asked.

She handed him the small card.

"Hmm. It says Erin Farraday. That must be your surname."

She laughed and started walking the long hall. "We call it our last name. What's yours?"

He shrugged, the same way as before. "I don't have one."

"What do you mean? I thought everyone had a last name."

"Actually, no one in the country does."

"You mean the kingdom, don't you? Surely the other people in Iceland have last names."

"No, just first."

She looked at him with a scrutinizing eye. His brilliant aura had not given him away, so he was clearly telling the truth. "How do they keep everyone straight, then?"

"It's just the way it is. I suppose we all know each other well enough to keep it straight."

"Wow. You're serious."

"Why wouldn't I be?"

"I don't know. I just didn't know there was a country anywhere where people didn't have last names."

"Welcome to Iceland, Miss Erin Fireborn Farraday."

"Why do you call me Erin Fireborn? I thought you all didn't have last names."

"We don't. You just have two first names."

Now she simply couldn't stifle a laugh. If he hadn't been telling the truth, it might not have seemed so funny. "So, Joel, do you have another first name as well?"

"No."

"Well, how did I get so lucky then?"

"We cannot ignore the name bestowed on you by your dragon. We would not extend such an insult to a potentially powerful ally."

"How did you know the name at all?"

"Pulsar has not been stingy with that information. Quite the contrary, he introduces you at every opportunity."

"So, does he talk to everyone?"

"Not exactly everyone. He reserves conversations with the most telepathically gifted. He doesn't bother with those who are struggling to even reach his thoughts."

"There is a lot I don't know about him still." She was saying it to Pulsar as much as Joel. Pulsar didn't offer any comment.

"I just thought of something." Her stomach suddenly twisted. "If Bain wanted his brooch to turn into fake ID or a plane ticket, it could, couldn't it?"

"Yes."

"So we are only going to be able to find him on a computer if he decided to use his own name." The thought was turning like a knife in her stomach. Why did she have to think of things? Something about the thought seemed revoltingly true.

"Let's start with the tech team and go from there."

She couldn't help it as she suddenly sprinted down the hall hanging onto Joel's hand for direction.

Chapter Thirty-seven

COMPUTER LAB

THE ENORMOUS ROOM REMINDED HER of a library, or maybe a university computer lab. There were desks spread through the center of the room with computers on every one. The team of experts roamed the room that was clearly open to anyone who wished to use a computer.

Internet access was available as well as top-of-the-line speed. It made her computer at home seem like a dinosaur. She wasn't surprised that they could not find Bain's name on any rosters. Even with unprecedented access to high security sites, there was no indication of his name to be found.

Their search seemed fruitless as they wandered from site to site. It was fascinating watching them work. The speed of the computers was no match for their lightning fast reading. Each screen would seem to only blink before passing on to the next frame.

I didn't know that some of their gifts extended to reading at the speed of light, she mused to Pulsar. He had gone back out to the forest instead of waiting for hours in her room. Their connection had not dimmed from the distance.

At least she hadn't been overly disappointed by their empty-handed search. After exhausting all their resources, the elves gradually dispersed, leaving Erin and Joel sitting at the desk alone.

She sighed as she swiveled the desk chair. "So that's that."
She peeked at his face to see his reaction.

"Actually, it isn't very surprising."

"What do you mean?"

"Most of our kind have an aversion to being traced. When
we do venture out into the world, we don't exactly use our actual
information. At least, most don't. We have the means of producing identification papers from around the world. Credit cards
and travelers checks are also easily invented in our labs.

"We don't really need money. The credit cards bank all the
way back to the kingdom where the stock market team use their
unnatural skills to raise enough money to pay them off. It actually gives them something to do. Right now the kingdom has so
much money they don't even feel needed unless someone goes on
an all-expenses-paid vacation."

"But Bain wouldn't have known any of that." She thought
for a minute. "So do you have traveler's checks just waiting in a
pile like cash for anyone to take?"

"Basically. You don't need to ask permission to take some, if
that's what you mean."

"And they can't be traced." She didn't ask, she just assumed.
"Wait, if you don't need money, than what were those colored
papers they used in the stores all about?"

"Service Slips. Our city uses the barter system. If you want to
purchase something, you trade for something else."

Her face was filled with confusion.

He spun his chair to face her as he continued. "So, say you
wanted to buy a new L bar for your shay."

"A what bar for your what?"

"Right, let's try something a little more familiar. A dress. You
go into town to buy a dress."

"What about a pair of jeans?"

"Don't interrupt," he said with false sternness. "You want to
buy a lovely new blue dress."

"Why do I want a blue dress?"

"That's not the point. Anyway, to purchase the dress you

offer your services in exchange for the item."

"What in the world would I offer?"

"I don't know. Maybe a ride on your dragon."

"No way. I don't think he would go for that."

"Well, that is the story of the Service Slips, take it or leave it."

She swiveled her chair back and forth absently. "Let's look at all the facts. Bain can't be traced on the airline rosters, but then neither can any of the other elves. He probably had someone with him that had as much money as they would have needed for their trip. And we are pretty sure he did ride in an airplane."

She stopped her chair as it faced Joel. "So we are no further ahead than when we started."

"I don't know about that. You've finally figured out how to pay for things in the kingdom. That's worth something. And you have your driver's license." He eyed the card in his hand.

"I completely forgot about that." She whipped it out of his fingers and transformed it into the golden leaf.

He watched her with a barely concealed smile. "There is something else you should know. Only the rightful owner can transform a Changing Brooch."

"Do you have one?"

"Sure." He reached into his shirt and pulled out a pendant on a chain. The clasp seemed to undo itself as he handed her the heavy silver.

She admired the shield with a lion's profile on the face. It didn't shimmer like hers did, but seemed antique. It felt like it was made out of lead instead of silver. "It's really amazing," she offered. The lion had so much detail that it could have been a real animal shrunk down and turned to steel.

She handed the pendant back. "I thought they were all brooches."

"Nah, that's just the name. Everyone's is a little different."

"There's something else I have been wondering. If you guys have all the best technology in the world, why do you use swords? It seems like you would just use guns."

His eyebrows raised in surprise. "What do you know about *wards*?"

"I know how to cast one, if that's what you mean."

"So, if you saw someone with a gun, you would simply throw your *ward* around you and save yourself from the shot. Is that right?"

"Yes, but what does that have to do with anything?"

"In combat, we could choose to simply shoot each other, but it wouldn't really work. It is kind of like the locks. Everyone has the key. Our wards protect us from such mundane weapons."

"Then how are the swords really any different?"

"Well, two ways really. First, and most important, eternal blades are embedded with magic. Our kind can only be killed by something that bears magic. Mere human weapons are made from metals that are not only easy to deflect, but also simple to heal from. We are also very resistant to the effects of bombs."

"And second?"

"Well, I guess you could say the second reason is pride."

"What do you mean?"

"It takes a great deal of skill to maintain a *ward* while in hand to hand combat. The amount of concentration needed to claim victory in a fight impedes the ability to effectively *ward*. So we appreciate the true talent such advancements in combat require."

"But you can't kill each other, or you lose your magic and your blade."

"No unjust killing. We still maintain the right to defend ourselves."

"I guess I was hoping to find a loop hole, some way of getting out of knowing how to use a sword. I have to admit, you really weren't any help."

He smiled and then stood and offered his arm. "Would you care to accompany me to the dining area?"

Resigned, she let him lead her through the endless halls once again. They wound their way to an outdoor patio. The setting was quaint with tiny tables for two. Warm sunrays greeted them as they found a place to sit. Before long they were served bread and salads, and they drifted easily into conversation.

"So what is this place?" she asked as she squeezed a lemon slice into her water.

"It is a common area for those who live in the Queen's house."

"Do you always eat here?"

"Mostly. I've always lived here, so I pretty much always eat somewhere on the grounds."

"You mean there's more than one of these little restaurant things?"

He smiled at her with amusement. "I never thought of it like a restaurant, but yes, there are quite a few scattered around."

Her thoughts involuntarily strayed to Bain. The riddle in her head was spinning in circles, never landing on an answer. She sat absently stirring her water with the straw. Suddenly her mind was able to grasp at the thought that had lingered in the corner of her mind for days.

"Carbonell!" she shouted.

Joel looked at her with a startled expression. "What are you talking about?"

"Carbonell. That's who Bain knows that I don't. He is the one who went with him."

And the words rang true in her mind.

"What do you know about Carbonell?" His expression had turned serious.

"Uh, nothing really. He sort of hung out with Bain back home, but I never actually met him. Why? What do you know?"

"He has a long history indeed." His face was thoughtful. "You said he met Bain while you were living at home?

She simply nodded.

"He was probably trying to spy, or win Bain over. I'm surprised he didn't try to get to you, too. Bain was much quicker about informing our world of his unusual gift than you were. Everyone in our world knows that he can see magic. No one has been able to do that for hundreds of years, maybe even thousands. It really does make him a target. Carbonell has probably been planning his meeting with Bain since your first day in the cottage."

"But what is there to spy on? Who does he work for?"

"There are some theories floating around, none of them have any concrete evidence, though. He has been around the world so many times and has so many alias names that even we can't track him anymore. He keeps his activity extremely veiled."

"I don't understand. So is he a bad guy then?"

"Some think he works for one, but no one knows for sure. We are careful about starting accusations with unfounded proof. In other words, we don't trust him, but we would never tell him that."

"So if Bain ran off with Carbonell, where would they go?"

"That is the scariest question of all. If he does work for someone, then they surely would head straight to his master. No question. We just don't have any idea who that is or where they might be."

She was surprised at how quickly they had arrived at another dead end. It seemed that with every new revelation, an even grander limitation would present itself.

Chapter Thirty-eight

THE HUNT

THE STREETS OF ĀLFHEIM WOUND meticulously around the quaint shops adorning the sidewalks. She found that without pockets, she really didn't know what to do with her hands. They ended up at her waist with her thumbs tucked into the belt of her sheath.

The air was pleasant enough, with a cool breeze brushing through every now and then—a perfect day for a walk. Erin had no problem blending in to the city life with her new clothes from the wardrobe, and most important, with Pulsar a considerable distance away.

The idea had come to her the night before, just as she was falling asleep. Maybe it was a long shot. While she drifted in and out of the shops, pretending to look at the goods, she was really searching out auras. Specifically, she was hunting the darkest ones.

Somewhere in the late hours of night it came to her. It was a combination of the memory of the horrible aura surrounding the man next to Bain and the mention of Carbonell. It might have been him. It probably was. The only way she could think of tracking him was to find his friends right here in the kingdom.

Pulsar hadn't been eager to agree to the plan. She was searching out the bad guys and trying to do it under the radar. But having a gigantic golden dragon following her around would complicate the inconspicuous cover she was trying to create.

So he agreed to stay out of sight but not out of sound. He assured her he would be listening very carefully. With the city center bustling with people, how dangerous could it be? Erin wasn't sure.

It shouldn't have surprised her to find a tavern tucked away at the end of an offshoot street. Something made her follow the road right up to its worn wooden doors. In another life, she wouldn't even dream of going into a place like this, but today was different.

There were no signs posted about age limits, no warnings about identification. The doors creaked open upon her command. Even if she were feeling brave, she had no desire to touch the splintery wood with her bare hands. Maybe no one ever did. After rummaging around town in search of the darkest souls, this place felt like a treasure cove of menacing auras. Not all were so dark, but there were a few whose auras would seem to almost match up to Carbonell himself, if that's whom she had seen on the plane.

She realized almost as soon as she spotted them that her plan did not qualify exactly what she would do once she found a bad guy. Maybe she should have watched more television after all. The inconspicuous plan kicked in, and she drew up a bar stool and proceeded to eat peanuts out of a bowl.

It was her luck that she had been noticed as soon as she entered the room. An elf that looked rather plain other than his impressively inky aura took up the stool next to her and leaned on to his elbow to look directly into Erin's face.

"So, missy, I haven't seen you around here before. May I have the pleasure of your name?" He leered at her, waiting for her response.

Just stay where you are, Pulsar. I can handle this. She knew he was on the verge of tearing the roof off to save her. Concentrating on what little training the movies had offered, she put on her best glamour smile. "I'm Erin, and may I have the pleasure of your name?" She hoped that he did not notice the nausea underneath the forced flirt attempt.

"Well, then. That wouldn't be the Erin who's forgetting her

whole name, would it?" He laughed a disturbingly knowing laugh and was quickly joined by a few others who managed to instantly surround them where they sat. "Don't look so shocked. There ain't no one around here that we don't know, is there?" He waved his hand to the others. "So, missy, you must think you're something special, walking into our bar and expecting to make friends. I say we put her to the test." He pounded his hand on the counter for emphasis and his friends shouted their agreement.

In what seemed like an instant, a ring of men stood around her, and she quickly stood to face them. "A challenge, I think. Little Erin here hasn't had a chance to get her blade dirty yet."

The ring of men parted to allow in a lady, whose aura competed with the men surrounding her. The locks of her hair shot in various directions, and her dark eyes bore into Erin's. It was good that Erin had practiced warding so much in the forest. Although she did not want to become invisible, a touch ward seemed more than appropriate.

The vicious looking älva took a step forward pulling out a purple and gray blade. "Don't worry, I won't kill you," she said in a singsong voice and slowly closed the distance.

Erin pulled her blade and waited for the attack. She didn't even see it coming. Somehow the purple blade was behind her, swiping low at her legs. The ward held, but she now understood how difficult it would be to keep up the ward and counterattack at the same time. It would take too much effort to effectively succeed at both.

Pulsar, I need you to ward me. He agreed, and just as they had practiced, he warded her from a distance using his mind and their shared magic.

Another blow glanced off her arm.

"Come out and play, Erin. Are you afraid you might hurt me?" A high pitched laugh sounded, followed by a heavy thrust to her abdomen.

"In all fairness, I suggest you protect yourself as well." Erin spoke calmly, surprising even herself.

Another laugh followed, and the älva raised her weapon to

attack again. This time Erin's green blade met hers before it could reach its destination. A blur of green and purple ensued. Erin was pleased that her eyes could match the speed of the lanky woman. As she focused on the fight, her blade velocity began to exceed that of the black haired älva.

But Erin did not go for the strike. Each slash of purple was met with an equal green blade until it looked like Erin was merely swatting flies around her. Although Erin knew how to go in with the offensive, she simply kept the defensive position, blocking every blow with complete precision.

A high squealing scream ensued, and the crazed woman flung herself at Erin, hoping to inflict at least a bit of damage. This time Erin stepped easily to the side, and the älva flew through the air and tangled into the bar stools.

Watch it. She heard the warning in her head as the circle of men rushed at her, swords out. But Pulsar's unyielding ward was no match for the flailing swords. She clasped her blade against as many as she could and let the ward do the rest.

She wasn't entirely sure when the fighting had branched out against each other in the bar, but the broken glasses, the hurled barstools, and the overturned tables littered the floor. Finally, she was able to dispatch her attackers and slip out the kitchen door under an invisibility ward.

That wasn't so bad, she crooned to Pulsar, hoping to avoid a lecture. *A girl walks into a bar, and walks right back out again. Not even a scratch. Thanks, Pulsar.*

She hadn't lifted the invisibility ward yet, hoping that she could remain in the vicinity. *Don't say it. I know. But I have to find Bain, and I bet one of those guys in there knows Carbonell.*

Fireborn, I think it's time we revisit your plan.

You're coming here, aren't you? Just stay invisible. I want to follow them home so I can keep an eye on them better.

Not alone, you're not.

No, I think I'd rather have you here anyway. I could let you keep us both undercover. Besides, those guys in there really creeped me out. I think I like the idea of having you here to watch my back.

It was hours before the tavern began to empty into the dusk. Erin watched it from the dragon's back. Pulsar was a very silent tracker after all. She couldn't believe how stealthily he could take off and cover the sky, watching the different elves make their way home. They managed to follow a few of them to their houses before calling it a day.

He flew Erin directly to her bedroom. It had grown dark already, and she was ready to find a meal. She bid him farewell, and he went off to sleep in a cove he had discovered shortly after arriving in the kingdom this last time. He had taken to the abandoned cave and had called it home ever since.

Erin washed her face and looked again at the stranger in the mirror. The unfamiliar eyes stared back at her. It was the face of someone strong. She smiled as she decided once again that she wore a mask—a face that protected her from the real Erin inside. Before she could begin to dwell on her missing twin, she headed out the door. If the queen's house really did have several eating areas, surely she would find one if she walked long enough.

As she wandered down the long hallway towards what she hoped would be near the "thinking room," as Joel had called it, a voice broke the silence.

"Just where do you think you've been?" Joel materialized directly in front of her. Clearly he had been using the invisibility ward since there was no sign of his sudden arrival.

Erin laughed. She supposed she should have been startled out of her mind, but Bain had pulled that stunt enough that she had become partially immune to it. "Why do you ask?"

Now it was his turn to be taken by surprise. His face showed a wave of embarrassment before he covered it with a carefree smile. "I haven't seen you today."

"So, were you looking for me? Was there something you needed?"

"I was hoping to talk to you." He looked into her eyes, and then glanced away. "Where were you going, anyway? It's getting kind of late."

She shrugged. "I don't have a watch. Actually, I was trying

to find somewhere to eat. You have any ideas?"

He smiled and held his arm out for her again. She couldn't help smiling at the floor as she wrapped her arm around his. She supposed she should be used to his formal way of leading her around, but it was so foreign still, and she couldn't help feeling self-conscious.

From out of nowhere she thought of the countries that kissed both cheeks in greeting, and she suddenly felt grateful that all she had to endure was being led by the arm.

It really must be late, Erin thought as she realized that Pulsar was already asleep. She was becoming so aware of him that she could tell when he was blocking her out of his thoughts, or, in this case, sleeping. Having her thoughts to herself while being led by Joel down the hall was a surreal feeling. She hadn't really dated before, but if this was like a date, she didn't really want Pulsar there as her constant chaperone. It might be fun having a two-way, rather than three-way, conversation with him for a change.

They ended up in a spacious kitchen where Erin found her way around and created omelets for two. Their conversation eventually wove its way into her strange day, and she found herself divulging her new plan to find Bain.

"You have got to be the craziest person I have ever met," Joel said as he stabbed a bite with his fork. "You mean you waltzed right into the center of *their* place. I know grown men who would think twice about doing that."

"Are you serious?" She was wondering if he was just teasing her. Maybe she expected him to be like Bain.

He leveled his eyes with hers. "Very. You have got to be more careful." He leaned back into his chair. "They must have been inebriated enough not to use their magic, but not enough to forget your dragon. I bet if it wasn't for Pulsar, you would still be at that tavern, and probably not exactly in one piece."

"Well, you're right about Pulsar. He wouldn't have taken it very well if they had damaged me, not that he would have let them. I don't think he worries too much about hurting their feelings, or anything else, for that matter."

"So, are you still planning to go along with this insane plan?"

"Do you have any better ideas?"

"I thought you'd never ask. How about you take someone with you who knows a thing or two about this place?" He watched her with a confident, yet serious expression.

"Like who?"

"Oh, come on! And they told me you were smart."

"Who told you that?"

"Never mind. Look, take me. I can be your guide. You obviously don't need a bodyguard with your dragon following you around, but I could help you find places with a lot less interaction." He waved his hands around with an imaginary sword for emphasis.

"So, you want to help me track down the bad guys, so I can find Carbonell?"

"I want to make sure you don't get yourself into too much trouble. As for tracking the bad guys, as you call them, we'll just have to see where that takes us."

Her face turned serious, and she stared at her empty plate. It was so easy spending time with Joel. She could tell him anything. And it almost made things feel normal. But things were never going to be okay with Bain missing. She didn't look up when she asked another question, this time in a softer voice. "Do you think we'll find him?"

"I may not approve of your methods, but you might actually be onto something. I hadn't really considered that Carbonell is in contact with people right here in the kingdom. It is as good a lead as anything I can think of." He reached over and touched the back of her hand as it rested on the table.

She let her eyes slowly rise to meet his. The look of sincerity held.

"I'll be waiting outside your door tomorrow. We'll go together, right after sunup if you want. You don't have to do this alone, and there's no way I am spending the day wondering what happened to you again." He said the last part quietly to himself.

Chapter Thirty-nine

NEW PLAN

ERIN TALKED JOEL OUT OF sunup; she really was exhausted. Even though she was eager to start the search again, she knew she had some explaining to do. Pulsar would most likely have an opinion about sharing the hunt with Joel.

It shouldn't have surprised her to be the last one awake. A soft knock on the door startled her out of bed, and she raced over to find Joel waiting. She asked him for a few needed minutes so he promised to return with breakfast.

She washed up and tried again for the thousandth time in her life to demand order over her unruly hair. It wasn't that she normally cared too much how it ended up, but somehow knowing that Joel was about to be her sidekick for the day made her care just a little more about the end result of her efforts.

Wishing she had thought to pack a baseball cap, and also wishing that her filthy clothes stuffed in her suitcase could find a washing machine, she settled for something out of the wardrobe again. She almost never wore dresses. Here, she felt as though she wore nothing else. Fervently she vowed to find some laundry soap. If nothing else, she could use the bathtub to wash her clothes.

She updated Pulsar with the new plans when he flew to the castle. He insisted on joining their adventure when Erin's thoughts randomly strayed to the conversation the night before. It wasn't hard for her to agree with him.

· · · 🦋 · · ·

"What do you mean? What did you think of between last night and this morning?" Erin asked

Joel had been relatively quiet through most of their breakfast, but was now doing his best to be persuasive. "Well, you don't even have to go out there. We can watch everything from here."

She searched him with scrutinizing eyes. "Are you talking about surveillance cameras? Satellites, or something?"

He awarded her with a lopsided grin. "Now you're getting the hang of it. We do have the world's best technology. It's almost embarrassing that we've managed to stay ahead of the humans in their own game."

"What are you talking about?"

"You have identified specific individuals, and now we will track them. If they have a visitor, we will know it even before they do. All calls will be screened. We've got it all under control."

"And you didn't think to mention this last night."

"Uh, yeah. I was a bit distracted. You had been missing all day. No one knew what you were up to until you came back."

She rolled her eyes. If she had known it could be this easy, she probably wouldn't have bothered surveying the town on her own. Maybe she was just as reckless as Bain after all. And yet, it was embarrassing. Here she thought of the kingdom of elves more like a free-from-worldly-influence-completely-relying-on-nature sort of place. Like a third world country without the famine. She was beginning to realize how much she still had to learn.

"So, you're going to have the tech team bug the bad guys to see if they come up with any leads?"

"Bad guys." He seemed to be mulling a thought in his head. "It must be television. We can get that here, but honestly, no one ever watches it."

"Well, what do you call them?" she countered.

He smiled again at her. "I don't know. I kind of like 'bad guys.' "

She was aware of Pulsar monitoring their conversation. This had been the first time he had actually met Joel in person. Their interactions had been free from the dragon's physical presence, until now. Somehow it made Erin even more self-conscious than before. And yet, for his towering, obvious presence, he was blocking her out of his thoughts so that her mind was free from his opinion for the time being. She knew it would be temporary. Soon enough she would know what he thought.

"Tell me the story of the eternal blades. Agnar said something about unjust killing stripping you of magic. I've been thinking about that lady at the bar. She said she wasn't going to kill me. What was that all about?"

Joel leaned back in his chair. "Do you like horror stories?"

"Not really. Is it that bad?"

He smiled quickly but seemed to sober even more. "If someone were to take another's life without just cause, the spells that surround the blade are undone. The very magic that holds it together turns on its owner. Then the metamorphosis begins.

"The owner's beautiful face and strong body warps into an unrecognizable imp. Each individual takes on the look and qualities of the worst parts of their personality. Every bad thought, every angry intention grows into a black furry leg, or a horned head. The nightmare they commit is what they resemble, each cruel thought visible on their malformed beastlike body."

"Oh," Erin said. She was having trouble imagining it.

"There's more," he said. His stare was on the distant hills.

Erin waited silently. He hadn't even glanced her way.

"The imps usually live in seclusion, by themselves somewhere in the world. They seek refuge from the memories of the past. But their dreams remind them of who they once were. No matter where they live, they cannot escape their past. And any solitary imp would not dare even approach one of the älvin races. Not only does their hatred of their beastlike appearance keep them from it, but the transformation into an imp is completed as the very magic they possessed drains from them forever, never to be restored. Even the most terrifying form of an imp could not match the magical ability of a tiny älvor. Their life span is not diminished, but without magic to aid them, they are left to their physical abilities to support themselves."

"Have you ever seen one?" Erin asked.

"Yes. Just once." His gaze did not lift from the distant hills.

"What did it look like?" She asked so softly that she wondered if he heard.

His answer was nearly as soft as her question. "Like a monstrous cougar. It could walk on two legs, or run on all fours. He was a terrible beast. And cunning, too, but then, I suppose he was always cunning." Joel stared off as if remembering something from a distant past.

Erin looked out to the hills too, waiting for Joel to come back to the conversation.

His hazel brown eyes caught the sun as he turned to her. "How are you with a bow and arrow? I noticed that your set hasn't even been touched since your first day here."

Her eyes flicked to the corner of the room where her bow rested. She hadn't even looked at it since she put it there. Guilt flooded over her. How many other things had she neglected since becoming an älva? She tried to arrange her features carefully to mask her feelings as she faced Joel. "I suppose it's about time I broke it in. I don't suppose you have an archery range?"

He made it to her bow and quiver and back before she even finished her sentence.

Chapter Forty

BLACK RAIN

Bain looked at the stark walls that stood cold and unwelcoming again this morning. How many days had it been? Somehow the number dial on his watch had lost its meaning. What month was it, anyway? He had never spent time in a hospital. He wasn't even sure that he had ever seen the inside of one, personally. Were they all so desolate?

Bain shook his head, trying in vain to clear it from the hazy buzz that seemed to be his constant companion. The headaches were killing him. He was hardly ever awake, but when he was, his head throbbed as though a train had tried to run through it. He knew his strength had dimmed since he had come here.

He stood from the small cot. At least the dreary room had a window. He wondered more than once why there seemed to be no view. All he could see was a misty gray as he gazed out the small frame. Before he could make out a clear thought, the door opened behind him.

Carbonell entered the room. Ever since he had come to this odd building, Carbonell had been his lone visitor. All the news, information, everything he knew came from Carbonell. Weeks ago, after waking up in the isolated room, Carbonell had explained everything to him.

Somehow he had contracted a rare and feared disease. Instead of risking the entire population, he had been sent to isolation.

Only Carbonell had the courage and the fortitude to accompany him on the voyage. On the days when he was awake long enough, Carbonell would assure him that he would overcome the disease eventually. But the headache would return, rendering Bain unconscious once again.

"How are you feeling?" Carbonell asked.

Bain rubbed his forehead with the heel of his hand. "I think I could use some Tylenol."

Carbonell produced two small white pills and set it next to the water on the tiny table. "Do you think you're up for a walk?"

Bain sat down on the cot and popped the pills into his mouth. The room temperature water did not aid his thirst. Somehow the thought pulled a memory into his mind. He saw a basin of water turning to ice. He did that. His wand! Maybe it was just a dream. He slept so much here he could barely decipher the truth from the dreams.

"Do you want to take a walk?" Carbonell tried again.

Bain looked up at him as if only just realizing he was in the room. "Carbonell, do you know magic?"

A surprised look and maybe a flicker of anger crossed his expression. "Sure, why not? Everyone knows a little magic."

"I don't mean tricks. Do you know how to do real magic?"

Carbonell studied him as if calculating something.

"I'm hallucinating again, aren't I?" Bain looked at the floor dejected. Even though he spent so much of his time sleeping, his dreams seemed so real. He used to tell Carbonell about Erin, the cabin, and the fairies. Somehow his whole past was weaving in and out of reality so that he could hardly decipher the truth. In his dreams, everything seemed normal, as if there really could be a world where all of those things existed.

Here in the stone-walled room, nothing seemed to really exist. Bain stood, trying to clear his mind. Another wave of pain shot through his head. Determined not to be ruled by it, he shuffled towards the door. "Let's go for a walk. I'm getting tired of these four walls."

He had to keep one hand on the wall for stability. His sense of equilibrium had been compromised since the illness had overtaken him. The hallway had almost nothing to offer. The walls were the same cold gray stones as his room, but at least he was moving. He was only vaguely aware of what Carbonell was saying. Somehow the effort to walk was affecting his attention.

"I have to go away for a while. It's business. I'll be back in just a few days."

Bain had to consciously make an effort to seem involved in the conversation as nausea hit him unexpectedly. "Where are you going?" He tried to keep his voice light. Maybe he could sleep for several days straight so he wouldn't notice how alone he was without Carbonell.

"Overseas, actually." Carbonell looked at him with concern. "You will be fine. I will arrange to have someone visit you while I'm away."

"I think I need to sit down," he murmured.

"Yes, well, I think you should enjoy your new visitor. He is an old friend of mine. You two should get along just fine."

Bain had slowly made it back to his cot and was rubbing his temples, trying in vain to cure the explosive headache. "Okay. You sure he wants to risk getting my terrible disease? I haven't seen anyone else that brave."

"Oh, you don't need to worry about him. He will take care of himself." He patted Bain's shoulder. "Get some rest then. I shall see you when I return."

Bain was scarcely aware of the light dimming; day and night had little relevance in this cell-like room. Sleep was never too far away as he spent most of his time there. The flash of a basin of ice burst into view in his mind. He could see his wand. The bright silver inlaid with a diamond tip felt warm and heavy in his hand. And he knew how to use it. Before he could turn the thoughts away he saw himself melting the ice and heating the water.

How could it seem so real? Like so many disconnected memories, he had been trying to regain his past, and outlaw the insanity. Carbonell assured him daily that these memories of his were a product of the tragic disease, warping his reality into meaningless impossible fantasies. If he were to hang on to the fantasy, he would never truly be sane.

It made sense. But the pictures in his head remained vivid. And then, there was Erin. How he missed her. He wouldn't dream of letting her expose herself to his terrible fate. But she was the one who brought happiness out of him best. She probably never realized that she was the reason he was funny. Here in the bleak room, he couldn't even remember what laughter felt like.

So many of his memories were connected to the impossible that it was painful to try to vanquish them. He wanted to see her spinning in circles on the grass, laughing with the fairies. Even if it meant he was insane, he never wanted to forget that moment. But then, who would know? He could pretend that he had overcome his bizarre past while protecting the incredible dreams.

For the first time in very long, he allowed himself a smile. Indulging in the forbidden memories, he decided he could afford to wallow in this small bit of fantasy. Carbonell would not be there in the morning to force a confession from him.

He closed his eyes against the darkened room. The bright golden flames of her hair danced as she dueled him with a sword. Even if it meant he was insane, this memory was worth a lot. Maybe he dreamed this too, but seeing Erin brandishing a sword was truly priceless. More random thoughts bounced through his mind, and for maybe just this moment, he felt happy.

It was almost like being home. He would try harder tomorrow, but today he would allow his thoughts to wander. He could hear the crickets buzzing and see the fireflies fluttering over the lawn. Basketball in the backyard, making the perfect shot with magic.

He was doing it again. Magic couldn't be real. When was he going to get it out of his head?

The fine line between reality and dreams faded as he drifted into sleep. Dreams were always better. Here no one could tell him what was impossible. But, most importantly, here is where he could see Erin.

· · · 🦋 · · ·

The door opened quietly as a tall stranger strode deliberately into the tiny room.

Bain had been awake maybe twenty minutes already. He lay there staring aimlessly at the gray ceiling. He was hoping that if he didn't move, maybe, just maybe he could stave off his headache a little longer. This was the first morning he had the privilege of waking pain free. He was sure it was temporary but enjoyed the reprieve, all the same.

Carefully he turned his head to see his visitor. Carbonell hadn't mentioned the man's name. Actually, he didn't think he knew anything at all about the stranger who towered over his bed.

"I see you are awake," the stranger boomed.

Bain waited for the headache to crash through his brain, but nothing happened.

The tall man continued, "My name is Xavene." He reached his hand across the bed and shook Bain's. "How are you feeling today?"

"Better. So far, so good."

"I have some food out in the hall. I will leave it with you and let you clean up. I think you could use some fresh air today."

"Okay."

The man stepped out of the room and returned with a platter of toast, fruit, and juice. It was eloquently prepared, as though it had been catered.

Bain was relieved to realize that he could sit up without the vertigo and pain he constantly battled. His appetite was unexpectedly ravenous. He easily finished the entire platter, and still, there were no signs of nausea. Maybe he was going to beat this thing after all.

It lifted his spirits considerably to find clean jeans, a T-shirt, and his shoes waiting in the bathroom for him. For weeks he had been wearing sweats. No shoes. He hadn't made it any farther than a few steps down the hall during his drawn out stay.

Bain looked at the final product in the mirror. His hair had grown out quite a bit. He hadn't shaved in a while and had better than a shadow tracing his jaw. But even with the long wet hair, having the familiar clothes made him feel like himself more than any other thing. It hadn't escaped him that the shoes were the only thing he recognized as his own. It seemed that Carbonell or his friend had gone the extra mile in buying him new clothes.

He was feeling good, too. Better. Maybe the whole night-mare was finally at an end.

He left the bathroom whistling.

He stopped immediately when he saw the new stranger sitting on his bed. Xavene was dressed more like a businessman with a black suit that matched the black light surrounding him. He reminded himself of Carbonell explaining that the light he saw surrounding people was a result of his affliction. It didn't mean much. He had gotten used to the plum-colored light that surrounded Carbonell.

He tried to put it out of his head as he looked at Xavene. He had an air of confidence much like that of a high-level CEO. His black hair was shorter than Carbonell's, but angled and waved more like a movie star's. The guy could have walked right out of a screen production.

He stood and faced Bain, his strong face proportioned too perfectly. "Are you ready to see the sights?"

Bain couldn't help but smile at the words. The complete lack of symptoms could only be improved by leaving the awful room he had been quarantined to. "Very ready," he responded.

The hall was familiar enough, but all this time he had been too preoccupied to notice much of anything about the building. They climbed a staircase for what seemed like endless levels. Bain couldn't help feeling surprised and pleased at his endurance. Shouldn't his muscles start burning by now? But the stairs reached on and on, and his legs proved to be stronger than he remembered them to be before.

In track, his coach had made them run the bleachers. It was designed to build muscle and endurance. Every year he would begin the season with this exercise, sure he was going to lose his lunch. His sides would burn, his legs would turn to jelly, but worse than that, his stomach would threaten to humiliate him in front of all his friends. Of course, the other kids faired equally. But somehow it was easier to forgive other people losing it behind the bleachers than yourself.

Eventually they reached an opening. It seemed they had climbed the entire structure and now stood high on a tower that oversaw the vast land. Bain stood against the railing taking in the view. Sand reflected the sunlight for miles around. The sight was breathtaking, but he was still aware of the normal pace of his breaths. How could he climb that many stairs without panting for air? He focused on the view, trying not to let his thoughts stray. He promised himself to be good today and to not think of things that were impossible.

"What is this place?" Bain asked, trying to focus his thoughts on something concrete.

"It is a city called Black Rain."

Bain looked out at the landscape. Not a single plant dotted the horizon. "Black Rain," he repeated. "It doesn't look like this place sees much rain." He caught Xavene's glance.

"Exactly," he answered, and didn't offer more.

Bain examined the building from where they stood. It was pretty big. Maybe the city was named after the black stone building that offset the otherwise ominous sand. "So, does anyone live here?" he tried. A place this big surely housed many.

"A few do. Mostly workers though. There really isn't anything nearby, so those who work here live here."

Bain studied the architecture of the surrounding building. A black smoke billowed out of one of the tall chimneys, a sure sign of life, even if it did seem dismal. The silence stretched on as Bain leaned against the railing, surveying the view. It felt good to be anywhere besides the small gray room. Even with the bleak terrain, the height offered a clear vantage point. He could get used to looking out from here.

Xavene cleared his throat, interrupting the silence. "So, there is something I wanted to talk to you about."

Bain turned and saw the serious expression on his face. "What's that?" he asked.

"Carbonell has told me you can see light around him. Is that true?"

This again, he thought. How long would it take him to truly be well? For a moment he had allowed himself to forget the horrible days he had just come through, and enjoy the sensation of freedom from the chains of pain. Now he let his answer come in an even tone. "Yes." He did not try to explain further. Xavene smiled slightly. "And can you see a light around me, as well?"

"Yes." He chose to look Xavene in the eye. There was no point in playing games with this.

Xavene laughed lightly. "Tell me, Bain, what color was Carbonell's light?"

No one had ever asked him this before. "Sort of a deep purple, I guess."

Xavene's bore into Bain with his stare. "And what color is my light?"

The question came out in almost a threatening tone. Bain was hesitant to answer, but decided to be direct. "It appears to be black, like an extension of your suit." Bain had never seen anyone with a black aura.

Xavene laughed at this and took the rail with both hands. Bain watched his reaction with confusion. What was so amusing about that?

"This could be enlightening indeed," Xavene said as his laughter faded. "Yes, I think there is much I could learn from your ability."

Bain did not respond. There was something odd about this man, and he wasn't entirely sure what to make of it. But the questions were intriguing all the same. "Do you think I will always have this problem, you know, seeing lights around people?"

"Yes, I'm afraid, young man, that you will be stuck with that for life. But don't worry, you will learn to cope."

Bain decided to focus on the miles of sand. It was disturbing to think that this illness would cause permanent damage to his sight. "So, how long do you think it will be before I go back?" Bain remained fixed on the sunlit sand as he asked. Somehow he knew he wasn't going to like the answer.

"Go back where, Bain?"

"Home. I want to go home. I need to see Erin. I'm sure she's worried out of her mind."

"No need to worry yourself. We have been updating her with your status on a regular basis. You really are better off here where she is not in danger."

"I know. But how long before I can go back?"

"I'm not sure. Perhaps you will find you want to stay after all. You haven't even begun to see the city, and haven't you always dreamed of seeing the world?"

What did the stranger know about his dreams? If he really knew, he would know that his dreams were filled with impossible realities: fairies, magic, elves, and most of all, Erin. That was where his dreams were. His escape from the nightmare of reality did not rest in seeing the wide world after all.

"Come," Xavene offered, "I will show you around."

Chapter Forty-one

CLOSER

THE KNOCK AT THE DOOR was unusually loud and urgent. The rapping persisted until Erin could finally wake up enough to realize that she wasn't dreaming the noise. "I'm coming!" she called as she wrapped a robe around her.

She wished she hadn't bothered to glance at the mirror as she walked to the door. She looked like a hurricane survivor. The knock came again so she closed the distance to the door.

Joel greeted her with an excited expression. "I think we found him."

"What are you talking about?" Her brain hadn't caught up with his statement. Then again, he was probably a morning person. Why else would he be knocking on her door at the crack of dawn?

"Carbonell. We traced a call to one of the suspected individuals. You were right. He's coming here. He'll be here today or tomorrow."

The news hit her, and suddenly she felt wide awake.

"Look, why don't you get dressed, and I'll take you to the computer room. They're trying to determine his location. He's been pretty tricky to find."

"Give me five minutes."

He smiled and nodded. "Okay. Five minutes."

The halls stretched into endless mazes once again. In spite

the days spent here in the massive building, her navigation skills were still catching up with the indoor landscape. They hadn't left the building and grounds at all since they had set up tracking devices on the dark elves. Joel had easily convinced her that she would be safer here than on the streets. Now that her face had become a target, she wasn't anxious to find out if she could win another battle with the elves.

A screen stretched across the wall displaying the different locations they were surveying. Joel pointed out the dwelling where a phone conversation had been tapped. Apparently cell phones were not entirely uncommon after all. Carbonell was definitely arranging a stay here in the kingdom, and since he did not suspect he was being watched, it hadn't been difficult to ascertain his intentions.

"So now what do we do?" Erin asked.

"Well, the team is working out the flight rosters. We think we can decipher which name he is using once he comes in. That will help track him in the future. As long as he doesn't know anything is going on, he is likely to use the same alias leaving again. Then, presto, we follow Carbonell and hopefully it leads to Bain." Joel had an animated voice as he explained the situation.

She let the words sink in. "Just like that?"

"Well, it's as far as I've worked things out."

"You mean we might find Bain as soon as next week?"

"It depends on how long he stays here, but things are looking good. If we determine his alias name for his flight in, we might be able to see what his return plans are as well."

She found a chair and let her body sink into the soft leather. Bain had been missing for so long that it seemed impossible to find him as soon as next week. What a change of luck. "Who will follow Carbonell? You said 'We follow Carbonell.' Who is we?"

Joel sat in the chair next to her and put his hand over hers as it rested on the arm of the chair. The gesture was simple, yet sent her pulse racing. She tried to force the blood away from her cheeks. He was looking at her with his genuine smile on his too dazzling face. *Why did she have to think about that now?*

"Who do you want to follow Carbonell?" he asked.

Her mind scrambled for a moment, and she tried to force her thoughts together. "Uh, I guess I hadn't thought about it."

He kept his eyes trained on her, and she had to look down. How was she going to keep a coherent thought with that face looking at her?

"Well, I know I'm going," she said. "Pulsar and I will find him. Maybe that's all we really need."

He lifted his hand from hers and buckled it under his chin. "So you're planning to go it alone, after all?"

She was trying to read into the question, but it was hard to tell where his thoughts really were. "I don't know. I'll talk to Pulsar and see what he thinks. Besides, it's not like Bain is in danger or anything. I'm just going crazy not knowing where he is."

Really she knew all along that it would just be her and Pulsar. How could she drag anyone else halfway across the earth to find her brother? And he probably was okay. She had determined already that she was the one who allowed his absence to crush her existence. Finding Bain was merely a selfish cause, and she had involved too many people already.

But Pulsar wouldn't feel that way. He was almost an extension of her own thoughts and feelings. She knew he would want to find Bain as earnestly as she did; if she was happy, so was he.

"I suppose you could be right," he said absently. "We have no indication of his current status. Bain could just be sightseeing." He leaned forward in his chair. "Of course, that doesn't exactly fit with the picture. Do you really think Bain and Carbonell just went backpacking in Europe? And even if they did, why would he come here and just leave Bain there?"

"What am I supposed to say? I don't really know what's going on." Erin started fiddling with her brooch. She turned it into a picture of Bain outside their home. As she inspected the photo, she tried to sort out the circumstances surrounding his disappearance.

It all went back to Carbonell. She wished that she knew for sure whether it was him she had seen on the plane. Maybe that would help her figure things out. Now that she was about to see him in person, she wasn't sure how excited she was about her plan. If it really was him, then Bain might be somewhere he shouldn't be. The thoughts were swirling around in her head, refusing to land on a right answer.

Suddenly she felt the same warm weight on her hand and looked up to see Joel watching her. She met his gaze and finally found her tongue.

"Look. I don't know how this is going to play out, but I can't expect anyone to get involved. I do have a dragon on my side. I'm not exactly alone, you know." She hoped she sounded more convincing than she felt.

A little help here, Pulsar! What do you want me to do? She knew he had been tuned into their entire conversation, but his own thoughts had been guarded. Now he opened the window of thought once more.

Ultimately, you must decide, Fireborn. But you realize that I will not be flying in a metal contraption, and neither will you.

Of course! Why hadn't she thought of that in the first place? Now a smile conquered her face as she began her new strategy. "I'll tell you what. I am going to be riding on Pulsar to find Bain. Anyone who feels the need to join the wild goose chase will have to do so by whatever means they can supply."

Joel's serious expression had not broken. "Fair enough," he answered.

"What? So that means you're planning on coming?" She had hoped she would change his mind. She wasn't exactly sure why she was so hesitant about involving Joel in this adventure. It was as if he didn't really belong in the same picture with Bain. She looked again at his photo in her hand and tried to unravel her confusing thoughts.

"Well, you just said that anyone who felt the need to join the search was welcome to do so." He had not lifted his hand from hers.

He had her. How did he do that?

"Right," she tried. "But why do you want to go?"

"I think everyone in the kingdom would like to go," he said and he leaned back into his chair and put his hands behind his head.

The loss of his hand on hers was too noticeable. It was nothing at all like Bain's. Somehow, when Joel touched her hand, a volt of electricity would race through her whole being. It should seem disturbing, but it had the opposite affect. Why was his hand so much different, anyway?

Pulsar was kind enough to pull her out of her thoughts. *So when do we leave, little one?*

She tried to clear her throat. "So, how long before we have a positive trace on Carbonell?"

"It shouldn't be much longer," he answered without looking at her. He was watching one of the screens in front of them.

"Well, if you'll excuse me, I want to check on something." She was hoping her casual voice was working. She stood and left the room.

Okay, Pulsar. I hope you've been paying close attention. How do I find you? Sure enough the pictures of the castle they had shared through their thoughts became a map in Pulsar's mind. He guided her to an outdoor garden where he waited for her.

I really need some sky under me right now, she said. Somehow he had known that before she did. His saddle was already in place. *How do you do that, anyway—the saddle?*

Material manipulation, of course. Fireborn, you might be getting a bit rusty.

Actually, you never told me you could use it.

He let a low rumble of chuckle escape. *It's true, I don't generally practice it, but I have been working specifically with the saddle. It seemed most convenient.*

She hadn't waited for his explanation to strap her legs into the soft fenders. They launched into the sky and watched the ground shrink underneath them. Once the altitude became sufficient, Pulsar pulled into maneuvers and let flames fly through the air. The familiar training was distracting and comforting at the same time.

Up here in the clear sky she could think. They were close. She could feel it. They were actually going to find Bain. But why couldn't she put Bain and Joel in the same picture? She fingered the brooch that she had transfigured. Bain was a part of her, like the other half of her own identity.

And Joel. She still couldn't understand. Why did she feel so awkward yet happy when she was with him? And why did she want to spend all of her time with him? She knew that she could go out on her own, see the town. She thought of the little bakery. That was another place she had completely neglected. And she still hadn't sought out the little girl from her first dream of the kingdom.

One thought leaped to the next and soon Adarae came to mind. She hadn't even talked to an älvor since arriving here. Not even in the forest. Somehow she felt lonely again. The past was haunting. Everything that was real in it was disappearing. Without Bain, and even the fairies, there was nothing left from the home she had not so long ago lived in.

She was going to find him. The hole in her heart would be filled again. Things would change. She hadn't known what to expect upon transforming into an älva, but nothing that had happened so far even came close to what she might have imagined.

Chapter Forty-two

CAIRO

ERIN WONDERED WHY SHE HADN'T thought of it sooner. With Pulsar's ability to cover ground at an enormous speed, she did not have to strictly rely on outside sources to inform her of everything. If Bain could reach out and discover the world outside of the small one they knew, why couldn't she?

Ultimately, it all rested in the identity of Carbonell. If it really was him she saw on the plane next to Bain, then she might have a better idea of what to do next. What if this mystery person was someone she had never seen? The trail would be cold. And why drag others into her chase of intuition?

Erin had never entered an airport before. She was surprised at the number of people shuffling their luggage to the counter. Using an invisibility ward she observed the system as close as she dared. Even though they couldn't see her, they were likely to bump into her in their rush. After considerable study of their documents, she took her turn in line at the security gate. This was even easier than she imagined. No wonder Bain had escaped so easily. With the right papers, you could do anything.

It seemed so much easier to just pull on the invisibility ward soon after she left the security screen and metal detectors. With a list of flights in her hand, another convenient transformation of her brooch, she began to watch plane after plane de-board.

Luck must have been smiling down on her. On just the third

plane, she noticed a dark aura in the crowd of people trudging from the gate. Even though she still could not see who was producing the menacing cloud, she could not help but feel that the shade was very familiar.

Feeling rather confident in her invisibility, she initiated her approach. The crowd began to thin out, and soon it was easy to make her way directly to the hard hateful black aura. From the side, she could see the same black hair she remembered and the ordinary clothes. She continued to keep in step with him until he stopped in his tracks and looked directly at her.

She felt her blood run cold. Every cell in her body froze as this man looked at her even through the invisibility ward. She couldn't take her eyes off of him. Could he really see her? In the terrifying moment she discovered two things. First, she couldn't remember how to do magic, and second, his face matched the one from her dream. He seemed to smile at her before shifting his backpack and continuing his way to the door.

Fireborn, you will find your way outside, or I will find my way in. Now!

But how am I going to track him if I don't follow him?

I will keep you invisible, you get yourself out. That is an order.

She hadn't taken advantage of her superhuman skills for a very long time. Running through the crowd seemed like an exhilarating release and the stairs were easily avoided as she merely leaped from one level to the next. She really hoped that Pulsar had thought to make her soundless as well, or someone was bound to wonder where the noise was originating from as she landed and kept her run.

It had only been seconds before the cloudy sky greeted her. Pulsar guided her to where he waited invisible on the lawn. She reached him and eagerly climbed on his warm back and to the saddle.

"How did he do that? He looked right at me. I thought I was invisible. I know I was. No one else was looking at me." She still felt shaken from the unnerving stare.

Hold on, Pulsar responded before jetting into the air. Before long the airport was shrinking below them and the familiar rush of air surrounded her. *Fireborn, I think that he will go back to the kingdom, and so should we. And as for why he could see you; that I cannot answer. But I was not foolish enough to let your ward slip. You were most certainly invisible.*

"Do you think he just knows? Like he can sense other elves or something?"

What do you think, little one?

She tried to let the words cross easily through her mind. Maybe she would sense the truth. "I don't know yet. I think I'm still too freaked out to tell. So, what about you? Did you catch him?"

Actually, I think he must have gone invisible. I haven't seen a trace.

She breathed out in frustration. If all of the elves had the same ability to go invisible, how did they track each other? Maybe the only time they can always be seen is in their sleep. But at least she knew who it was. And she knew what flight he was on. The tech team would be able to do the rest.

She hit her forehead in frustration. "I probably just messed everything up! Now he knows I was there! He will probably change his name again and make it impossible to find out his flight plans. How could I be so dumb?"

This is not finished. I am not finished. If you have to follow him from my back for a week, we will find him. We will not give up.

She wondered how to get around telling Joel about her latest adventure. She supposed it would only be fair to let them know that she probably interfered with their success in tracing him. Maybe she should have left all of this to the experts in the first place. But as much as she appreciated their help, she wished she could do this without involving others unnecessarily. The thought of finding Bain was the only thing driving her now. And maybe she would solve the mystery from Pulsar's back after all.

It wasn't long before the castle loomed into view once again. She entered her elaborate room and quickly changed into something more elflike. Maybe Joel hadn't noticed her absence, and she really didn't want her jeans to be giving her away.

Pulsar guided her to the vast computer room. His navigation skills were like having a personal GPS. She entered the computer-lit room and scanned the screens for any hint of Carbonell. She caught her breath as a pair of hands gripped her upper arms. In her mind an image of Joel flashed before her, but as she looked down, she could not see the hands that were still firmly at her sides.

"Be still and be quiet," a voice said softly in her ear.

The hands never left her arms as he guided her out of the room. She realized that it would look as if she were walking on her own accord. She reached out to Pulsar with her mind, but he was blocking her thoughts. That seemed so unlike him. Pulsar had been in contact with her just moments before.

"Where are you taking me?" Erin asked the stranger. He was still guiding her with his firm invisible grasp.

"To see your brother, of course. Isn't that what you have been searching for?" He gave no hint of menace in his voice.

"Why won't you let me see you?" she tried. If she could just see him, she would know whether to trust the stranger by his aura alone. But she could not see the aura of anyone using an invisibility ward.

"I wouldn't think you would wish to ruin the surprise." His voice seemed genial and soft with an almost imperceptible hint of humor.

"Is Bain very far?" She was hoping that he would release his grip, which thus far he had maintained with perfection. The path they were taking was familiar. They were indeed heading straight to her room. The hallway stretched on, and with each passing step, an icicle seemed to form in her chest, and she realized she could hardly breathe.

She tried to manipulate his hands off of her shoulders, but her ability to concentrate was slipping away. Everything around her began to spin.

"Help!" she tried to call, but her voice was lost in her throat. Her legs began to feel like jelly underneath her, and the walls swirled. Before she could reach the door to her room, everything went black. She felt herself falling, but something caught her and carried her into the room. She was aware of her bed underneath her before all sensation left, and she drifted into unconsciousness.

··· 🦋 ···

A low rumble was the first thing she was aware of. Her arms balked at the sensation produced by a scratchy blanket that was draped over her. The rumbling noise was loud, and yet she could hear the sounds of people talking. It was familiar somehow. She tried to force her eyes open, but so far, they refused to obey.

So she sat still and listened. Where had she heard this before? She was vaguely aware of someone walking past her. Someone else was talking, but she couldn't understand a word. The language was garbled and had a choppy accent. An image of a tall lady with russet skin flashed in her mind.

The airplane! She listened more carefully, trying to hear every sound, any hint of information. Maybe she was dreaming. But in her dreams she could open her eyes. Why weren't they working now?

Pulsar! She screamed it in her mind, as if she could somehow intensify the volume of her thoughts. *Pulsar, are you there?* She was focusing with every part of her mind. She thought she could hear his voice.

Fireborn! But then it faded.

The silence was horrifying, so she tried again. She called and called in her mind. Where was he? And where was she? Finally she surrendered. If she couldn't reach him, maybe there was something more constructive she could do, like open her eyes.

She chided herself. She could perform magic that could transport objects, and yet her own eyelids refused to obey her commands. Maybe she could force them open with her hands. She hadn't tried moving yet. As she thought about moving her arms, she realized that they felt distant and unattached.

She slowly lifted her hand, but it felt as if she were moving through congealed mud. Eventually, her hand touched her face and she awkwardly felt her way above her cheekbone and to her eye. With one eye forced open with her fingers, she adjusted to the light and tried to focus.

In front of her a seat back held magazines and a plastic tray tacked to the top. Erin experimented to see if she could keep her eye open without her hand, but it proved too difficult. So she settled for examining her surroundings with her right eye partially opened.

The seat next to her was empty and she gazed out the window. The sky outside looked blue, but she couldn't make anything else out from her position. A woman's voice startled her as she tried to peer out the window.

"Do you speak English?" the lady was saying in an accented voice.

A jolt of energy surged through her and she was able to focus her gaze in the direction of the voice. A uniformed lady was holding a basket out to her with small steaming towels.

"It is to freshen up with," the lady offered.

Erin took the hot moist towel and unfolded it. She put it to her face and let the hot steam soak in and rejuvenate. Too soon the heat dissipated and she folded the small towel. The lady was still standing there.

"Would you like another?" she asked, her voice was smooth and friendly.

"Where are we going?" Erin asked as she handed the lady the damp towel.

She smiled sweetly at her. "You must have been sleeping well. We are due to arrive in Cairo," she glanced at her slender watch, "in twenty minutes."

"Egypt," Erin breathed. The lady seemed to accept her reaction as a jog in her memory. She nodded and went on to the next seat.

Erin's mind tried to catch up with the events. The last thing she remembered was the invisible hands guiding her to her room.

She couldn't help looking down at herself. She was wearing the same dress she changed into just before leaving her room.

Egypt. Why was she going to Egypt? A familiar voice caught her attention. He was speaking a foreign language, but it was the same voice that came from the invisible hands. He was coming closer. She tried to decide whether she dared peek out into the aisle to see him.

It wasn't going to be necessary. He was nearly to her seat already. Almost instinctively, she closed her eyes and tried to relax into the upholstered seat. She could feel him climb over her and into the seat next to her. The click indicated he had fastened his seatbelt. She was stuck sitting next to this man for the remainder of the flight.

Erin tried to come up with a plan. How was she going to leave the aircraft without him detecting her awareness? Did he already know she was awake? She wished she could understand Egyptian, or whatever language they conversed in.

In high school one of her friends had talked her into taking a drama class to fill a curriculum requirement. Erin earned her grade with high test scores, not with her acting ability. The most pronounced thing Erin learned in drama class was that she was never going to pursue a career in acting. She couldn't act to save her life.

At least that's how she felt at the time. Now she tried to remember everything her teacher had tried in vain to teach her. Once she had been given the role of a sleeping girl. It was probably due to the terrible time she had at delivering lines convincingly. All she had to do was sleep, and yet she couldn't even get that right. Her teacher emphasized that sleeping individuals breathe slowly and deeply, and they don't generally blink.

She honestly never thought that she would ever depend on the skill again, but now she found herself willing her breaths to draw slowly in and out. Her eyelids relaxed enough for her to not feel as if she were forcing them shut. Sleeping Beauty would be proud.

And while she was at it, she tried once more to reach Pulsar with her mind. This time she repeated her destination over and over, as if her waves of thought might somehow connect with his over the distance between them.

The air pressure in the cabin began to change, indicating their descent. Erin couldn't help but be pleased with her ability to adjust without yawning. Flying with Pulsar had granted her a few advantages. She wondered how her captor had managed to get her into the plane while she was sleeping. Her stomach began to tie in knots as she felt the plane taxi to the gate. It would only be a few minutes before she would be leaving the plane.

Something was announced several times over the intercom. The cabin filled with the sounds of passengers retrieving their luggage from the over-head compartments. Her seat-mate had climbed over her once again and was shuffling through the cabinet just above her head.

The noise gradually dimmed, and it seemed that she and the stranger were the only individuals left on the plane. Erin felt a touch on her shoulder and her seatbelt unbuckled. Suddenly two strong hands hefted her out of her seat and she was draped over the man's shoulder like a sack of potatoes.

He walked off the plane and into the airport. With her head behind his back, she dared to peek at her surroundings. The airport was filled with bustling people carrying bags, eating at tiny restaurants and rushing through the crowds. She wondered why no one seemed to notice her dangling over the shoulder of a man. Why was no one staring at the spectacle?

Of course! She was invisible, and most likely, so was he. That made things less complicated for her. As long as she let her body hang limp, she should be free to look around as much as she wished.

Watching from an upside down perspective, they passed gate after gate. She couldn't help but wonder how far they had to go. He wound his way to the doors exiting the airport and kept walking.

The hot sun hit her with unexpected force. Iceland had been extremely mild in comparison to the heat that now radiated off the blacktop of the parking lot. She wondered if he was headed to a car, but he passed through the parking lot and took off at a full run. From her limited view, she couldn't be sure where he was headed. She didn't want to chance him suspecting her conscious state merely so that she could get a better view of the field.

So she hung limply over his shoulder while he sprinted on. She cried out to Pulsar in her mind, trying, and failing again, to reach him. She didn't know which was worse, being kidnapped or getting cut off from Pulsar. Either way, it left her lost and alone.

She watched the ground speed by under the stranger's feet. He said that he was taking her to Bain. If that was really true, then all of this might be worth it in the end. Her only goal for weeks now had been to find him.

Chapter Forty-three

THE INSIDE STORY

HER CAPTOR'S FEET SLOWED WHEN he hit asphalt once again. Soon they were boarding a helicopter and she was flopped into a seat and strapped into place. Erin tried to keep her breathing slow and unaffected by the change. Carefully, she let her head tilt towards the window. From her position, she should be able to look out the window with one eye without being detected.

The blades began to rotate into a flurry of noise and they lifted off the ground. There was no one in the aircraft besides the two of them. This had to be a good thing. Erin watched out the window as they traversed the land when his voice pierced the engine noise unexpectedly. Only this time, she could understand the language.

"This is B Cliff, do you copy?"

Something sounded in his headset. She could hear the voice, but the words were too broken up for her to understand.

"Affirmative. The diamond is on its way. Over."

The other voice spoke in a muffled sound.

"Yes, she looks like the journey hasn't worn her too badly. Over."

Another phrase garbled in his ear.

"Copy that. We are expecting to arrive in thirty minutes. Over and out."

She watched the ground underneath them turn into endless

sand. Where vegetation once graced the ground shrewdly, now drifted sand created the landscape. The sound of the engine and rotors were interrupted once again with another sound.

Was he whistling? She listened as the man patterned out a strange lullaby. It had a mesmerizing quality, and in spite of her fear, she felt somehow comforted by the unexpected music. It was familiar, and the melody was catching as it repeated in his impromptu serenade.

His whistling was replaced with humming as they continued their journey. Erin watched the sand below, the only thing visible for miles around.

Exiting the helicopter proved to require more acting than she had been compelled to provide thus far. Erin felt someone's hands settling her into a gurney and now it was bumping along on an uneven floor. Other voices were present, but the thought of peeking was too terrifying. They entered an elevator where the sensation of falling backwards through the floor made her already knotted stomach turn.

Another hall was crossed and finally the bed came to a halt. The voices disappeared and so did the light at the sound of a door shutting.

At long last, Erin carefully opened her eyes.

The room was dark and small. The walls were of gray stone and in the corner was a bathroom with its door slightly ajar. Other than her bed, the only furniture to grace the room was a tiny table.

She sat up and tested the cot for squeaking. It seemed silent enough, so she crept to the bathroom. She was grateful for the opportunity to freshen up, as much as practice her invisibility ward. It was a trick Bain had taught her. A mirror was a pretty accurate indicator of how well an invisibility ward was holding up.

Maintaining the ward, and adding a sound one to it for

good measure, she opened the bathroom door. Although she half expected someone to be waiting there for her, the room remained empty. She commanded the door to open, and to her surprise, it obeyed.

Her fingers reached to her throat where her brooch was pinned. Miraculously, it was still in place. Her sword was missing from her side, but having her brooch was more than she had hoped for.

The long hall led to a set of stairs where she climbed level after level. An open arch came into view eventually and she followed it out onto a balcony. The sight before her was daunting and magnificent; a city of black smudged on an endless sea of sand. Erin scanned the layout of the buildings trying to guess which way was out. Voices broke the silence, yet she vigilantly preserved her ward before slowly turning around.

"Yes, I'm sure she was out the entire flight. She must be more vulnerable than her brother." The voice was familiar and coming from an unseen room.

"Have you bound her with the migrainous spell?" It was a male voice—sharp and commanding. The sound of his voice made her cringe. Even from a distance she could feel his malevolence.

"I thought we might try a different approach. Perhaps we should ascertain what gifts she bears before breaking her."

The sound of footsteps ensued. "What do you imagine she can do, Carbonell?"

"If her brother can see magic, perhaps she will have a skill that will prove useful as well."

"It is true. Superior to any weapon we could create, a magic seer can see every spell. Nothing will be invisible to us, and with this gift, there is nothing that can stand in our way. The possibilities are endless. I very much doubt, however, that she could have such a worthy talent. We may do well to eliminate her. It would make things a bit less complicated."

She listened to their words and began to panic. The pieces were rushing into place from a thousand different directions, like glass from a broken chandelier flying together to mend itself. She could see Bain and Carbonell on the plane. The same plane she had been on. He was here, and she would find him.

Without waiting another second, she leaped off the balcony and landed on the soft sand below. Quickly she manipulated the sand to cover her landing before sprinting along the outer ledge of the boardwalk. At least she wouldn't have to cover her entire trail.

As she ran, she screamed for Pulsar in her mind. No answer came. The cruel silence was maddening.

Chapter Forty-four

HIDE AND SEEK

SHE HAD COVERED THE ENTIRE length of the city in such a short time. The tar black buildings that edged the towering castle offered no imagination in their design. Erin felt surprised not to meet a single living being in her rushed exploration. Maybe it was too hot outside.

Even with her high tolerance for temperature extremes, she could still feel the heat radiating off of the sand and sucked into the black exterior of the ugly buildings. She wondered why anyone would paint something black in a place where the heat was already suffocating.

A door stood slightly open, and she took the invitation carefully. Even if she were invisible, someone might notice the door opening. Inside, the room held no charm. The heat seemed condensed in the poorly lit space of what appeared to be an entry room. A hallway led her to a staircase descending into darkness.

The sound of machinery greeted her as she picked her way through the old wooden stairs. The sounds grew until they were as loud as the rotors on the helicopter. Metals clanged and screeched as if they were being mercilessly beaten. The stairs finally ended and an enormous shop came into view.

The sight was paralyzing. Monstrous creatures manned fire pits, metal wheels, and anvils along with other unnamed machines. No two creatures appeared the same with the exception of their sickening oil black auras. The room was as doom black with auras as the outside of the tar buildings had been.

A tall spiderlike creature was using its many arms to hammer a bright hot piece of metal. As one arm would ding the steel with a hammer, the next arm would follow in rapid succession. Its head bore several eyes, and its entire body was covered in black spiking hairs. In spite of the arachnid appendages, two stocky black legs supported him.

A lizardlike creature shoveled coal into a fire pit. Erin winced as she watched a long blue tongue whip out of his mouth and lick his bulging eye. For every station, another horror, portraying mutated animal characteristics, worked and labored to produce various metal pieces.

It took Erin a few minutes to pull her eyes off of their abhorrent figures to notice the piles of weapons they were creating. Blades of steel, spiked clubs, and unfamiliar weapons of war lined the walls of the room. Crossbows seemed like a popular choice as well. She reached down to her side where her blade should have been. Faced with the piles of armory, she felt naked without her sword.

She crept back up the flight of stairs and continued to explore the winding buildings. Hunger began to settle in, and she realized how much time must have passed since her last meal. If she didn't find food soon, her ability to focus on magic would suffer and she would lose her invisibility.

No vegetation burst from the sand surrounding the city. Any hope of securing food would come from inside the ominous black buildings. Erin followed the sounds and smells until she was sure there was no alternative than to re-enter the hated castle. There had to be a kitchen in there somewhere, as the outer buildings held no hope for food.

She found her way through doors and halls until the unmistakable smell of a cook fire tantalized her. Voices could be heard coming from the kitchen as well as clanking dishes and sizzling pans.

"Their sayin' she got away. Bet they underestimated her, they did." More voices added in to the conversation.

"Carbonell has himself a hot head, he does. I reckon he thought she was under his mighty power without a fuss. Knew it was gonna catch up to him someday. Always actin' like the hero, he is."

"You better not let them hear ya. You'll be on sand patrol for a month. Old Jamie ain't been seen for 'bout six weeks. Had a mouth on him, though, didn' he?" Laughter followed and the sound of dishes continued.

"Yeah, but that was priceless, what he said to Carbonell. I don't think I'd have the guts."

Erin determined that she might be able to sneak into the kitchen without their detection. As engrossed in conversation as they were, she might even pick up a decent meal and leave without them the wiser.

She commanded the door to open just wide enough for her to slip through. No one seemed to notice, so she let herself in. For the depressing state of everything she had seen since arriving to this horrid place, the kitchen was impressively cheery. Skylights in the ceiling let in plenty of sunshine, and the walls were not coated in gray or black.

The cooks even shone a lighter aura than she had seen since the airplane. Each had their own shade of gray, but there was enough light in them that it lifted her spirits. Carefully avoiding contact with the bustling cooks, she investigated their pots and pans. When one would turn around to attend to another area, she would quickly jab a piece of sizzling meat or a boiling potato. Thermal control was a lifesaver as she shoplifted her lunch directly off of the fire.

"Don't suppose any of you heard if they're offerin' a reward for finding the little devil."

Erin froze in place and concentrated on remaining invisible.

"I imagine the master would be right pleased if someone were to turn her in."

"Can't say that I'd mind a raise myself. Maybe I could

afford some paint for my bunker. Gettin' right tired of all the black. It's like they found a sale on black paint and bought the store out."

More laughter followed. Erin slowly edged her way to the door. She couldn't help noticing the short haircuts on the men. Their ears indicated their human state. It was a strange combination, the horrible creatures working metal in the deep cellars while ordinary humans cooked in the kitchen.

She closed the door behind her and moved silently away. Her entire life she had relied on others to help her navigate. Even so, she hoped that a lifetime of exploring might prove to have its benefits.

She couldn't help but wonder why the place seemed mostly deserted. She would expect guards or even residents to be wandering the halls, but they stood empty as she ran aimlessly through them. A plan began to form in her mind, and Erin familiarized herself with the layout. If she were in charge around here, she would want a place high in the castle, somewhere she could see far out into the distance.

So she raced upwards, cheating as much as possible by leaping over steps, and reached a corridor that showed promise. Plush carpets lined the halls and tapestries hung on the walls. It wasn't her taste in décor, but it seemed someone important occupied this level. She crept along the hall listening for any signs of life. Instantly, she froze as familiar voices pierced the door.

"Have they scoured the dungeon?" It was the same haughty voice that spoke earlier.

"They have checked everywhere, my liege. There is no sign of her." The voice was gravelly and low with a churned accent that made him difficult to understand.

"You have your orders. I will accept no failures."

"Yes, my liege."

The sound of footsteps ensued.

"Report to me immediately after she is captured, Clawzhia. That is all."

The door swung open and Erin cemented her invisible form into place. A creature towering well over a man's height exited the room and now was walking down the hall straight towards her. Its head looked like that of an oversized hyena with dirt brown spotted fur and a blackened snout. The face was completed with the semi-round ears protruding straight out of its head and black-brown eyes. Below the hideous head was a thick warped neck extending into an oversized, fur covered chest. Its arms bore the same ugly fur and dangled longer than a man's, ending in a mutated paw with five discernible digits.

It walked on two legs and wore some kind of clothing over the bottom half of its form. She noticed him sniffing the air as he passed by her and slightly baring his teeth. Erin was almost certain it would find her by smell alone. She hadn't learned a ward for smell yet. She flattened herself slowly against the wall, hoping the open window next to her would help her out.

The creature let out a cackling howl and raced from her view. Erin tried to catch her breath and darted into an empty room across the hall. Someone was already walking past the room, and instinctively, she crouched behind an oversized chair.

"Ah, Carbonell, do you have news?"

"It is only a matter of time before she surfaces. There is nowhere to go in this forsaken place. She will be easily managed." Carbonell's voice was familiar to her now.

"And what do you have to report about our other honored guest?"

A low chuckle preceded Carbonell's answer. "This has worked even better than we predicted. He has been vigilant in putting every magical thought aside. He is cleansing his mind even more thoroughly than I would have hoped. I think he may be ready for the next step soon."

"Do you think it would be safe to re-introduce magic? Don't you think the memories it would stir would be irrefutable for him?"

"We could always wash his mind completely clean."

"The consequences may be too severe. We cannot afford to have him lose his gift. Without that, he is nothing to us. Perhaps it would be best to leave things as they are for now."

"Perhaps."

"Our priority concern is to find the girl. I have briefed the imps. I am confident that she will be in our hands by sundown."

The sound of their feet and fading voices indicated their departure. Erin waited until she could no longer hear the two before she let herself out of the small room. The leader's room stood empty and the temptation was too great to ignore. Holding her breath, she stepped in.

The spacious office was an odd sight in the otherwise dreary, foreboding structure. Light beamed into the room through unobstructed windows. Broad leaves sprouted from a tall plant potted in the corner of the room. She was surprised to remember its name from her lessons in the Door of Vines. A grand, shiny mahogany desk graced the center of the room accompanied by a soft leather chair.

In elementary school, her friend had dared her to sit in the teacher's chair during recess. Everyone else was out to lunch and recess, but she and her friend had come back to the room to grab their jackets. She took the dare and sat at the teacher's desk. They never were caught, and she pulled herself out of the seat almost as soon as she sat down, but Erin had felt so guilty about invading her teacher's space. It was as if the desk held personal meaning for her teacher, and she had violated it.

As she sat in the soft black leather chair, she experienced a completely different sensation. Rather than encroaching on the owner's personal space, she felt she was exacting justice. One by one, she commanded the desk drawers to reveal their contents. The deep bottom drawer slid open last, and her stomach leaped into her throat.

Shining out from the drawer was a silver wand with a matching sword, and by it rested her green blade. With quivering hands she quickly belted the sheath to her waist and brought her beloved eternal blade to rest in its proper place. Bain's wand and sword hung on the opposite side of her waist and were noticeably heavier. She wondered if wearing the two sheaths would slow her down. Erin pushed the drawer shut and with trembling limbs, raced from the office.

Chapter Forty-five

NOT-SO-SWEET DREAMS

Having no one to talk to made the time drag slowly on. Erin changed her brooch into a cell phone. It really didn't help. Not only did she lack a signal, she had no one to call. Why didn't Joel have a cell phone? It would be nice to hear his voice right now.

But there was a benefit to having a phone. The time read 11:24 PM. It really had been a long day. For some reason, pretending to sleep for a few hours did not award her a rested body. The stress of the day was finally wearing on her, and the adrenaline rushes were fading out.

She had found an abandoned room and had created as comfortable of a space as the limited scraps she found could provide. The kitchen seemed to be gold around here. It was virtually the only place where food could be secured. Earlier she had snagged a cup from a cupboard and had been inconspicuously filling it throughout the day. Water seemed another rare commodity in the overheated city.

Other than hiding from every living creature and trying to find Bain at the same time, things really weren't so bad. Erin let her invisibility drop while she rested in the corner of the cell-like room. As long as the door was shut, no one could see her. For a while she listened for footsteps, or any sign of visitors to her hide out. It wasn't the easiest way to pass time. Maybe the castle was large enough after all. Surely they didn't know every room.

She smiled as another thought crossed her mind. Holding the cell phone in her hands, she changed it again. This time it was a tiny ipod with skinny white wires leading to ear buds. And it was programmed with all her favorite songs. The music was soothing and familiar. It was amazing how much this simple luxury changed her mood.

Erin stopped counting songs and let her eyes close while she lost herself in the rhythms. Somewhere in the hypnotic melodies, sleep won the battle. Dreams bounded off and on through her mind, but the last one was more like reality, as if it were simply an extension of her long day.

Somehow she had missed this staircase in her earlier explorations. It brought her to a previously undiscovered wing. Unlike the hot black and gray walls that dominated everywhere else, this section of the building seemed more modern. A bentery tree graced the corner with its delicate bright green leaves and white bark, and yet it was strictly endemic to the älvin presence.

She strode across the soft white carpet. It felt familiar somehow, as if she had been here before. The realization flashed before her mind. It was like the palace in Älfheim, as if a tiny spot of the world had somehow been transported here. A door opened, and Bain stepped out. Close behind him followed Carbonell.

Erin didn't have time to ward herself, but it probably wouldn't have mattered. Carbonell had seen through her invisibility at the airport, what was to stop him now?

She stood exposed in the center of the beautiful room. But neither Bain nor Carbonell so much as glanced her way. It was as if she were not there at all.

"I thought you might be ready for some fresh air—maybe see more of the country." Carbonell was patting Bain on the back as they walked.

"Do you think it's safe? Are you sure I'm not still contagious?" Bain was looking at Carbonell as if he trusted him unquestionably. Erin wanted to shout at Bain and tell him to run, but her voice refused to work.

"Don't worry. We'll be very careful. Besides, you have been

doing so well. I think you may have kicked this after all."

"Carbonell, I want to go home. If you really think I'm better, then just take me home. I need to see Erin. I can see the world later."

"Sure, sure, I'll see what I can do. It would take some time to arrange things, though. Why don't you enjoy the sights while you still can?"

"So where are you taking me?" Bain asked so casually, she wondered if he truly trusted Carbonell.

"I know a little place that isn't too far from some pyramids. Do you think you're up for some sightseeing?"

Bain looked at Carbonell without a smile. "I suppose. But you really have to get me home."

Carbonell gripped Bain's shoulder. "All in due time, Bain. You must be patient."

Bain watched the floor as they exited the room.

· · · 🦋 · · ·

She felt something electrical shock her cheek. Her hand reached to soothe her face when another electric zap hit her other cheek. Erin opened her eyes. The music still played dutifully into her ears and the room was just as unsavory as it had been earlier, but her eyes could not make the sight before her fit into reality.

There, in all her splendor, stood the elegant, if tiny, Adarae. She was not alone. Many of the älvor she knew fluttered in the dingy stone room. Accompanying them was Riken. His bright wings folded against his sides like a Spanish fan.

It was too much. Erin jumped into the air, but before she could utter a sound, Adarae was at her face sending a modest jolt of electricity to her lips. Confused, Erin looked at her silently and transformed the ipod into a watch. It was already morning, 8:30 AM.

Adarae flew to her ear. "You must leave at once. The imps are nearly to your door. Make yourself invisible and I will guide you to a safer place. Do it now!"

With that, all of the magnificent fairies presently disappeared under wards. Not a sound could be heard, but the door seemed to open on its own. Erin was scarcely aware of Adarae fluttering near her ear.

"Take a right and run as quickly as you can."

Erin shot down the corridor. She wondered if Adarae could fly as fast as she could run when she heard the hallway behind her fill with monsters. One was giving orders and soon two thick beasts were bludgeoning her door down. Adarae must have bolted it shut after she left.

"Up the stairs!" came an urgent command in her ear. Erin leaped with all her might skyward, wishing that she too had wings. Why hadn't she thought of a sound ward? It was too late now. Maintaining invisibility and running for her life were all she could handle at the moment anyway.

Adarae continued to guide her through a maze of halls and doors. At last they came to rest in a room high in a tower. The windows gave a view of endless sand in all directions. Being this high off the ground felt so familiar, like being on Pulsar's back. She noticed the bedding stationed around the room in miniature proportions.

Skyla, the black and white fairy who took on the role of second in command, addressed Erin. "Adarae is securing the area. You are to wait here for her return. Please make yourself comfortable."

Erin looked around the stone floor. Like nearly every other room in the vast castle, it stood largely vacant. The small tufts of bedding were only sufficient for the älvor to settle on. She chose an empty spot of floor and sat with her back against the warm, gray stone wall.

The älvor went about tidying their areas, and she noticed that they were gathering small bits of food from their beds and filling a cup in the center of the room. Skyla presented the cup to Erin. "Please eat. We need you to stay strong." The black and white fairy flitted away, leaving Erin holding the cup of morsels.

It was an assortment of fruits and nuts. Some were exotic

varieties that had been dried, while others, such as dates and figs seemed more locally acquired. Her stomach agreed with the admonition, and she slowly emptied the cup.

The room was abnormally silent for the many fairies that occupied it. No singing or talking filled the air with sweetness. If there was one thing the älvor were especially adept at, it was making beautiful sounds. Their songs could make Erin laugh, cry, think, relax, dance, or anything. Each tune was a masterpiece. Even when they spoke, music came through their speech, in every word.

The Living Garden had been her grove of peace, a place where everything tasted and sounded heavenly. There she could think and ponder. Her magic ability had grown just as much there, where she had time to mentally review and recharge, as it had in the Room of Magic and practicing with Bain.

She smiled at the memories. They had practiced magic in the garden as well. The älvor never displayed their own abilities, yet gave the two of them pointers regularly.

The door opened and Adarae zoomed in before it quickly shut again. "The area is secure. The wards should keep out any visitors."

As soon as Adarae made the announcement, the room began to buzz with their sweet familiar voices. Erin watched the älvor, and realized that their numbers came to twelve. It seemed like a lot of fairies for such a confined area.

Adarae stood on the floor facing Erin. "I am sure you have many questions. I would be honored to tell you all we know."

Erin pulled her feet under her cross-legged. She really wished she could hug Adarae. She had missed her so much, she couldn't begin to explain. "Adarae, thank you. I am so glad to see you. All of you." Erin looked around the room. Each of their delicate faces looked up at her. Her eyes watered as she turned to Adarae. "You can't imagine how much I've missed you." She wiped her eyes and tried to level her cracking voice. "Please, tell me all you can."

Adarae floated on her deep blue and black wings and began.

"We came here to this dreadful castle nearly two months ago. As you know, we accompanied your party to Älfheim. We were there for your inauguration into the älvin world. As is custom, we did not make our presence known to you or Bain.

"We did keep watch over you, however. Perhaps it was out of habit, or more for our fondness for the two of you. It was trickier to stay out of Bain's sight than yours, but fortunately, you both were much too preoccupied to study the corners of rooms for our presence.

"Then we caught sight of Carbonell and Bain leaving the queen's house, so we followed. I had hoped to give the entire kingdom Carbonell's location. We were certain we could turn the situation in our favor quickly. Once we arrived in the city, we launched an attack, but I should not have waited.

"By then, Xavene was present and their combined evil magic was savage. We escaped the battle and I made the mistake of sending a party outside the grounds to go for help. Soon after they left, all communication ceased. They were not able to come back into the city, and we have been isolated here with no hope of aid.

"At first we tried to tend to Bain, but Carbonell thwarted our efforts by making Bain believe that he was delusional. Carbonell utterly convinced Bain that magic was a product of his imagination and illness. Yet Bain is not truly sick but held captive by Carbonell's spell.

"He was moved to a secured floor, one that we could not penetrate. Since then, we have lived here, stealing food to survive like rats. We might have abandoned our efforts, if it were not so completely irreversible. If the two we sent for help could not return to us, we thought it was likely we would find ourselves unable to return here as well.

"Imagine our joy and horror when we learned that you had arrived here. We celebrated upon hearing of your escape and hoped to find you before they did. You didn't make things very easy. Your warding has reached mastery level. It wasn't until you slept that we made your discovery."

Erin jumped to her feet with a start. "Bain!" she gasped. "Carbonell is going to take him away from here. They're going to see some pyramids." She spun around and groaned in frustration. "But I don't know when they leave."

Adarae was eye level with her. "How do you know this?"

"I saw it in a dream. It was the real kind though, I'm sure of it. Do you think we could track him?" She watched Adarae gather some of the älvor together in the corner of the room. Apparently they were discussing strategy.

Erin twisted the Changing Brooch in her hands. She wished she could turn it into a crystal ball or a live video feed. She let herself sink once more to the floor. The brooch transformed into a picture. She was surprised to see not only Bain looking back at her, but Joel's face as well.

Chapter Forty-six

A TEAR

ERIN CROUCHED BEHIND THE OVERSTUFFED chair. She had been waiting here for nearly a half hour already. The sounds of the hallway made her heart race. Imps were regularly pacing the floor. It had been a miracle she had made it to the room without being discovered.

Already she had overheard Xavene's meeting with Clawzhia and their discussion of the night's work. The imps had systematically searched every room in the entire city. No door had been left unopened, and yet she still had not been found. Silence ensued after the meeting with the imp. Maybe this wasn't such a good idea after all.

Once again, the office door opened and closed as another meeting began.

"Xavene, I have heard the reports. It seems impossible that they haven't located her yet." It was Carbonell's voice.

"We will resume the search. She can't stay awake forever. And she can't escape." Erin soaked in the new information.

"I've searched the entire perimeter. It seems we have succeeded in capturing two spies. Two älvor are caught in the barrier. For now, they remain in a paralyzed state. Perhaps we could retrieve them when you are ready to interrogate.

"Or I suppose they could remain there indefinitely. I must say, Xavene, the barrier has worked impressively well. Nothing can enter or exit the city. It is simply genius, a work of art from the master himself." Carbonell spoke with a confident casual voice.

"What of Bain? Have you finished preparations for the transfer? Our satellite training field was an intriguing idea. It shows possibility. I believe you are going to need a couple of things to truly be successful though. It may be difficult to present relics of the past without him recognizing them. Perhaps I should bind his tools with a coating so they do not stir familiar memories."

Erin thought her heart would stop when she heard the drawer of his desk open. A murderous scream, like an animal ready to overcome its prey, ensued. Erin covered her ears as the howl rang through the room. At her waist Bain's wand and blade were still secured, as well as her own sword. She wouldn't have guessed that their absence had not yet been revealed. Erin gripped the sheaths at her waist. They might have Bain, but they would not touch his wand again, nor his blade. At least she had rescued this much.

Xavene was shouting orders to nearby imps and soon the floor was pounding with the sound of running feet. Erin did not dare escape yet. Carbonell was likely to spot her no matter how well she warded. It was mysterious indeed that he was able to see her at the airport.

At least her reconnaissance efforts were not without assistance. Adarae had assigned two älvor to accompany her on this mission. Papen and Kaon had been silent and invisible, but knowing they were there was a comfort. She wished she could communicate with them without speaking, transferring thoughts as she did with Pulsar. Even so, the frenzied activity increased the possibility that she wouldn't be overheard.

"Someone has to follow Carbonell. If he gets away with Bain, we'll lose him," Erin whispered into the back of the chair hoping they were listening.

A tenor voice came into her ear. "Erin Fireborn, we will attend to Carbonell. You must find your way back to the secured room. Do you remember the way?"

Erin nodded her head and wished she could see the

two chasing after Carbonell. Slowly she stretched her legs, remembering to secure her wards. The hall was a madhouse of circus-worthy creatures rushing about. Sheer numbers threatened to expose her, even if they couldn't detect her visually.

She couldn't help but wonder which creatures had the keenest sense of smell. Should she be more afraid of the tiger-man or the gorilla? Maybe they all were the same. Flattening herself against the wall, she inched her way slowly along. Her mind tried to imagine that she was in no danger, she was playing tag. If she let herself look at the monsters rushing mere inches from her body, she risked losing it all.

The stench that filled the corridor was overwhelming. Each imp magnified the sweaty odor of the animal their bodies emulated. It was like a zoo of oversized beasts walled into a tiny room. For not the first time, Erin wished that her senses were a little less acute.

Eventually she made it back to the fairy outpost without incident. The door opened after she knocked quietly. Papen and Kaon were absent, as well as Adarae and others. She found the cleared spot of floor against the wall and took a seat.

"Loden, can you mind-speak with the other älvor here in the castle?" Erin watched the tiny fairy, her emerald green wings matched the color of her bright eyes. The fairies were such a welcome sight to her. The days spent in the Living Garden allowed her to become familiar with many of the älvor. They had offered so much to her during the summer that their acquaintance extended far beyond her ability to remember their names. All of the fairies here in this dismal city were old friends.

"Yes," she answered in a voice of bells.

Erin looked at the floor. "Then you know. The two that were captured in the barrier—I'm so sorry."

Erin felt something as soft as a rose petal on her hand. Loden was sitting on the back of her hand, wiping her eyes. "Yes. It is much worse than we imagined. We are all prisoners here. Adarae has already gone to see if there is anything that can be done for Jauk and Derris. She has not given us her report."

Erin felt the limitation her disproportionate size presented. Had she been equal to it, she would have wrapped her arms around Loden and offered all the comfort a sincere hug could provide. As it was, she could only watch while the miniature girl shed quiet tears on her hand.

A warm sensation began in her hand and spread up her arm and through her shoulder. Erin looked at her arm. Nothing appeared to have changed, but the feeling grew, radiating through her chest and then up into her head and through her legs. It reminded her of the circlet the queen had placed on her head, and yet there was a distinctly different quality to it.

Loden sat on her hand as before, but even her small weight bore a strange sensation, as if she could feel the emotions of the grieving älvor. But it was more than that. Her magic seemed replenished, as if she had just touched Pulsar. The sensation fed into her muscles, soothing them from the tight springs they had become since she had come to this awful city. But it was the weight of the älvor's grief that she felt more than anything else. It was as if she now bore every ounce of the burden Loden was feeling. Anger, sadness, determination, and despair mixed itself together in a heavy weight.

She looked at the tiny fairy with questioning and sorrowful eyes. Loden stood and faced Erin, wiping her cheeks with her fingers.

"Oh, Erin Fireborn! I forget myself. Please forgive me for grieving so. I do not wish to force this burden upon you."

Once again Erin felt the poignant limitation her comparatively enormous size presented. She longed to reassure the fairy and wrap her arms around her. "Please don't apologize. Your loss is my loss, your grief is mine. I just wish there was something I could do, some way to fix everything." Tears spilled down Erin's cheeks and dropped like rain onto her hand, threatening to splash the älvor.

She let the moment capture all of her losses. Bain was still under the enemy's control. She missed him so dearly. And Pulsar's constant presence had been ripped away from her heart as well.

She missed Joel more than she imagined she could or should. And then there was the two captured älvor. For a few moments, she allowed herself to feel the great losses and despair as she cried softly into her hands.

Loden reached out her hands and caught a tear. The single drop shimmered in her palms and began to crystallize. Within a few seconds, a stone cast light where the tear had been. The tear shape remained, but the liquid had been replaced by a diamond.

Loden lifted her arms letting the light reflect prisms on the walls and floor. "A token of the tears you shared." The delicate fairy placed the diamond in Erin's palm and took to the air. "Only the tear of a true friend could do that. Erin Fireborn, you warm my heart."

Erin gazed at the sparkling jewel in her hand.

"Let me help you," Loden said. "Pull out your eternal blade."

Erin carefully unsheathed the marbled jade sword. Loden lifted the diamond from Erin's palm and brought it to the ornate hilt. A bright surge of light beamed out from the tear as Loden fused it to the sword.

The diamond glinted brighter than the other stones delicately placed on the swirling hilt. Erin watched as the light reflected off of it.

"A forever blade with a forever tear, Erin Fireborn." Loden was floating above the green blade.

Erin looked at her with confusion, tears still streaking her cheeks. "I don't understand."

Now Loden smiled and swooped back down to the sword. "The magic in the tear will increase your healing power and strengthen the magic in your sword."

"Why have you given me this? I have given you nothing." The tears were still dripping off of her cheeks.

"Please, I did not think to bring an umbrella." Loden was flitting in front of her once again.

"Sorry," Erin replied. She wiped her cheeks and tried to set her emotions.

Loden's tiny hand rested on her arm, in a comforting gesture. "Erin Fireborn, all is not lost. We have much to hope for." She landed once more on the hilt of the blade. "And do not think of this as a gift, but a token of friendship." She was seated before the twinkling tear-shaped diamond, her small hand resting on its smooth surface.

Wiping the remainder of her wetness onto her sleeve, Erin tried to smile back. "Thank you, Loden."

The morning passed slowly into afternoon when suddenly the door opened and several älvor jetted into the room before it shut again. Their flight was so fast it was hard to count the butterfly-winged fairies. Riken was spinning tight circles around the ceiling.

She watched the flying frenzy and wondered how they avoided colliding in their lightning flight. Erin caught glimpses of älvor kissing cheeks in greeting. Their buzz of speech was too quick and trill for her to understand, so she sat back and waited for the commotion to settle.

At last Adarae hovered before her. "Erin Fireborn, we have done it! Riken assisted us, and we were able to free Jauk and Derris. They are here!"

Erin tried to discern which blurring wings represented the two rescued älvor. She turned her attention back to Adarae. "Are they okay?"

"The spell only held power over them while they were caught in its web. It took all of our strength combined to free them. If it had been you caught in the barrier, I'm afraid the results would have been much worse. The magic was strong, and evil. We have never seen such a net as this before. Edina brushed too close to it and instantly froze into a paralyzed state. We had to rescue her along with the other two."

Adarae flew into the center of the room and immediately the swirling colors of wings came to a hovering halt in the air. All eyes were on their leader.

Adarae spoke with all the authority of a queen. "My brothers and sisters, we all have cause to rejoice in the return of Jauk and

Derris. Our hearts are mending already." With that statement all the fairies applauded. Adarae lifted her hands to continue. "We have another to save. Bain is still under Xavene and Carbonell's control. We will not give up until we have found a way to free us all from this vile place."

Her words were met with silence. One by one, the fairies flew to Adarae and kissed her hand. Erin watched with wonder as each älvor gave their bond with a kiss. The ceremony seemed ancient and full of strength. With each kiss on her delicate white hand, the feeling of unity grew. As the last älvor finished, Erin stood. Pressing her fingers to her mouth, she kissed them and reached out to Adarae.

The regal fairy understood, and reached out her hand so Erin could touch her fingertips to her hand. Adarae nodded as she bore into Erin with understanding blue eyes. Erin smiled back. No matter how impossible things seemed, she would rather be imprisoned with a room full of älvor than free in a world without Bain. If there was to be a rescue, she wanted nothing more than to be an active participant.

Chapter Forty-seven

Silver Tray

THE NOISES FROM THE POTS and pans clanked merrily. Even though Erin was quite sure she would not be considered a welcomed guest, she enjoyed the jovial, if rogue company of the bantering cooks. Their busy hands and joking demeanors lightened her heavy mood.

"You hear about that too, then?" One large man stirring a pot of sauce was talking to the others. "They're getting ready for a big trip. Guess we'll all be leavin'. Looks like the big bosses can't cook." He got a peal of laughter out of the others.

"Aye, but I can't say I ain't ready for a change. This place'll getcha down faster than a boat with a hole in it."

His comment was met by murmurs of agreement.

"So Joey, you think they's ever gonna catch that girl? Betcha she's not even alive no more. No one can survive out there in the sand. It's a cryin shame, really." Someone raised a spatula in agreement.

"But a fine meal they're planning for tonight. Looks like we'll be cleanin out the kitchen after this. You boys maybe should think about taking a swag or two of the food. Doubt anyone would notice if a steak went mysteriously missing." It was the bigger cook making this address.

Erin was desperately hoping she could filch a piece of paper from the kitchen. She hadn't seen any paper since entering the dismal city. But maybe there was something here. It wasn't especially easy to weave in and out of the cooks searching for a recipe card, or even the corner of a cookbook. Her efforts were at last rewarded when she found a stack of blank cards accompanied by a few pencils. Jackpot! She carefully found her way to the hall and began writing. It was a long shot, but so far, it was the only thing she could think of.

With her note gripped tightly in her hand, she re-entered the kitchen. This was going to be the tricky part. The conversations she had eavesdropped on earlier suggested that Bain ate separately from Carbonell and Xavene. All she had to do was figure out which tray was destined for Bain, and slip the note into it.

It sure would have been easier if she could just ask someone. How to do it? She hovered around the three trays and waited. Of course! She would just have to put the note in while she followed the trays. Thanks to the fairies, she knew now where his room was. She would just have to follow the procession, and Bain's tray should likely be the only one entering that way.

Erin hated waiting. She was so excited about her brilliant idea, but her hands were shaking in anticipation. *If this worked . . .* She could hardly think about it. To see Bain would be such a miracle. It had been so long.

Her stomach tied in knots as she stood by the food waiting impatiently. The least she could do from here was snatch a few things while she waited. When no one was looking, she lifted a large silver lid. The smells wafted towards her making her stomach growl. One roll fewer could hardly be noticed. She snatched the light steaming bread and ate while she kept her eyes on the cooks.

One opportunity after another arose, and soon she had filled her famished appetite. At long last, though truthfully it was only a few minutes, the trays were hoisted on shoulders, and the meals were paraded to their destinations. It was easy to keep up with the cooks, and Erin's hope nearly burst from her chest. This was going to work!

When one of the cooks turned left and proceeded to ascend

the stairs, she followed. Stair by stair the two of them climbed. How was she going to get the note inside the tray? She followed the cook wondering how she would lift the lid without arousing suspicion. There had to be a way.

She focused on the heavy silver lid and commanded it to lift ever so slowly from the tray. It should have been easier than it was. The silence in the staircase was sure to give away her efforts if they were not executed perfectly. The note in her hand floated above the cook's head and settled on top of a plate. Ever so carefully she set the lid back on to the tray.

But it still insisted on clanging slightly as it set down on the metal. The cook stopped climbing the stairs and looked behind him. His stare passed right through Erin and he turned again, resuming the climb. Erin wanted to jump up and down in victory, but she noiselessly followed him instead. She was surprised to see the cook walk right through the spell impeded door. She could not enter the room, but the cook's pace did not even slow. He left the door open behind him, so she was able to watch him deliver the meal to a table in the room.

Bain came into view, and her heart leapt into her throat. She nearly screamed out his name. How she longed to run to him and throw her arms around him. He was just there, only a few paces from where she stood.

"May I set your meal for you, sir?" the cook asked, motioning to the large lidded tray.

Erin hadn't considered that her plan could have been destroyed this way. If the cook saw the note, which of course sat on top of the plate in plain view, there would be no hope. She wrung her hands in terrible nervousness.

"That's okay. I'll get it in a minute." Bain stood and waited for the cook to nod and exit the room.

The portly man nearly walked right into Erin as he exited. She was still standing there staring at Bain; she didn't want to lose sight of him. The cook pulled the door shut and left. Erin waited until the man was out of sight before reaching out to the door. Her hands could not even grasp the handle. It was as if an invisible wall barred the surface.

She knew there was a spell guarding the door, but she was hoping for a flaw. Erin sat against the wall and waited. Hopefully Bain would be hungry soon. She wouldn't even know if her plan was going to work unless she waited here for him.

Her hands felt cold in nervousness. She wondered how much stress she could handle before she gave up and tried to beat the door down. Knowing Bain was only a few feet from her was eating up every ounce of willpower she had left. She began pacing the floor. Sitting still was not an option anymore.

Then, like an angel straight out of heaven, Bain appeared in the doorway. He looked around and his eyes stopped on her. But she was still invisible. He shook his head and started to close the door.

"No!" she yelled. She had become so accustomed to invisibility that she had forgotten to turn it off in the heart stopping moment of his appearance.

He looked back up at her and a smile grew on his drawn face. Stepping out into the hall, he looked every bit the Bain she remembered, if a little thinner. He was wearing his old tennis shoes with jeans and a T-shirt. It was like seeing him on any other day of the week.

"Erin, is that you?"

She raced at him in a blur and hugged him fiercely. He nearly fell over from the impact, but regained his balance and embraced her back.

"Oh, Bain! I can't believe it!" Erin couldn't even think of words. She had so much to tell him.

"What are you doing here?" He looked at her with a strange expression, worry mixed with confusion.

"Bain, you have to come with me now. It's not safe. We have to go somewhere we can talk." Erin held his wrist and tried pulling him along.

He still looked dazed and confused. "Erin, what are you talking about?"

She set the full power of her green eyes onto his. All her life this look had worked miracles in getting her way. "Bain, come with me. If you have ever trusted me in your whole life, you need to run now." She smiled mischievously. "And try to keep up. I might be even faster than you."

He smiled crookedly back at her; the look nearly melted her heart. "Never!" he said.

She kept his wrist and fled as fast as her feet could carry her. She knew that her invisibility ward would probably only cover herself, but she used it anyway. Bain kept right behind her, although she was certain she would have carried him out if he seemed unable to run. She might not let him out of her sight for a very long time.

They made it to the älvor's safe room without seeing anyone. Erin hadn't let them slow their pace the entire journey. When she turned to Bain, she was pleased that he wasn't out of breath in spite of the excruciating speed she forced them to run. She watched him take in the view of the cell-like room.

Most of the fairies had gone to keep watch over Carbonell and Xavene. It was their part in her "last hope" plan. They assigned themselves to their posts while Erin had been adamant about her role in the operation. So there were only a few in the secured room to ensure the spell guarding it remained stable.

"They're just like my dreams," Bain said as he watched the flitting älvor. He shook his head as if to clear it. When he reopened his eyes, he let his mouth fall into a small smile. He reached his hand out as if to touch them. "Am I still dreaming?"

Erin set her hand on Bain's shoulder. "If you're dreaming then I don't ever want to wake up." She turned so she could look into his eyes. "Bain, this is as real as it gets."

"Then why do I still see fairies?"

"The älvor? Why wouldn't you?"

Bain looked at her with a serious expression. "Because they're not real, of course."

"You better watch what you say or one of them will zap you." She slugged him playfully on the arm. "Bain, you've been in this horrible place a little too long. What do you say we get out of here?"

He let his eyes settle on hers. "Yes. I would like that." He let his gaze follow the butterfly wings around the room, his smile growing ever so slightly.

"Oh, I almost forgot!" Erin pulled at the buckle and let the sheath fall from her waist. "I believe this is yours."

He took the sheath and held it in front of him as if it were a strange piece of art. His face did not register. He glanced up at Erin as if to ask what the thing in his hand was suppose to be.

"I think I can help you with that," she said, taking the sheath back into her hands. She tried to mimic Agnar's speed and grace as she swiftly secured the sheath into place.

Bain looked at his sides. He touched the pommel of his sword experimentally, and then let his fingers wrap around the grip, pulling the blade from its case. Erin watched his eyes light up in recognition.

"I know this sword." He turned the silver and white marbled blade letting the sunlight glint off its edges. "It's so bright," he murmured. Soon he was replacing the sword and pulling his wand.

Bain flicked the silver wand as if he were pretending to direct music, but then a serious expression replaced his half smile. "All of this," he held his wand out and spun slowly in place. "I have seen this before in a dream." His eyes landed on Erin's.

"Bain, it's all real. The wand is really yours, the eternal blade; that's your magic you felt. It's just as real as I am. You're not dreaming."

He watched her with a pained expression. "I want to believe you."

She reached out her hand and grasped his in it. "Then do. And if you think that this is all a dream, just believe in me long enough to prove it to you. Look, just see if you can remember anything."

She tried to remember how Master Ulric had commanded them in the use of magic. Where she could, she used his exact expressions. Bain was a bit more than rusty—he was practically a beginner. She took him through some rudimentary skills and tried to encourage him along the way.

"A little help!" Erin was looking up at the älvor who were occupying the space above their heads. "Please, I don't think I am cut out to be a magic teacher."

The älvor joined in the lesson, reminding Erin of their days in the Living Garden. Soon Bain became a little more confident as he tried to obey their instructions.

"Look, I appreciate all your help, really," Bain was saying after he succeeded in a few tries. "But sooner or later I'm going to wake up from this dream, like I have from all the others." He was shaking his head. "It's not like I haven't seen all of this a thousand times in my head."

Before Erin could respond, the door opened and a burst of color flashed into the room. The door shut just as suddenly and the room now held twelve fairies and Riken.

Bain looked at them in surprise.

Adarae flitted at eye-level in front of Erin. "They're coming. It's now or never."

Chapter Forty-eight

FLIGHT

"They know where we are stationed. The imps have marked off on a map every room they have searched, and now Xavene has identified which room they missed. They are sure you are hiding out here, and the entire imp army is now coming with Xavene and Carbonell. They want to ensure you will not escape this time." Adarae was flickering around the room as she spoke. It seemed the stressful energy prohibited her from a stationary flight.

"Do they know about Bain yet?" Erin was sick with anxiety. She didn't expect their escape to be simple but had no idea how they would leave the city. She had been counting on having more time with Bain before they were forced to make critical decisions.

"Not yet. Carbonell and Xavene were meeting with the imps when you rescued Bain. As of now, their plan is to find you. If we don't leave at once, they will."

"But how are we going to hide Bain?"

Even as she asked, the älvor were gathering around him. It looked like a whirlwind of color with each fairy streaking ribbons of speed around him. Bain looked stunned. Erin reached out and took his hand before they both disappeared.

Erin manipulated the door open and she pulled Bain into the hall. She could hear the approach of the innumerable imps. If

Carbonell was there, it wouldn't even matter if she were invisible, he somehow would be able to see her.

The tower room had offered many advantages with its lofty view and open windows. Even the isolated location in respect to the rest of the castle had been convenient. But there was only one exit. It was the very stairwell that led to their recluse that presented itself as their only escape. The same staircase that now shook with the weight of hundreds of beasts charging straight towards them.

Erin felt herself being pulled back into the same isolated room. Without warning, Adarae appeared and placed a spell on the door before disappearing again. Erin felt her hand being tugged towards the wall. Were they simply going to wait here for the army to beat the door down?

Her heart was racing as she felt herself moving across the room. Already the angry howls could be heard through the door. It would only be moments before something overcame the piece of wood that separated them.

Erin continued to move closer and closer to the window. Suddenly, her hand was jerked through the opening. She was holding Bain's hand, and yet their hands were being lifted upwards through the window. Erin flung her other hand upwards and grasped Bain's wrist just in time for her feet to lift off the ground. In only a moment, she was lifted out of the building like a helium balloon. She was still hanging from Bain's wrist, but now they were steadily floating away from the castle wall and towards the perimeter of the city.

Erin loved to fly, but being suspended in the air made her feel helpless. She watched the black city drift under her feet. It was like dangling from the basket of a hot air balloon. Their movement was slow and deliberate.

An explosion interrupted the silence of their flight. She twisted around to see the tower room fill with yellow and orange flames. She looked away. The thought of their target was too much to take in, and now it was impossible to know what to expect next.

They had drifted across nearly half the length of the black looming castle when the ground began to fill with the dark aura of the imps. They were flooding out of the castle like ants attacking something outside their nest. Black seeped out of every entrance until it filled the sand.

"No!" She yelled. At least she had already thought to put up a sound ward.

They were armed with crossbows, and were shooting the sky. Arrows rained upward like an upside down storm. She tried to focus on her touch ward while keeping herself invisible. But it was hard to think while floating through a sky of hissing arrows. She wasn't sure how long her magic would hold.

She was almost surprised to notice when the cooks began to fill the sandy courtyard. They were looking around as if in confusion. Some were pointing at the imps, while others searched the sky in vain. Erin was sure the imps couldn't see them either. If they connected with their deadly arrows, it would be as a result of their quantity, not accuracy.

As they floated away from the wall of arrows, she began to worry that their escape might be drawn short by hitting the barrier. All of this would be for naught if they ended up paralyzed against a magical web. It was invisible. There was nothing to see but the great expanse of sand. How would they know?

"Down a little," Bain's voice broke through. "A little more."

He can see it! She wanted to shout for joy. How could she forget? Bain could see magic. Slowly they descended at a careful angle. The ground was soon under their feet, but she still kept her hand fastened on to his.

"How are we going to do it?" Erin asked, still unable to see the fairies or Bain. "How do we cross the barrier?"

There wasn't time for an answer. Already the army of imps was surging towards them with Carbonell shouting orders in the lead.

Keeping one hand in Bain's, Erin drew her sword. If she were going to die, she was going to go down fighting. As soon as her hand touched the hilt, it seemed that time slowed down. She could see the army pounding towards them, but she could hear their very breath, see every movement of their muscles, every hair on their deranged bodies, and every drop of sweat and saliva that fell from their faces.

She gazed at the green sword in her hand. And she knew. It wasn't hers to defeat the entire imp army, or even to spill a drop of blood.

"Bain, draw your sword!" she yelled. "On three I want you to sink your blade into the barrier." She still couldn't see it, but she was certain it was just behind them. She turned to face the invisible net. "One! Two! Three!" Her voice was a raw scream.

The green blade in her hand obeyed her very heart's desire and thrust forward into the unknown. She could hear herself yelling as she forced herself into the wall. Every possible corner of her will was drawn to the tip of her blade.

Her sword was met by a physical wall that seemed to give under the pressure of her blade. It was sinking forward, and yet she was not paralyzed. A blinding flash of light burst out. Erin squeezed Bain's hand. With one hand on her blade and the other in Bain's, she watched the sky light up.

An enormous dome enveloping the entire city became visible with bright cracks winding their way through the crystal ceiling. The soprano screech of breaking glass filled the air as the entire dome shifted under the fissures spreading throughout the clear structure.

"We have to get out!" Erin yelled. It looked like the entire city was going to be buried under the breaking dome

Carbonell and Xavene were in the lead as they raced towards Erin and Bain. She screamed as Xavene produced a magical ball of swirling fire bigger than he was, rushing straight towards them. The impact of the crushing fireball hit them like a charging tank, filling their ears with a detonating roar and throwing their bodies into the barrier.

The dome surrendered to the pressure of their impact, hurling them through the sharp edges of crystal and onto the soft sand. The resulting hole immediately began to fill as clear shards plunged to the earth.

To the sound of crystal falling to the earth, Erin lifted Bain off the ground. She pulled him into a run, her hand steadfastly in his, as the crystal dome collapsed behind them. She didn't dare look back at the ruin. She didn't want to know if Carbonell, Xavene, and their imp army were following them. And she didn't want to know if she had been responsible for the demise of an entire city.

She kept her hand in Bain's and ran. Images of the cooks flashed through her mind. Tears washed across her cheeks, but she kept running. She never meant to harm anyone, but the sight of the enormous dome crashing to the earth seemed inescapable. She wondered if there could be survivors. She couldn't run fast enough to escape the sound of breaking glass and the tones of pieces shattering when they hit the city below.

She was vaguely aware that Bain was visible, and that he ran with his hand in hers while his other hand gripped his silver sword. She could see the älvor streaking through the sky with Riken far above them.

They ran, as fast and as free as their älvin bodies could carry them. Like an arrow from a bow across the stretching sea of sand. Maybe if they ran far enough, she wouldn't be able to hear the falling crystal or imagine what destruction befell the city.

The älvor knew the way. It had taken over an hour in the helicopter, but, with help from the troupe of fairies, the twins managed to find their way to Cairo. Erin couldn't imagine what they would do from here. Their clothes were charred in some places from the ball of fire Xavene unleashed at them. Their faces still showed traces of dirt and Erin was sure her cheeks were tear-stained. Beads of blood traced her skin where the jagged crystal caught her when she was blown from the city. Bain had fared much the same. She supposed her wards must have been compromised in those final moments of fear.

Her passport, clothes, everything she owned was gone. And so were Bain's things. She thought of his blue suitcase Grandpa

Jessie had given him before they left for Iceland. How were they going to explain that? She wasn't sure if Carbonell had bothered packing her things before kidnapping her. She didn't remember seeing her purple suitcase anywhere in the castle. He had probably been in too much of a hurry.

Sooner or later, they were bound to see normal people, and in their present state, Erin and Bain were sure to draw attention. Maybe the älvor could make Bain invisible again, but how were they going to get home? They had nothing on them other than their swords, and Bain his wand. She knew her changing brooch could do something, but it wouldn't be enough. More than one document was required at a time to board a flight.

"We need to make a plan," Erin stated as they plodded on. "We've got to find a way to get back."

"In my dreams we had some amazing things," Bain answered, a far off look set on his face. "We had our own Fairy Godmother, and you," he set his eyes on Erin, "you had a golden dragon." He turned his stare ahead of him. "Kind of crazy, huh? I had the most amazing dreams. But, you know, since I'm probably still dreaming, why don't we see if we can get someone out here?"

He laughed softly. "Let's see, if I remember this right, all you have to do is call her. What was her name? Oh, yes. Ella! If you can hear us, we are stuck out here in the middle of nowhere with no money and some incredible fairies. We would be ever so grateful for your assistance." He had stopped walking and now had a lopsided smile on his face.

Erin watched him warily. "Bain, that wasn't a dream. Ella is real. So is Pulsar. I hope you don't act like a fool if she really does show up."

"No worries. You keep reminding me that I'm not sleeping. I'll just have to be Prince Charming himself."

"Bain, you're acting really weird."

"Now that doesn't sound like a dream at all. You always say that."

"Well, it's probably true then."

The älvor had kept their silence high above their heads. It

was easier than becoming invisible to simply camouflage as butterflies. Riken was no where to be seen, however. He was probably under an invisibility ward.

Bain drew his wand from his sheath. "You know, I dreamed of this every time I slept. There were so many things." He flicked his wand and created a small whirlwind of sand. "It feels so real."

"Bain, don't you think if you were sleeping you wouldn't feel so much?" She touched a scratch that ran along his neck. "Can't you feel that?"

He just looked back at her and nodded.

"I don't know what they did to you in that awful place, but there are some things you need to know. You are an älv. You have been able to use magic for some time now. You used to be even better at it than me in some things."

"That sounds reasonable," he said smugly.

"Don't interrupt." She pointed to the wand in his hand. "Ella gave you that wand." She looked at his sword. "And that, Bain, is your eternal blade. And have you felt your ears recently?"

"Why would I feel my ears?"

"Well, just do it." She bore her green eyes into his in all seriousness.

He traced his fingers over the edges of his pointed ears. A small smile crept onto his face. He reached up and carefully lifted Erin's locks. A flicker of light reached his eyes as his smile grew. "Your ears are adorable."

She could see the real Bain in his eyes now. His smile was right; it went all the way through his soul. Tears welled up unexpectedly in her eyes. "Bain, I missed you so much." Her voice was cracking. There were too many emotions boiling under the surface for her to contain them all. She looked down, a little embarrassed. Why did she have to start crying now?

Warm arms were suddenly pulling her in and Bain was holding her against his chest. For just a moment, she thought she could feel subtle shudders before she heard him sniff.

"Erin, I missed you too."

He held her close, and all of the fractures in her heart some-how began to mend. The nightmare was finally over. He pulled her away from him by her shoulders and searched her face with his blue eyes. "I didn't keep my word, did I?"

She looked at him in confusion, trying to sniff away the flow.

"I told you we were in this together." He squeezed her shoulders. "I think I have some making up to do."

She laughed and wiped her dripping nose on her already filthy sleeve. "I'm sure you'll think of something," she answered. "Meanwhile, it appears we have some company."

Ella had arrived but kept her silence. Now she made her graceful approach. A broad smile spread across her face.

"There's someone waiting to see you," Ella said and turned around.

A golden glow appeared behind Ella, reflecting the bright sunlight and casting it in every direction.

"Pulsar!" Erin ran to him and threw her arms around his neck. The magic that filled her made her want to never let go. He rumbled a deep purr while she soaked in his presence.

Ella cleared her throat. "Actually, Erin, there is someone else waiting to see you."

Erin reluctantly let her hands slip off of Pulsar's neck as she slowly turned around. Joel was standing there, as dashing as any of her memories could recall. She walked steadily towards him, unsure of how she should greet him. Did elves run and hug each other?

She reached him, waiting at arm's length. He lifted her hand in his, took a knee, and kissed her hand before standing. The gesture was done so gracefully that he seemed like a royal knight honoring a princess. She thought of the älvor kissing Adarae's hand. There was still so much she didn't understand about this strange new world.

"Erin Fireborn, you are a balm to my weary heart. It pleases me greatly to see you."

She was too overwhelmed to think of an appropriate response.

She knew she would never figure out how to be an älva before the moment passed. "I missed you too, Joel."

She threw her arms around his neck, and after a second, she felt him reach his around her back to return the gesture.

Now it was Bain's turn to clear his throat.

"Uh, Bain, there's someone I'd like you to meet." Erin smiled as Joel took her hand.

Chapter Forty-nine

RETURNING

ERIN WAS IMPRESSED WITH THE jet Queen Āldera sent for Joel and Bain. But, in spite of the luxurious interior, she wasn't about to board the aircraft. Pulsar had been absent from her mind and sight far too long.

The long journey home allowed her time to recount the details. Pulsar had the advantage of seeing everything that she experienced in the black city. Once she began to tell her story, it came out in a rush, and she let her mind flood into his.

Pulsar was very apologetic for letting her down. No magic should have allowed them to be separated. That Carbonell had the power to interfere with their communication was disconcerting. He assured Erin he would find a way to overcome the dark spell.

They traveled over land, invisible to the world below. She was sure the jet would make it back to the kingdom well before they did, but it was worth it. She thought of the many countries she was seeing from the sky, and how far from home she was. From her view, there were no boundaries on the land below sketching out the countries. It was impossible to tell which places she was seeing for the first time in her life.

Pulsar flew so fast. The land and the water sailed under them. When the ocean stretched on for endless miles, she knew they were almost there.

Pulsar, is Bain going to be okay? She had been worried about him. Even though he seemed to snap out of his daze, she had no idea what he had been through. She worried it might affect him for a long time to come.

He will be with those who love him most. Time can heal all wounds, and there are those in the kingdom who would be more than happy to offer their assistance to him.

Like learning magic again? She thought about his diminished skills. It had taken them so long to get to where they were in the first place. It seemed like they would have to start all over. *I'll just have to help him.*

You will, and you already have.

She could see images from Pulsar's mind, a reflection of the events she had just shared. It was strange to see it through his eyes. With it came the inflections of his thoughts, like a running commentary. She could see how incredulous he was at her bold, straightforward approach. He was almost angry and proud of her at the same time. If he were there, he would not have seen her take so many risks and be so unprotected in the face of immense danger.

But Pulsar was not there, and she had saved the day anyway. It was a complex range of emotions that raged through his mind to hers. He was deeply upset by her disappearance. And to be completely cut off from her was unbearable. Erin sympathized with his feelings. They had been hers only days before.

It was impossible to ensure that it could never happen again, no matter how they vowed to not be separated for so long in distance or thought.

How is Joel doing? She could only imagine what he might have said after learning of her part in the mess. He must have been so disappointed in her. It was too late to say she was sorry, too late to take her actions back. She hadn't even asked his opinion, but ran after her own ideas. It could have ended so much worse.

Pulsar was following her range of emotions. *I told Joel of our trip to the airport. All attempts to find you failed, and he took it rather hard. But he never relented. The whole kingdom was placed*

*on high alert. The barrier must have been incredibly strong to resist
the search that followed your disappearance.*

It was amazing to snatch the limited pictures out of Pulsar's
thoughts. His entry into the queen's house was rare, and she was
sure he was keeping some of it from her as well. She did not see
the conversation he had with Joel. Maybe things were too difficult. Maybe Pulsar didn't really want her to know everything.
Her mind raced to fill in the many blanks.

What are you thinking, Fireborn?

She hadn't even realized she had blocked him out of her
mind. But maybe it was for the best. Some of her thoughts should
be her own, just as his were. *Oh Pulsar, why do I care so much
about what Joel thinks? Why am I more terrified of breaking his trust
than I was of being chased down by super smelly giant imps carrying
swords? There must be something wrong with me.*

A deep rumble of chuckle erupted from Pulsar. *Fireborn, you
may be right about that. I will just have to keep my eye on you.*

From on his back, he couldn't see her roll her eyes. And
punching him would be a lost cause. *Thanks, Pulsar. It's good to
know I can count on you.*

Pulsar seemed to be enjoying the banter. *Anytime,* he
answered.

Ahead, a shock of green appeared on the horizon. Iceland
was so close.

· · · 🦋 · · ·

A counsel meeting had been convened. The queen and all
of her advisors were present. A large circular table with chairs
wrapped around it sat in the center of the enormous conference
room.

Erin sat next to Bain, feeling small and young. It was an
overwhelming audience. Joel was there, though, and his familiar
face was a welcome sight amid the strangers. He winked at her
quickly without breaking his formal demeanor. This was business, after all.

Queen Äldera called the meeting to order. All voices hushed, leaving a solemn mood in the room. "As you know, we have information that affects the entire kingdom. It is unprecedented to have a gathering of imps. It is troubling news, indeed. They gather under the leadership of Xavene. Carbonell has also been implicated." She turned to Bain and Erin. "I will now give the floor to these two."

The queen took her seat. Erin gripped the armrest of her chair. All eyes were on them. The first question came from across the table and the session of questions and answers began. After the first few questions, Erin settled into the meeting. It really wasn't so difficult. Most of the questions had to do with her visual scope of the city, her estimation of the imp army, Carbonell's involvement and other strategy-minded affairs.

Bain answered some questions, but his experience was so altered by the mind spells that he was spared from most of the questioning.

Even as Erin told all she could, she wondered guiltily how much of this information could still be true. Hadn't the whole city been buried under the broken crystal? Could the imps have survived the shower of dagger-edged glass? She didn't know. The questions ran through her mind.

"Tell us how you managed to break the barrier." Heads were bobbing in agreement to the query. "It was powerful magic that held such unyielding protection. It prevented all communications, physical passage, and visibility from crossing its border. It is astonishing that they were able to create a nearly invincible structure."

Erin reported their final moments in the black city. She really didn't know why she had decided to run her blade through the barrier; it just came to her at the moment. She hadn't even stopped to wonder whether it would work, she just knew it would.

Hearing the story out loud from her own lips made it seem ridiculous and not very well thought out. There they were, two teenagers and a dozen fairies, up against a whole army of horrible creatures and two master sorcerers. And she just decides to plant her sword into a paralyzing wall. It didn't sound like such a smart plan. What if it hadn't worked? She wondered if she was in for a lecture after all. She had endangered many lives, not to mention her trip to the airport that resulted in her own abduction.

She finished the tale and stared at the floor waiting for her well-deserved rebuke. She didn't want to see an audience of disappointed faces, so she kept her gaze down, concentrating on the colored flecks in the thick white carpet.

It was the queen's voice to break the unbearable silence. "So it happens, Erin Fireborn, that not only did you prove your strength in the face of overwhelming odds, but you were able to utilize the very gift that would set you free."

Erin's eyes came slowly up to meet Queen Āldera's, her mind filled with confusion.

Queen Āldera continued. "It was your gift of sight and the combined strength of you both that brought the wall down. In the end, Erin Fireborn, it was your ability to see truth that led you to your escape."

"I don't understand. I didn't feel like I was using my gift at all." Erin was surprised at her own boldness.

"You came to the conclusion that the two of you needed to attack the barrier. Your gift helped you realize that the idea was true and instead of questioning your own judgment, you acted on your inspiration."

"But why could our swords take down the wall if no one else could penetrate it? It doesn't make sense that it even worked." Erin had been thinking about it since they overcame the wall. "We should have been paralyzed like the älvor. I really don't know why we were able to get through."

The queen stood and walked around the table. "Your strength combined with Bain's produced a force that was too much for the barrier to withstand. It seems you two have proven the legend of synergy. It has always been believed that twins are able to create very powerful magic when they unite their efforts—a power that is well beyond that of any one of our kind. When you choose to unite your magic, a new form of energy is created, often producing unpredictable effects. Even we are not familiar with all of the possibilities of your combined power. But it seems clear that it was your joined force of magic that shattered the spell."

Erin tried to absorb her words. She hadn't thought of it like that. Under the scrutiny of the table of onlookers, she simply nodded. She really needed to learn elf culture. She had no idea how to take a compliment from a queen.

"Bain," the queen turned to him. "You must realize that your part was crucial in the miraculous escape as well. Even in your weakened state, you must have shown great faith in assisting Erin with little to no knowledge of your true strength. It shows that you have a heart that is true, and for that, I personally commend you."

Bain stared at her with a blank expression.

At least Erin wasn't the only one who didn't know how to take a compliment.

"And now, brothers and sisters, if there are no further questions, this meeting will be adjourned."

The chairs began to scoot back as one by one, the room emptied. Bain and Erin, not sure what to do next, remained in their chairs, waiting for the room to clear.

Joel made his way over to the two of them, a broad smile filling his face. "You two must have made quite an impression. She doesn't extend praise unless it is well deserved. You should feel quite honored." Joel was leaning casually on the glossy table.

"Yeah, and then I blew it by just staring back at her like an idiot," Erin answered. "So when do we get to learn how to be proper?"

"You make it sound like it's difficult."

"I just haven't been around long enough to have a clue."

"I'm sure I can think of something." Joel turned to Bain. "Are you up for some magic lessons? I talked Master Ulric into some practice sessions. Thought I'd go myself. I imagine there is a lot I could learn too. What do you think?"

Bain had been unusually silent since returning to the

kingdom. He didn't crack jokes, and he didn't try magic. It was as if part of him was still lost.

He looked up at Joel. "Sure, no worries."

Joel seemed to be gauging his response. "I'll pick you up at your room tomorrow. We'll go together."

Erin appreciated that Joel was reaching out to Bain. It made her feel as if she weren't alone in trying to help him come back. She might know magic, but she had never taught it. And she was pretty sure she was mostly a beginner herself. Maybe Bain would turn a corner soon.

They left the conference room and wandered through the endless corridors. The fact that she was no longer guided by Joel's arm was blaringly obvious to her. She almost missed it, but was grateful for avoiding the embarrassment she might feel in Bain's presence.

It was odd and yet heartwarming to see Bain and Joel in the same building. It seemed so impossible and wonderful.

"Joel, do you really think that there is still a whole army of imps out there. Do you think Xavene and Carbonell survived?" Erin was haunted by the sound of crashing glass. It weighed heavily on her, flashing through her mind often.

"It is almost certain. If Xavene was powerful enough to create such a complex ward around an entire city, surely he would have been able to protect his followers in the face of physical threat. There is no doubt that Xavene and Carbonell would have survived, but it remains to be seen how they chose to react for their army." Joel continued his measured stride down the hall.

"So what if Carbonell comes back to Álfheim?" Erin shuddered at the thought. She could almost feel the invisible hands on her arms.

Joel must have sensed her reaction because he was suddenly standing in front of her, the full force of his honey brown eyes searching hers. He spoke with a solemn air. "Erin Fireborn, so long as I live, I will do my best to keep you from ever falling into such evil hands. Carbonell would have a lot to deal with if he decides to enter our kingdom." He reached up and touched her cheek.

Before Erin could respond, he spun and continued his path down the hall. She could feel the spot on her cheek where his fingers had touched. His hand left a warm buzzing feeling that she was sure had little, if anything, to do with magic.

She caught Bain's eye. He looked like he had a few questions to ask himself, questions that he would save until they were alone.

Chapter Fifty

HOME

ADARAE HAD RETURNED TO HER colony, along with her small platoon and Faerie dragon soon after arriving at the kingdom. Although their time with Bain had been short, he had been melancholy since their departure. Erin wondered if the älvor had somehow connected him to the reality of the fantasy world he was trying to understand. It didn't seem to help having the elves teach him. He did as he was directed, but his heart wasn't in it. It was as if Carbonell had won the battle of his mind.

And Bain wasn't much help in discerning the extent of magical manipulation he had endured. He still counted Carbonell as a friend, and suddenly translating that relationship into an enemy was beyond his reach. For months, Carbonell was the only friendly face in his isolated world.

Erin tried again and again to assure him that he had been under Carbonell's spells, but the bond was difficult to break. And Bain just couldn't place himself in the impossible world of the älvin kind.

It hadn't been hard to talk him into visiting home. Erin was sure that if he could see the Living Garden and the fairies again, his heart and mind might begin to mend.

And she thought he needed to see Grandpa Jessie. They both did. Thanksgiving was just around the corner, and a surprise visit would definitely boost their spirits.

Pulsar had been eager to assist them in their journey. Bain

hadn't complained at all as they soared over the endless trees, as though he had forgotten his dislike for flying. He had told Erin about how exhilarating it had been to look out from the lofty tower in Black Rain. After spending endless days in a gray stone cell, the tower view had been supernal.

Even though it had only been months since their departure, it seemed as if a lifetime had passed since they crossed the Door of Vines. Bain's excitement grew steadily as they raced through the underground maze and up the stairs. He burst from the cabin and out into the clearing. The familiar earthy aroma and the November frost of their homeland greeted them as his eyes searched the trees expectantly.

... 🦋 ...

"I think you have done more than grow taller, Erin. You look like your mother." Grandpa Jessie said as they stood in the entryway.

Erin and Bain had decided to ring the doorbell instead of just walking in. Surprising him was just too good of an opportunity to pass up. And they were right. Grandpa Jessie opened the door with a confused look. Bain broke the silence with "Hi, Grandpa" and it was all over after that.

"It's good to see you too, Grandpa." She threw her arms around his neck.

After a tight squeeze, he pulled her to his arm's length. "I can see why my son couldn't keep his eyes off your mom. She was like no woman I have ever seen, but looking at you is like seeing her all over again. You're growing up, love."

Erin tried to keep the tears from coming to her eyes. She was happy to be home, but Grandpa's words had caught her off guard. There were so few pictures of her mother. She had only seen a couple of wedding pictures. Her parents married only months after meeting each other, and for some reason, her mom didn't like her picture taken. All these years she had only a few details of what her mom looked like. She loved the fact that her mom had the same red curly hair and fair skin as she did, but the photos were always profiles, like someone had taken them without her noticing.

The next thought hit her like thunder. She had seen her Mom, in the horrible dream. The red hair flying around her face as she screamed her father's name, she just wished she had a more pleasant memory of her.

. . . 🦋 . . .

Thanksgiving had been filled with homemade rolls and turkey. The house still smelled of dinner as they sat on the floor in Erin's room. Each had a roll with cold turkey and mustard. It was practically tradition. The only thing better than the dinner itself were the turkey leftovers.

As Erin watched Bain she thought of how he had been almost normal since they had been home. At least here he wasn't expected to know magic, or come to terms with an impossible reality.

Mrs. Hammel and her husband had been out of town visiting their son's family, so Thanksgiving was just the three of them. But it couldn't have been better. Grandpa Jessie had them laughing most of the day, and even though Erin cooked a lot of the food herself, the day was not spent alone in the kitchen, but surrounded by her sweet family.

Grandpa Jessie wasted no time in digging out the old Christmas albums and before long they were singing about snow as they worked. That's when she saw the Bain she had always known. While he sang along to the tunes, the sparkle came back into his eyes. Coming home really had been a good idea.

In spite of his longer hair, Bain could almost pass for the little boy she grew up with as he sat there on the floor licking stray mustard drops off his fingers. She couldn't help but giggle as a piece of turkey landed on his lap and he turned his roll upside down to catch another drip.

"What are you laughing at?" he countered as he salvaged the escaped turkey.

"Nothing!" She smiled back at him.

For another minute a comfortable silence elapsed. It was so easy spending time with Bain.

"Do you think they can grow plants in the fall?" he asked suddenly.

"Who?" she asked. All around their home stood empty fields. Even the pumpkins had all been harvested. Through spring and summer the earth was worked steadily into production, but as the frost settled in, the ground was left barren for the winter months.

"The älvor," he answered simply. "We haven't seen the Living Garden in forever."

"I'm not sure," she answered. He was finally talking about their world as if it were real. She didn't want to overreact and send him off into another denial phase. She waited quietly for him to continue his thought.

"So, I've been meaning to ask you about something else."

She looked up at him, a little curious. "What?"

He returned a look that made her feel like the little sister rather than his twin. "How long have you been seeing Joel?"

She couldn't help but laugh out loud. "Why? Are you worried?"

"You didn't answer the question."

"Okay! Uh, actually, I'm not entirely sure."

"What do you mean, you're not sure?"

"Well, I don't have a watch, for one, or a calendar. I have no idea how long I've known him."

Bain impulsively looked down at his watch. Although he had lost his suitcase and clothes, the watch had made it through the long journey. Something seemed to light up in his eye, as if he remembered something.

"This one tells me what time it is here," he pointed to a dial on his watch, "And this one . . ." He didn't finish. He looked back up at Erin. "I don't believe it. All this time I knew what time it was where you were. All this time." He was looking at the wall as if calculating something. "It's like starting over, isn't it?"

Erin watched him silently, unsure what to say.

"All this time I didn't know I was living a lie. And now that I'm living the truth, I think it's a lie. Sometimes I wish I had your gift instead of mine."

"But you know now. You're going to be fine."

He looked back at her with an expression of questioning and sorrow. "Erin, I'm so far behind. How am I ever going to catch up again?"

She reached over and unfastened his sword pin. He had worn it every day. It was a miracle it hadn't been lost in the city as well. She pulled his hand out and placed the pin in his palm. "This is your Changing Brooch. Just by thinking about it, you can change it into whatever little thing you want." She shut his fingers around the pin. "Think of something," she commanded.

He sat there staring at his fist. She wasn't sure if he really was concentrating but decided to wait. A smile crept over his face as the metal in his hand began to transform. Soon he was holding a piece of paper and inspecting his work.

The suspense was killing her. "What did you make?" She was surprised at how fast he transformed his brooch. Maybe his magic was stronger than she thought.

He handed over the stiff paper. Her heart skipped a beat as she grasped the image on the front. There, in the background, was the queen's house and standing in front on the magnificent lawn was Pulsar with Adarae and nearly a hundred other älvor filling the sky. But smiling back from the center of the photo was Bain and she. The image was breathtaking and as clear as reality.

She looked up at him in surprise, speechless.

"It seems we have more than one home." He smiled at her, and suddenly was on his feet, pulling her off the ground. "Come on, you can tell me all about Joel while I eat pie and decide whether or not I need to be your own personal stalker."

"Don't worry, I have Pulsar to keep me in line. Besides, I think Joel would be more afraid of a dragon than my brother."

"I wouldn't be too sure about that." In his impossible speed, he was already to the kitchen raiding the cherry blueberry pie.

BOOK CLUB QUESTIONS

1. Erin isn't sure she should take the step of becoming an elf, but Bain is. Have you ever found yourself at odds with someone, especially when both of you could be right? What do you do in this kind of situation?

2. If you were Bain, would you have kept training in the cottage even if Erin had decided not to? Why?

3. Erin finds herself lying to Grandpa Jessie to protect him from the truth. Do you think she did the right thing? What would you have said to Grandpa Jessie?

4. Bain enjoys Carbonell's company from the start. Is it always easy to know if your friends are going to be good for you right away? How could Bain have discovered the truth about Carbonell sooner? What were some of the tricks Carbonell used to make Bain like him?

5. If you could choose to enter just one room of the cottage, which room would you enter? What would you do there?

6. Erin and Bain are given superhuman abilities in speed, strength, hearing, sight, taste and smell. Which of these gifts do

you think you would like the most? What would you do with it?

7. What abilities and talents do you think Erin and Bain had before they entered the cottage? What are some of your talents and how can they help you?

8. Erin made the right choices when she believed in herself. Why does it matter if you believe you can do something? Can it change the outcome?

ABOUT THE AUTHOR

NEARLY A NATIVE OF IDAHO, Laura Bingham was born in Iowa and moved to Idaho at age four. She graduated from Ricks College with an associate's degree and from Boise State University with a bachelor's degree in biology as well as a certification to teach all science subjects in secondary education in the state of Idaho. In her backyard stands a dance studio, where she teaches youth of all ages the lesser known, but much loved, sport of clogging.

Her grandparents and other relatives live in the beautiful Pennsylvania hills where she adores visiting and eating home-grown blueberries. She lives in Boise with her husband and five young children, including her own set of boy-girl twins.

0 26575 52729 2